Storm Testament IV

Storm Testament IV

Lee Nelson

Council Press
Springville, Utah

ISBN 13: 978-1-55517-413-2

Published by Council Press, an imprint of Cedar Fort, Inc., 2373 W. 700 S., Springville, UT, 84663
Distributed by Cedar Fort, Inc. www.cedarfort.com

LIBRARY OF CONGRESS CATALOGING-IN-PUBLICATION DATA

Nelson, Lee.
[Storm testament]
The Storm testament I / by Lee Nelson.
p. cm.
Originally published: Storm testament , 2001.
ISBN 978-1-55517-413-2 (alk. paper)
1. Rocky Mountains—Fiction. 2. Ute Indians—Fiction. I. Title.

PS3564.E4675S76 2007
813'.54—dc22

2007026687

Cover design by Jeremy Beal
Cover design © 2008 by Lyle Mortimer
Edited by Melissa Caldwell

Printed in the United States of America

10 9 8 7 6 5 4 3 2 1

Printed on acid-free paper

Prologue

A weathered bronze tablet in a deserted mountain valley about an hour's drive west of Cedar City, Utah, carries the following:

Mountain Meadows

A favorite recruiting place on the old Spanish trail.

In this vicinity September 7th, 1857, occurred one of the most lamentable tragedies in the history annals of the West. A company of about 140 emigrants from Arkansas and Missouri led by Captain Charles Fancher, enroute to California, was attacked by white men and Indians. All but 17 small children were killed. John D. Lee, who confessed participation as leader, was legally executed here March 23rd, 1877. Most of the emigrants were buried in their own defense pit. This monument was reverently dedicated September 10th, 1932, by the Utah Pioneer Trails and Landmarks Association and the people of Southern Utah.

Chapter 1

I knew something was wrong the instant I saw Porter Rockwell. It wasn't that his face gave anything away. On the contrary, he had a face of stone, occasionally smiling to indulge friends, but otherwise a face that never gave away the thoughts and feelings of the man behind it. Port could stand face to face with the Devil himself, look the old man in the eye without blinking, and call him an egg-sucking hog.

That was Port, all right, the man who had gunned down the leader of the Carthage mob that had killed the Prophet Joseph. Though it had never been proven in court, Port was the man who had shot Lilburn Boggs, the notorious governor of Missouri who in 1838 ordered that all Mormons who refused to surrender their arms, sign over their property, and leave the state would be exterminated. There's no telling how many men had fallen before Port's smoking guns in his efforts to help Brigham Young turn the Utah wilderness into a thriving, civilized community. Had Port cut notches in his gun handles, like other lawmen and gunfighters often did, there's no doubt but what the stocks on his guns would have been notched entirely away.

There was nothing in Port's personal appearance, either, that caused the hollow feeling in the pit of my stomach. He wore the usual buckskin shirt, greasy and torn from years on the trail. His long hair was tied in a bundle under his sweat-stained hat. He sat straight in the saddle, though it appeared he had been on the trail for many days.

I knew something was wrong from the condition of his horse. I had seen the stylish bay stallion before, in Salt Lake City. Port loved fine horses, and this bay was one of the finest west of the Mississippi, also one of the fastest horses in the territory. But as it trotted toward me across the rocky flat beside Silver Lake at the head of Big Cottonwood Canyon, it appeared to be favoring at least two, if not three, feet. As it got closer I could tell from the sound of the hooves on the rocks that two shoes were gone, allowing those hooves to be worn to the quick on the rocky trail. The animal was wet with sweat, and the dirt stains streaking down from the saddle blanket and around the bridle told me it had been sweating a long time. The bay's ears were not forward anticipating the trail ahead or back to pick up signals from its rider, but drooping sideways in total exhaustion. Not caring what was ahead or behind, its only concern seemed to be to keep going. And it didn't appear that it could go much farther.

I knew cruel men—even mean boys—who would abuse a horse like that for no reason. But not Porter Rockwell. For him to wear a horse down like that, he would have to have a good reason. And that's what worried me.

I nodded at Port as he rode by, followed by three other riders on fresher horses. The riders had apparently joined him somewhere down the trail; it was obvious that neither they nor their horses had traveled as far as Port and his horse had.

"Dan Storm, good to see you," he said without slowing the big bay. He continued on toward Brigham Young's tent, where he dismounted and quickly disappeared inside without bothering to tie up his horse. But that wasn't necessary. The bay was too exhausted to even graze on the rich mountain grass. It just stood where he had dropped the reins, its head down, its rear foot cocked, too weary to even swat at flies with its tail.

Chapter 2

Brigham Young didn't make the announcement right away. Maybe he didn't want to spoil the festivities for the nearly twenty-five hundred people who had made the trek to the head of Big Cottonwood Canyon. Maybe he just wanted to fully analyze the situation before he made any public announcements.

Either way, it was evening, just before the final night of dancing, that Daniel H. Wells, acting under Brother Brigham's direction, called the people together.

He began his remarks by announcing that the United States government mail contract with the newly established pony express had just been canceled. No further mail would be coming from the East. But that wasn't the worst of the news. Port and his friends hadn't nearly killed their horses to bring word of a canceled mail contract.

The President of the United States had dispatched twenty-five hundred troops to invade Utah and put an end to what many Easterners referred to as the Utah rebellion. An army supply train consisting of seven hundred wagons full of supplies and a walking larder of over five thousand head of cattle were already on the plains heading for Utah.

The formerly jovial crowd suddenly became silent. No one seemed quite sure how to react to such shocking news.

I looked toward the American flag flapping briskly in the

cool evening breeze at the top of a newly peeled pine pole. At the beginning of the two-day celebration there had been an elaborate flag-raising ceremony, complete with patriotic speeches and a brass band playing the national anthem. Now the same government that we had pledged allegiance to was sending troops to put the Mormons in their place.

I'm sure some in the stunned crowd were thinking back to the persecutions in Missouri and Illinois when the government sat idly by while angry mobs had attacked the Mormons, driven them from their homes, and taken away their property. Now that same government was invading their promised land for no legitimate reason that anyone in Utah could understand.

Everyone knew the recently departed federal judge, William Drummond, had had nothing good to report about the Mormons. The judge had created a scandal in Utah, having left his wife behind in coming to Utah, and often having his mistress sit with him on the bench. Mormons had taken their disputes to the bishops' courts, leaving the federal court nearly empty and the non-Mormon judge without influence or status in Salt Lake City. The judge was on record as telling two reporters that "money was his God." The man was without respect among the Mormons and left the territory in disgrace. But no one suspected his tales of rebellion and disobedience among the Mormons would have such an effect on the President of the United States.

Knowing the judge wouldn't have anything good to report about the Mormons when he returned to Washington, some enterprising Mormons had taken a good portion of the judge's court records, intending to pass them on to the next judge at a later date, figuring the less ammunition the judge had on his return to Washington, the better. The trick backfired, however; the angered judge reported how the Mormons were stealing and destroying federal court records.

As I found out later, Congress was not in session when President John Buchanan and Secretary of War John Floyd ordered a regular army force mobilized at Fort Leavenworth to march on Utah Territory. The mission was to unseat Brigham Young and put Alfred

Cumming in his place as territorial governor. Cumming was formerly an Indian agent on the upper Missouri.

Daniel H. Wells's remarks were brief. When finished, he turned and reentered President Young's tent, leaving the silent crowd to speculate on future developments. Gradually the shock wore off and people began to talk more freely. The band began to play in preparation for the dance.

I returned to my tent and wagon, where Caroline and Sarah were preparing the children for bed.

As I approached I could see Caroline's silhouette against the last rays of the setting sun, which turned her loose blonde hair into a spray of gold as she tossed her head to one side, her arms reaching high to hang articles of wet clothing over a new hemp rope stretched tightly between the wagon seat and an aspen tree.

She was wearing a loose white blouse that only showed her womanly figure more when she raised her arms high into the air. Below the blouse was a gray skirt that extended nearly to the ground.

Caroline looked amazingly good for a woman who had spent nearly ten years on the frontier, bearing three children during that time. She didn't wear a bonnet or hat all the time like the other women, allowing a tanned healthy look to her skin. The hard work of the pioneer life had kept her figure trim and youthful—had not burned her out and worn her down as it had so many pioneer women.

Caroline was unaware of my approach as I walked up behind her, seizing her firmly around the waist. She spun in my arms, slinging a wet pair of trousers behind my neck, pulling my face down to hers.

"I'm so glad we came up here," she said when she finished kissing me. "We need to get away like this more often." I nodded my agreement, reluctant to share the recent news from the East, not wanting to spoil the holiday.

After throwing the wet trousers over the line, I took her by the hand and led her into the tent, where Sarah was bent over our seven children, all in a row between two big blankets. The two oldest, Pat and Sam, were on the outsides to keep the smaller children from rolling out. None of them looked very sleepy. Sarah had been trying to quiet them with a story.

Sarah wasn't as strong as Caroline. The frontier life had been harder on her. She had been ill more often and had tired more easily. But she seldom complained. She couldn't work as hard as Caroline, but her patience with the children seemed endless. Over the years, while Caroline had assumed more of the work responsibilities, including working side by side with me in the fields, Sarah had assumed increasing responsibilities in tending and caring for the seven children of both women.

I dropped to my knees and fell forward across the children, some of them beginning to squeal in delight as I gave them their goodnight hugs and kisses while their mothers began getting ready for the dance.

"Don't get them all wound up," scolded Sarah. "And don't let them get out of bed."

"Pat says that man in the buckskins is Porter Rockwell," said Sam, now eight. "But I know he isn't."

"How's that?" I asked.

"Porter Rockwell has long hair. Joseph Smith promised him he would be strong like Samson if he never cut his hair. The man in buckskins didn't have long hair."

"Wasn't the man wearing a hat?" I asked. He nodded. "What do you think was under the hat?"

I explained how Port frequently braided his hair like an Indian and coiled the braid on top of his head under his hat.

"I tol' you so," said Pat condescendingly.

Sam sat up. "I got to see him."

I pushed him back down. "You'll have plenty of time for that tomorrow. He's spending the night."

"Has he really killed over a hundred men?" asked Pat.

"I don't know," I said. "Good night." I stood up in spite of the protesting children and motioned for Caroline and Sarah to follow me outside. It was time to give them the news, before they heard it from someone else at the dance.

"But what does it mean?" demanded Caroline after I had related the details of the recent announcement.

"What will happen?" asked Sarah.

"I don't know," I said. "We may have to defend our land against federal troops. Perhaps we'll have to flee. Maybe the whole thing will just blow over. I don't know. I suppose many things could happen. We'll just have to wait and see. We'll head home tomorrow as planned and see how things go from there."

"Has the dance been canceled?" asked Sarah.

"No," I said. "Hurry and get ready."

Sarah turned toward the tent, but Caroline remained where she was. "We have company," she said, looking past me. I turned to see who was coming. It was Porter Rockwell. We didn't know each other well. I had been in his posse on several occasions. He knew I had lived with the Utes before the pioneers came to the valleys, and he was aware of my skills in the mountains.

"Can I see you alone?" he asked while still walking toward me. Port was not a man of many words. He always got directly to the point.

Caroline joined Sarah in the tent, where I could already see the faces of little boys peeking under the canvas.

Port and I shook hands. "Good to see you, Port," I said. He nodded. "Some of the boys and me are heading east in a few days," he began, looking me directly in the eye. "Going to check out that supply train, find out what we can on what the soldier boys is up to."

He looked down at his cowhide boots as he kicked at a clump of bear grass. "Brother Brigham's still not sure what to make of the situation. But one thing's for sure. Can't let them get in the valley this year. Me and the boys may do some things to slow 'em down."

Port looked up again, directly into my face. "Want you to come with us."

I hesitated, thinking for an instant of all the farm work back home that required my attention. The potatoes and corn that needed to be tended to. The second crop of hay. The livestock. A new fencing project I was determined to finish before winter. My boys were still too young to be very much help. But even more important, with an army about to invade the land, I was reluctant to leave my families alone.

"Can I tell you in the morning?" I asked.

"Any problem?"

"No. Just want to discuss it with the women."

"Let me know in the morning," said Port as he turned and walked away.

Chapter 3

After buying the last of the supplies for our journey eastward, Port and I walked out on the porch of the State Street dry goods store. We were heading out the next morning. Caroline, Sarah, and the children had prearranged to pick me up in front of the store.

As I looked up the street to see if they were coming, I saw, instead of one wagon, an entire train of wagons coming in my direction. Word was out that two gentile trains were in town, one from Arkansas led by a man named Charles Fancher, the other from Missouri, the men in this group calling themselves the Missouri Wildcats. Both groups were headed for California and had apparently joined forces in Salt Lake for their mutual protection.

"Brigham Young, may your stubborn heart burn in hell forever and ever," shouted a tall, thin man walking through the gray dust next to the lead ox team.

The man had a sparse red beard that offered his sunburned face little protection from the summer sun. His felt hat was dirty and stained with sweat around the band. His blue cotton shirt was also dark with sweat under the arms and in the center of the man's thin chest. His mouse-colored trousers were wrinkled below the knees and grease-stained on the thighs and hips. The man wore a long-barreled horse pistol on his left hip, backwards, so he could draw it with his right hand.

"Git moving, Brigham," he shouted, loud enough for everyone

along the street to hear, "or I'll kick you in the belly. If you hadn't been castrated, I'd kick you where it would really hurt."

The big brown and white ox wiggled its ears and flicked its tail but did not hurry up its plodding pace.

"Damn you, Brigham. For two cents I'd skin you alive and feed you to the Mormons," shouted the man, louder than ever. Then referring to the other ox, he said, "Heber Kimball here may be dumb enough to try to pull the whole load by hisself, but he can't do it."

A small crowd was beginning to gather to watch the man abuse Brigham and Heber. Mormons were accustomed to this form of heckling from California-bound settlers and normally tried to ignore such taunting. Non-Mormon settlers naming their oxen after Mormon leaders was nothing new. But this man was more creative, more colorful than most, and certainly more vocal.

Noticing the gathering crowd, the man took a step back, hands on hips. He wasn't about to let an opportunity pass to perform for an audience. He turned to the crowd.

"Brigham Young here is too lazy to put in an honest day's work," he shouted. There was no response from the crowd, all of whom were now aware that Port and I were standing on the porch. Some were looking toward Port to see how Brigham Young's personal bodyguard would respond to the taunting. Port did nothing.

"And oh, how Brigham smells," continued the man, gaining confidence. Not only did the gathering Mormons appear weak and cowardly to him, but he had nearly sixty armed companions to back him up in case of trouble.

"He stinks as bad . . ." He paused, searching for the right comparison. "He stinks as bad as Heber here. Smelliest buggers I ever saw."

"You don't like Mormons?" ventured one of the spectators.

The man in the street began to laugh, then said, "No, no. I love Mormons." He paused, then continued. "I love the feel of a Mormon beneath my boot. I love to see a Mormon in my rifle sights. I love Mormon women . . ."

"Seth Stevenson, shut your dirty mouth!" shouted a female

voice. I hadn't noticed the woman before. She was sitting on the seat of the man's wagon. She had long brown hair and was wearing a clean blue dress. Even in her anger she was uncommonly handsome as she looked straight ahead, shouting at the man in the street.

The man spun around in surprise. He hadn't anticipated an attack from his own group. He pointed at her, his hand shaking.

"Woman!" he screamed. "You be silent."

All was quiet for a moment, with everyone, including the man in the street, waiting to see how the woman would respond to the challenge. She continued to look straight ahead, her jaw firm. It seemed she was about to say something, and finally she did. Her voice was calm, but firm.

"If you want silence out of me, Seth Stevenson, you'll have to be more careful about what you say, at least in public."

The man didn't finish his comment about Mormon women. But he continued his tirade against Mormons in general.

"See this here gun?" he said, turning back to the crowd and placing his left palm on the butt of the revolver in the holster. "Worth a lot of money. Know why?" He paused, allowing the crowd to think about his question. "It's one of the guns that killed old Joe Smith. Mighty proud of this ol' piece. Yes sir. Bought it from a man in Carthage for fifty dollars. Said a slug from this ol' piece tore right through old Joe's . . ."

"That's enough, Mr. Stevenson," said a voice from the crowd, a quiet voice, but everyone heard it. It was the voice of Porter Rockwell.

Chapter 4

I was more than a little surprised when Port motioned for me to accompany him into the street. He certainly didn't need my help putting the smart-mouthed Missourian in his place. Nevertheless, I complied with his request, walking at Port's side as we approached Seth Stevenson.

"No barbers in Salt Lake, squaw man?" asked Stevenson, noticing Port's long hair and buckskin shirt. Port was not wearing a hat and his hair was hanging loose about his shoulders.

Port didn't respond. Stevenson swelled with confidence.

"You don't like me naming my oxen Brigham and Heber?"

Port surprised me by looking down at the ground. His arms were folded across his chest, his hands a long way from his guns. He kicked at the dust with his boot. "Say anything you want about the Mormons," said Port, surprising everyone, including me and the tall stranger. "It don't bother me."

Port continued to look at the ground. Stevenson was grinning over his apparent victory.

"But my friend here, he's plenty upset," muttered Port.

"Wait a minute," I began, looking over at Port, who ignored me.

"Said to me over there that he'd like to black both of your lying eyes," continued Port. "But he's too bashful to ask you to fight him."

"That so?" said the Missourian, looking at me for the first time.

I was just about to try to explain that Port was the one who wanted to fight when Port cut me off.

"He don't want to embarrass ya in front of all these people. He thinks all you hogbrains got outhouse slush in yer veins and yeller streaks down yer backs. No guts to toss yer gun in the wagon box and fight a real man like Storm here."

Before I could say anything, Stevenson had drawn his pistol and tossed it into the wagon box in front of the woman in the blue dress. In almost the same motion he was throwing one of his bony fists toward my face.

As I thrust my arm forward to parry his blow, I swore to myself that someday Porter Rockwell would pay for his trickery. He was a man accustomed to fighting and violence, and perhaps thought his little trick very funny. I did not. It had been many years since I had fought a man, and as I grabbed the Missourian's fist, a sick feeling welled up in my stomach. But as I noticed Port's laughter, I became angry.

Though I was not used to fighting, I was not in poor physical condition. A man does not get soft clearing land, building fences, digging ditches, and wrestling cattle and horses. I was strong and soon had the tall, thin Stevenson wrestled to the ground. But before I could rub his sweaty face in the gray dust, he wiggled out of my grasp, kicking me in the side of the face as he scrambled to his feet.

Hoping not to give him a chance to catch his breath, I lunged forward, head down, hoping to get a hold on him again. I had no intention of boxing him at arms' length, not when his arms were probably six inches longer than mine.

But this time he avoided my efforts to grab him by dodging to one side, delivering two vicious blows to my face. Holding both of my hands over my face, as though I were hurt bad, I watched him through my fingers, waiting for him to come again.

I didn't have to wait long. Still holding my hands over my face, I waited until just the right moment to grab an arm and begin twisting while I kicked his feet out from under him. He hit the ground hard this time, and I could feel what seemed to be the cracking of a rib as my knee thrust into his chest. He wiggled free again, but not before I delivered several solid blows with my fists and elbows.

As he scrambled to his feet, holding his ribs, I was expecting him to come at me again. I was totally surprised when he turned and lunged toward the safety of his wagon. I hadn't expected the fight to end so quickly. I had thought this loud-mouthed Missourian had more fight in him.

But that sick feeling suddenly returned as I realized he was not running from me, but going after his gun, the one he had thrown in the wagon box. I charged after him, figuring my only chance was to beat him to the gun.

Stevenson was stepping from the wheel into the box when I reached the wagon. Using the big wagon wheel as a ladder, I leaped after him, grabbing him from behind before he could get to the pistol. Over we went into the back of the wagon, taking the surprised woman with us. Over the sound of bodies crashing against boxes and boards I could still hear Port's laughter.

The lanky Missourian was no match for me in the close confines of a cluttered wagon box. I was soon on top, punching him repeatedly in the face when suddenly, without warning, someone grabbed me around the neck from behind. At first I thought friends of the Missourian from other wagons had decided to join the fight, but when fingernails began digging into my flesh I realized it was not another man, but the woman in the blue dress who had attacked me.

I reached back with my left arm and tried to brush her away, but she wasn't about to be pushed aside. As I struggled to shake her free, my grip on the man was loosened and he began reaching for the pistol by our feet. Outside I could hear Porter Rockwell's shrill laughter. My life was in danger, and he was laughing.

I became angrier than before, reaching back over my shoulder with one hand while trying to hold the man with the other. Finally, grabbing the woman's hair, I jerked her around to one side and backhanded her solidly across the face.

With the woman finally out of the way, I delivered a solid blow to the man's jaw, feeling his body go limp. The fight was over, except for Port's continued laughter.

I looked over at the woman. Her hands were covering her pretty face as blood oozed from her nose. I felt terrible for what I had done to her. At least she wasn't crying.

"I'm sorry," I said.

"Seth?" she said, looking straight ahead. There was alarm in her voice. "Seth, are you all right?"

Something was wrong. The woman was not looking at the man she was calling to.

She was blind. I had hit a blind woman. And it was Porter Rockwell's fault.

Chapter 5

Her name was Susannah Stevenson and she had been blind since birth. The blow from my hand had broken her nose. And how she ended up in my wagon with Caroline and Sarah, I still don't quite understand.

It happened after the fight while I was giving Porter Rockwell a piece of my mind. Caroline and Sarah had arrived to pick me up, as previously arranged, but finding the woman with the bleeding, broken nose, and learning that I was responsible, they somehow convinced her they could provide the medical help she needed. By that time Seth had come to his senses, and except for his badly injured pride and a sore jaw, was unharmed.

While that was going on I was telling Port I wanted no part of an expedition led by a man who could not be trusted. While he may have thought the whole situation was very funny, I did not. I could have been killed. Besides, I felt that with just a little diplomacy the fight might have been avoided.

I asked him how he would have felt had he been the one to strike the blind woman. I told him that if Brigham Young needed my help to scout the approaching army, I would still do so, but not under the uninspired leadership of a man like him. For the present I was returning to American Fork, and he and his men could go to hell for all I cared.

Without a word to defend himself, Port let me say my piece.

Then he invited me to walk with him in the street where we could be alone. Reluctantly, I agreed.

"Some of the boys were concerned when I told them you were coming with us," he began. "You being just a farmer and all, they didn't want somebody along who would wet his pants at the first sign of a fight."

"They wouldn't take your word that I was all right?" I asked.

"What could I tell them? You and me have been in the same posse a couple of times, but we've never been in any real scrapes together."

"Why did you ask me to come along, then?"

"Just a feeling you get around some men, that they can handle themselves when the killing starts."

"But you didn't trust that feeling. That's why you set the Missourian on me."

"You're making too much of it," said Port. "When it was obvious the buzzardmouth was looking for a fight, it just seemed like a perfect opportunity to give you a little test. That's all."

"Did I pass?"

"Except for belting the blind lady in the face. I mean, there's some things a man just shouldn't do." He was grinning.

"I know," I said, "like setting a trap for a trusting friend where he might get killed."

Port started to laugh. I was beginning to believe Brigham Young's personal bodyguard had a warped sense of humor.

"Actually, I figured Stevenson was a coward, that when it came right down to it he wouldn't fight you. I was as surprised as you when he was so quick to let that first fist fly."

"Do you know what bothered me as much as anything about the fight?" I asked, changing the subject a little.

He shook his head.

"Your laughing. Nothing funny that I could see."

"Been wondering about that myself," confessed Port. "Usually nothing funny about a fight, especially a street fight with a Missourian.

"But this one was different," he continued. "Someone besides me, for a change, was taking the heat. And that felt good. So good I just had to laugh."

"I don't understand."

"Ever kill a man?"

"Many years ago."

"Seems I'm doing it all the time," he said thoughtfully. "Some got it coming," he continued. "Like Frank Worrell. Pulling the trigger on old Frank felt downright good, like getting your back scratched after a long day of hauling dusty hay." Frank Worrell was the man who had led the mob on Carthage Jail, where Joseph Smith and his brother Hyrum were killed.

"But I hate killing a man just because he has a big mouth—like this Stevenson," he continued. "When he crossed over the line, and I figured there was going to be a fight, I figured I'd have to kill him, make a widow out of that pretty lady in the blue dress. Made me sick to my stomach. Always does when I get ready to kill a man."

"You'd have killed the Missourian?" I asked.

"Couldn't have fought him like you did. I'm too old. Don't take my guns off anymore. I'd have killed him."

"Then why did you laugh?"

"Because I was happy," he responded quickly. "When the fight was shifted to you, I could see that I would no longer have to kill him and make that pretty lady a widow. That made me so happy I just had to laugh. Storm, I owe you one. Do you understand?"

I wasn't sure what to make of Port's comments. He seemed sincere.

"I'm still not going with you to scout the army," I said, feeling my heart soften to the professional killer, but determined to maintain distance so I would not be used again.

"We're gathering at my stable at seven in the morning," said Port. "Hope you change your mind." After a brief handshake, he turned and walked away.

I was surprised he didn't try harder to get me to change my mind. I liked his style. I liked Porter Rockwell. I didn't like the trick he pulled on me. I got to thinking that if I didn't go with him, I'd probably never have a chance to get even with him.

Chapter 6

Susannah was laughing when I arrived at the place where my family was camped in a cottonwood grove on City Creek. It was almost dark.

She was sitting on the wagon tongue, holding my three-year-old Elizabeth in her arms. The rest of the children were seated on the ground in front of her. It appeared they were playing some kind of game.

It seemed strange to me that this woman from the Missouri wagon train seemed to be having such a happy time in my camp, with my family. That she was part of a group where so much anti-Mormon feeling existed didn't bother me as much as the fact that just a few hours earlier I had smashed this woman's face during a fight with her husband. Any normal person in those same circumstances would have considered me and mine their enemies. At least, that would seem natural. But this woman was holding my three-year-old as if the child were her own.

A white bandage as wide as the length of her nose reached around behind Susannah's head. Both of her pretty eyes were blackened, too, though I had not struck her above the nose. Apparently the blow had caused sufficient internal bleeding to affect the eyes.

To my surprise, Susannah was the first to become aware of my approach. "Someone's coming," she said, turning her head in my direction.

While little Elizabeth remained on Susannah's lap, the rest of the children ran to greet me. Caroline, who was stirring a kettle of stew over the fire, was the first to speak.

"It's the man who broke your nose," she said coolly.

"Heaven's sakes, Dan, how could you strike a woman like that?" demanded Sarah, stepping from behind the wagon.

I felt like turning around and walking away. At least the children were glad to see me.

"Oh, that's him," said Susannah.

"Don't worry," continued Caroline. "We won't let him hit you again."

"That's right," said Sarah, offering her support.

I knew they were teasing. Still, I didn't like it.

"How's the nose?" I asked Susannah as I walked closer, ignoring the taunting from my wives.

"Getting sorer by the hour," she said calmly, "but I'll be fine, thanks to the doctoring from Caroline and Sarah."

I couldn't get over how familiar and at home she seemed to be with my family, even with me.

"Don't you feel a little uneasy?" I asked. "A blind gentile among the Mormons, like a lamb among wolves?"

"I think it's the blindness," she said, shaking her head. "I sense things people with eyes can't seem to see."

"Like what?" I asked, remembering that she was the first one to hear me coming.

"Like the way your children ran to you when you came into camp. The eagerness of Caroline and Sarah to care for my injury. Even the way they joked about you hitting me again. Your family tells a lot about you, Dan Storm. You're not a man to fear, at least not by me."

"Thank you," I said sincerely. "But you don't seem to be a woman with many fears. Seems to me it would take a lot of courage to head west without the use of one's eyes."

"You have no idea what it's like," she said, her face becoming very serious. "Hearing approaching footsteps and not knowing if it's a friend, or perhaps an Indian. Knowing fear and helplessness as constant companions. Not being able to see stumps or holes that make the wagon jolt sharply from one side to the other. Gathering firewood, wondering what you would do if you grabbed a snake, perhaps even a rattlesnake. Trying to set up camp and preparing to cook in a different, unfamiliar place each evening."

"That would be hard," remarked Sarah, who was now seated beside Susannah. Elizabeth was asleep in the blind woman's arms.

"Walking along a riverbank, hearing the rushing water, not knowing how close you might be to a steep drop-off," continued Susannah. "Even some men in our wagon train frighten me. I can feel their eyes staring at me, encouraged by my blindness to think that they can take advantage of me, if you can believe that."

"What about your husband?" asked Caroline, a tone of anger in her voice.

"Oh, he would kill any man who tried to harm me. But he's not around all the time. Sometimes I wish I were old and fat. I hate going to the bathroom and not knowing who might be watching."

"That would be horrible!" exclaimed Sarah.

"Stay here in Salt Lake," said Caroline, obviously disturbed by Susannah's account of her hardships.

"I belong with my husband," she said simply.

"Is Seth good to you?" I asked, hoping her response would be favorable.

She hesitated before answering my question. "He loves me," she said, "and he puts up with a lot, with my blindness and all. But sometimes I wish he could be more patient when I get sand in the biscuits, or let the wagon get too far behind . . ."

"You cook biscuits over an open fire?" asked Sarah, amazed that a blind woman would attempt such a task.

"But I usually get sand or dirt in them."

"Surely you don't drive the wagon," remarked Caroline.

"Only when Seth's off hunting, caring for the stock, or talking to the other men. It's hard to judge distance from the sound of a squeaking wheel on the next wagon."

"You're an amazing woman, Susannah Stevenson," I said.

"I'm sorry if I talk too much," she apologized.

"Not at all," said Caroline.

"Seth and I don't talk much. Seems so good to have someone to talk to. And to be with your children." She began to rock from side to side, holding the sleeping Elizabeth tighter in her arms.

"Do you have any children?" asked Caroline.

"No," said Susannah, hesitating. "When I was first married, I was afraid I would have a child and not be able to take care of it. Then when it became apparent I could not have children, I began to feel really bad that I would never have a child like this of my own. Thank you for letting me enjoy your children this afternoon. But Seth will be looking for me. Can you take me back?"

"Be glad to," I said. Then in an attempt to turn the conversation to a more cheerful vein, I asked, "Would you rather ride on Buchanan or Boggs?"

"What do you mean?" asked Susannah.

"Please explain that comment to me too," said Caroline. I was grinning.

"Just renamed our horses," I explained, referring to the two draft horses tied to the nearest two cottonwood trees. "Got the idea from Susannah's husband, who calls his oxen Brigham and Heber."

"Which one is Buchanan?" asked Sarah.

"The bay," I said. "He's the dumbest and clumsiest horse we have. A good namesake, don't you think, for a president stupid enough to send federal troops to Utah?"

"Excellent," laughed Sarah. "And the sorrel is just about mean enough to deserve to be called Boggs. I like the names."

"When you say Boggs, are you referring to the former governor of Missouri?" asked Susannah.

"No," I said, "the governor's cousin—a filthy one-eyed, one-legged rascal who would trade his mother into slavery for a bottle of rot gut."

"Is his name Dick Boggs?" asked Susannah.

"You know him?" I asked, hoping she wasn't a relative.

"He's traveling with the Missouri Wildcats."

I could hardly believe my ears. My old enemy was in Salt Lake City. He had lost his foot as a result of being caught in my bear trap.

He had lost his eye in an attack from my dog. The last time I had seen him, he had sworn to kill me.

"Where is the train headed?" I asked.

"West to California."

"To the Humboldt and over Donner Pass?" I asked. She nodded.

Good, I thought. The Wildcats would go directly west, avoiding my home in American Fork. Just a few days and they would be away from the Mormon settlements.

I was just about to tell her to say nothing to Boggs about me and my family when Susannah looked past me into the darkness.

"Someone is coming," she said. "One rider."

Normally such news would not be alarming to me, but the recent news of Dick Boggs suddenly made me cautious. Could my old enemy be approaching in the dark? I could expect no kindness for me or my family from such a man. Quickly I stepped away from the fire, out of the circle of light, reaching for my pistol, searching the darkness to see the mounted rider whom I could now hear.

My caution was not necessary. It was Porter Rockwell, accompanied by a huge wolf-like dog with piercing eyes and a gaunt belly. It was gray like a timber wolf and lanky like a greyhound. It did not wag its tail as it entered the circle of our firelight, but glanced quickly from side to side before dropping on its haunches as Port brought his bay stallion to a halt.

"Susannah," I said, "I'd like you to meet Orrin Porter Rockwell."

"Oh, the Porter Rockwell!" she exclaimed. "Joe Smith's personal bodyguard, leader of the Danites, the man who shot Governor Boggs?"

"He's the one," I said, "though he might deny some of those charges. Also, you might add to that list that he is the man who almost killed Seth Stevenson today."

"What?" asked Susannah.

Port remained silent, gloomy, not liking the conversation about him but unable or unwilling to do anything about it.

"He's the man Seth first tried to pick a fight with, the man who got Seth more interested in fighting me."

"Seth could have been killed," she said weakly.

"Yep," said Port, finally speaking. "I's just gettin' ready to gun your man down when Storm here stepped in and saved me from havin' to do it."

Suddenly I became aware of a loud growl. I glanced over at Port's wolf dog just as it snapped out at my son Sam's hand as the boy tried to pet it. The boy was all right. The dog's growl and snap had been merely a warning.

"Stay away, son," said Port. "Old Abe don't let strangers, or friends, pet him. He's not a pettin' dog."

The next thing I remember, Susannah handed the sleeping Elizabeth to Sarah, then walked toward the dog, finally dropping to one knee, hand outstretched.

"I'd get back if I were you, ma'am," said Port. "You'll get a bloody hand to match your nose if you get any closer."

Susannah stayed where she was, hand outstretched, saying things to the dog in her soft, feminine voice. I could not make out what she was saying.

The dog was standing, ears flat back against his massive skull, a deep rumble in his chest, the hair on his neck and shoulders stiffening. Susannah didn't back away but continued talking to the animal.

Without warning, the beast dropped to his belly and began inching toward the woman's hand. His ears were still back, but the hair on his back was beginning to settle back in place. And the growl was gone.

A short minute later Susannah was scratching the dog's ears while the dog looked back at Port, a look on its face as though it were anticipating scorn from Port for allowing this gentle woman to pet it.

"Wouldn't have believed it if I hadn't seen it," said Port, reaching unconsciously for a strand of long hair on his shoulder.

"I've always had a way with animals," said Susannah. "They don't frighten me, and for some reason I don't frighten them. Petted lots of skunks. Even a bear once."

"Come here, Sam," she said to my boy. "You can pet him now.

He won't bite you." Without hesitation my boy walked up beside Susannah and placed his hand on the dog's head. Other than look at him, it did nothing.

While Susannah and Sam were petting the dog, Port explained the reason for his coming. There had been a change in the purpose of his expedition. The objective was no longer merely to scout the enemy's strength and position but to harass the army to prevent it from getting to Utah before winter.

"We'll be burning feed, stealing livestock, pulling out axle pins in the middle of the night, anything short of killing to slow them down. Need you more than ever, Storm," said Port. "Are you with us?"

It felt good having Porter Rockwell in need of my services.

"On one condition," I said. He nodded for me to continue. "That you take this blind woman back to her husband."

"Do you think she would go with me?" said Port. "She a traveling companion of the Missourians and me the so-called leader of the Danites? After dark?"

"Will you let this Danite take you home, in the dark?" I asked her.

Susannah stood up, turning to face me and Port. "I don't suppose he could be any worse than his dog," she responded, smiling. "As for the dark, it's always that way for me."

After saying good-bye to my wives and children, Susannah reached out and took Port's hand. He had already mounted his horse, and he pulled her into the saddle behind him.

As the horse trotted into the darkness, the big wolf dog to one side, I couldn't help but wonder what would become of this remarkable blind woman.

"Every time I go to the bathroom I will think of that poor sister out in the woods wondering who is watching her," said Sarah.

"I think we should include her in our prayers," added Caroline.

Chapter 7

The crowd that had gathered in the Tabernacle on Sunday, July 26, began to get excited when parts of Indian agent Garland Hard's report to Washington were read from the pulpit, especially the part about Mormon missionaries being "rude and lawless young men, such as might be regarded as a curse to any civilized community."

But the congregation was on its feet when Heber C. Kimball vented his wrath from the pulpit. With red face and clenched fists, he shouted, "Send twenty-five hundred troops here . . . to make a desolation of this people! God Almighty helping me, I will fight until there is not a drop of blood in my veins. Good God! I have enough wives to whip the United States . . ."

But Kimball was only joking about his wives going out to do the fighting. Instead of sending out women, Brigham Young was sending out Porter Rockwell and a dozen or so men, including me—not to fight, but to harass and slow down the advancing army. In the meantime, fortifications were to be built in Echo Canyon. Messages were being sent for missionaries to return early from their missions. Mormons in Samoa, San Francisco, Carson City, even up on the Salmon River, were ordered home to help in the defense of Zion.

Someone had uncovered a statement made by Brigham Young upon entering the valley exactly ten years earlier. It read as follows: "If our enemies would give us just ten years unmolested, we would ask no odds of them; we would never be driven again."

Now, after ten years, everyone felt the statement was prophetic. They would not be driven again. What had happened in Ohio, Missouri, and Illinois would not happen in Utah. This time the Mormons would stand and fight in defense of their homes, farms, and freedom.

The militia, under the leadership of brigadier general Franklin D. Richards, was ordered to readiness. In every community dusty rifles were readied, saddles repaired, and horses shod. Utah was under martial law. Richards ordered that not a kernel of grain be wasted; furthermore, that none be sold to gentile merchants or wagon trains passing through to California or Oregon.

Brigham Young invited all Indian chiefs in the territory to attend a special powwow. His purpose was to win the Indians to his side in the war against the United States.

Sermons in the churches were more fiery, discussions in the street louder. Editorials in the papers were more inflammatory, and prayers more earnest. The spirit of war was in the air.

Still, there was humor. When a messenger from the East naively suggested that President Buchanan might call the whole thing off if Brigham Young would give permission to leave the territory to all—especially plural wives—who were being held in the territory against their wishes, Brigham Young made an interesting counterproposal. "Tell the President," he said, "that I will gladly pay the way for anyone wishing to leave Utah, if the President will pay the way for anyone wishing to come to Utah." Of course Brigham Young was aware of the thousands of poor immigrants in the East without enough money to come west to Utah who would eagerly accept help from the President. Washington ignored the offer, but the Utah Mormons loved their leader's clever answer to the unfounded charge that many of them were forced to stay in the territory against their wishes.

On the morning we left Salt Lake, less than a week after Heber Kimball's speech, crowds lined the streets to shout encouragement and wave farewell to Porter Rockwell and his men heading east to harass President Buchanan's army—a dozen men against twenty-five hundred. Port, Bill Hickman, and Lot Smith were in the lead.

My family had left for Utah Valley earlier that morning. Caroline was going to contact my old friend, Ike, to help with the hay. An escaped slave, he had come west with me the first time in 1838 and had become chief of the Gosiutes in the western desert. Ike usually helped with the haying anyway, always bringing some Indians with him. The women and children would be able to handle the rest of the chores until I returned sometime in the fall.

We hadn't gone far when Port pulled his horse in, letting the others go on ahead. When I caught up with him, he reined his big bay stallion over, saying, "Got to tell you what happened when I took the blind lady home last night." He was grinning.

"As soon as her man saw us coming he ran up, swearing, cussing, and hollering like a wild man. He was about to grab the horse's reins when she said, 'Shut up, Seth, and shake hands with Orrin Porter Rockwell.' Never seen a man shut up so fast in my life." Port looked away toward some people who were calling to him from a street corner.

"Did he?" I asked.

"What?" returned Port.

"Did he shake your hand?"

"Nope. Soon as Susannah got down, he grabbed her hand and headed as fast as he could drag her to the safety of his viper friends."

"That Susannah is a remarkable woman," I said.

"And so is that lady over there," said Port, changing the direction of the conversation and nodding up the street to a woman in a red dress standing on the front porch of a big house.

Even from a distance, I could tell this woman was not an officer in the Mormon Relief Society organization. Her dress was too short, well above her high-topped shoes, almost to the knees. Downright shameful for a woman to dress like that in public. I mean, how could men be expected to behave themselves when there were women who exposed their naked calves to all who would care to look? Her arms were naked too, three or four inches below the shoulder. Add to that what appeared to be almost unkempt sorrel hair falling loosely about her shoulders, and there was little doubt but what she was one of what Heber C. Kimball called street women, who were finding their way to Zion.

"Storm, do you have any idea what that woman has in her bedroom?" asked Port matter-of-factly.

"No, never been there," I answered quickly. I was surprised he would ask such a question because it implied that he had been in this woman's bedroom, not particularly something a Mormon in Zion would want to advertise. But Porter Rockwell wasn't by any means the average Mormon, either.

"Law books, big brown law books. A whole shelf full of 'em."

"You're joking," I said.

"Nope. Her name is Molly Skinner."

"But why would a woman like her study law?"

"Don't know," answered Port, "except it keeps her out of jail. Knows more than most lawyers. Can tie some in knots. Because she's a woman, they won't let her hang out a shingle to practice law, so she makes a living doing something that comes more natural."

By this time we were almost alongside the big house. The woman ran down the steps and into the street, straight for us. Most men, I think, would try to avoid recognizing a woman of her profession, at least in public. But not Port. He pulled his horse to a halt, tipping his hat.

"Good morning, Molly," he said warmly.

"Greetings, Elder Rockwell," she said in a clear, articulate voice. Before continuing, she cocked her pretty head to one side, a slight twist to her mouth as if she were getting ready to scold.

"I understand you've named another mountain after me."

"In Skull Valley. That's five now," said Port, leaning forward in the saddle, looking directly at her.

"I don't think you should do it. A lot of people take offense."

"Going to sue me?"

"Now that would be stupid," responded Molly. "The free advertising is good for business."

"Then I'll stop doing it," said Port, loosening his horse's reins, allowing the horse to start walking again. Then looking back over his shoulder at Molly, he added, "More business you don't need."

"Why do you name mountains after her?" I asked after we had gone a short distance. A day earlier I would never have dared asking Port such a potentially personal question. But after the trick he had pulled on me, I welcomed the chance to put him on the spot.

"Elder Rockwell, why do you name mountains after Molly Skinner?" I repeated when he didn't respond.

"Can't do what I'd like, so I name mountains instead," said Port as he spurred his bay stallion, galloping ahead to catch up with Hickman and Smith.

Chapter 8

The big pink pig rushed from an open meadow into a patch of mesquite just as we reached Willow Springs, located on the Oregon Trail between Fort Laramie on the North Platte River and Independence Rock on the Sweetwater. Apparently the pig had strayed from a recent wagon train. Two of the men dismounted and ran after it. A minute later there was a loud squeal, then a shout of conquest from one of the men. My mouth watered at the thought of having roast pork for supper.

"Watch where you dip up the drinking water," warned Port. "No telling where that hog has been wallering. Don't want nobody getting the diarrhea from pig water."

Everyone was thirsty, as this was the first fresh water since we left Independence Rock early in the morning. It had been a long and grueling ride. My knees had a fierce ache, both of them.

"Don't forget to salt down the geldings' dongs," barked Port.

Sometimes when a gelding is pushed long and hard without water it is unable to urinate and, if the situation persists, the animal can become ineffective because of the pain and even die. Rubbing salt in the right place causes urination almost immediately. The Utes had a similar cure for the problem, using wild onions instead of salt.

Advance scouts had informed us that General Haney's seven-hundred-wagon supply train and twenty-five hundred teamsters and soldiers were somewhere near the upper or last crossing of the North Platte and headed our way. Shortly we would be meeting the enemy, and the men were anxious to hear Port's battle plan, but so far he had been silent on the matter.

About an hour later the pig was strapped to a huge cottonwood log and was roasting slowly over a blazing fire. We had been on trail rations of hard biscuits, jerky, and dried fruit for nearly ten days. None of us could wait three or four hours for the pig to finish cooking, so as soon as the flames licked the outside of the carcass to a dripping golden brown, we began slicing off hot chunks of dripping flesh. There was no doubt that all of the meat would be gone before the carcass finished cooking.

I was seated on a nearby rock, chewing the last of the flesh from a front leg bone, when Port approached me, his mouth full too. He dropped down on the ground beside me without saying anything, still chewing.

"Like you to forget what I said about that woman as we left Great Salt Lake," he said when most of the pork in his mouth had been swallowed.

"The lady in the red dress, the one you name mountains after?" I asked.

He nodded. "Molly Skinner," he said. "Feel like an old fool, letting a woman like that get under my skin. A woman of the streets who studies law books. Young enough to be my daughter. Probably just playing games with me, trying to stay thick with the law. Still . . ."

"Why don't you ask her to marry you?" I asked. "Maybe she'll repent, change her ways. In Utah, a man like you can always take another wife."

"Got two already. Hardly ever home. Never know when some outlaw might get me instead of me getting him. Don't want another wife. Don't want a woman that'll stir up a lot of talk and bad publicity for Brother Brigham and the Church."

"Then forget her."

"Don't intend making a fool out of myself, not over that woman. Just do me a favor and don't say anything."

I nodded my willingness to respect his wish.

Port reached inside his buckskin shirt and pulled out a round clear bottle nearly half full. He pulled out the cork. I declined when he offered me the first drink.

"Brother Brigham says that someday a man won't be able to drink or chew and still stay in good standing in the Church. Hope that day is a long ways off. A man in my business needs a good snort now and then." He drank deeply from the bottle.

"Storm," he said, after swirling the brown liquid around in his mouth and swallowing it, "do you think a man like me can get into heaven, into the celestial kingdom?"

"I suppose so," I said without thinking.

"You do?"

"Why not?"

"I've killed a lot of men, over fifty."

"You do it in the line of duty. You're a peacemaker."

"That's what everybody says," said Port. He took another drink. "Killed a kid last month, only seventeen years old, hardly a man, certainly not a hardened criminal," continued Port, stretching out on his back, looking up at all the stars that were beginning to appear in the blackening heavens.

"What did he do?" I asked.

"Stole a couple of mules, was headed for Las Vegas."

"Can't have horse stealing," I said. "People's livelihoods depend on their horses and mules. Stealing them is so easy, penalties have got to be tough." I knew the right answers, but they didn't seem to comfort Port, who was taking another drink from the bottle.

"Caught up with him at Nephi. When he saw me coming he started galloping the mules toward Salt Creek." He paused, saying nothing for what seemed a long time, just looking up at the stars.

"What happened?" I asked.

"Shot him out of the saddle. When I got to him he was still alive, blood running out of his mouth. He was crying about how he didn't mean to steal the mules. Didn't even have a gun. Died in my arms. Took him home to his ma and pa over the back of one of the mules. The lady was wailing like a squaw when I left."

"Someone's got to do it," I said, my words feeling shallow and useless.

"That's right," he said. "But don't talk to me about the pearly gates swinging wide for me. I don't believe it."

Port got to his feet, his knees a little wobbly from the drink.

"Do you believe the gospel is true?" I asked, sensing that perhaps the testimony of a killer was somehow different than what the rest of us believed.

"I don't cut my hair," was his only response. It was common knowledge among Mormons that, just before his death in 1844, Joseph Smith had given Porter Rockwell a special promise that the Lord would make Port's arm strong and protect him if he did not cut his hair.

"What are we going to do tomorrow?" I asked, changing the subject.

"Think we'll steal some of Uncle's mules," he said, beginning to laugh. He was still laughing as he wandered away into the darkness.

Chapter 9

It was almost morning when Port finally passed out, falling in the ankle-deep grass on the sloping hillside a short distance from the spring, the empty bottle at his feet.

A short time later most of the men were up and about, preparing their gear and horses for another day's travel, though nobody knew for sure how far we might go because we were already very near the approaching wagons and soldiers.

There was nothing but a pile of bones and ashes where the pig had been roasted the night before. Most of the men were avoiding breakfast, still full from the pork feast.

I was resetting the shoe on the left hind leg of my horse when I became aware of a commotion at the spring. Three men had a long pole, which they were shoving into the spring, laughing as they worked.

Curious, I dropped the horse's hoof and walked over to see what the men were doing. I wasn't very far away when I noticed the pile of pig guts at their feet, the entrails that had been removed from the big pig the night before.

Without my asking, one of the men, Lot Smith, began to explain what they were doing.

"When Uncle's troops get here in a day or two, their drinking water will be polluted with rotten pig guts. Them soldier boys ought to get mighty sick drinking this filth."

With the help of the long pole, the men were pushing the entrails into the depths of the spring, hoping to poison the water as the pig flesh began to decay. Seemed like a great idea to me, an effective harassment technique. If the soldiers became ill they wouldn't be able to travel as fast. On the other hand, it would be too bad if an Oregon- or Utah-bound wagon train, or a band of Indians, became afflicted with the poisoned water.

"Give us a hand, Storm," said Lot Smith, who was holding onto the long pole with both hands, pushing entrails into the hole. I bent over to grab some of the guts, but as I began pulling them apart, the sight of the pig's bladder triggered a strange idea in my mind. I began to chuckle as the idea took shape. Kneeling down and removing my knife from its sheath, I laughed as I carefully cut away the bladder.

"What's so funny?" asked Lot.

"Anyone ever pull a practical joke on old Port?" I asked.

"Not and lived to tell about it," he said. "Port's not a man to fool around with."

"Ever since he got me into the fight with that fellow with the blind wife," I said, looking up at Lot, "I've been looking for a way to even the score."

"What are you going to do?" he asked.

"Come and see," I said, standing up, the empty bladder in my hand. Lot and his companions followed as I began walking toward Port. By the time I reached him, all of the men were gathered around, speculating in whispers what this farmer from American Fork was planning to do to the famous gunfighter.

As a kid I had had a lot of good times playing with bladders on hog butchering days. Pig bladders made fine balls when inflated with air. But I had no intention of playing ball with Porter Rockwell.

As I knelt on the grassy slope above Port's head, I watched his chest rising and falling very slowly, evidence he was still in his drunken stupor. So far so good.

Cautiously I arranged his long gray-brown hair in a sort of knot at the back of his head, then very carefully worked the bladder over his head as if it were one of those rubber bathing caps advertised in the mail-order catalogues.

When finished I stood up to admire my work. The rest of the men still hadn't figured out what was happening.

"He'll think his head's been shaved," I said softly.

Now the men knew what I was up to. When Port woke up and felt the pig bladder he would think his hair was gone. Everyone knew about the promise Joseph Smith had given Port, that he could not be harmed if he did not cut his hair. Here we were about to take on the United States Army, and Port would be waking up thinking his head was shaved and Joseph's promise was no longer in effect.

It was a great practical joke, or so I thought. The only question remaining was how Porter Rockwell would respond.

The anticipation was too great. There was no telling how long it would be before Port came to his senses. One of the men fetched a canteen full of cold water and began pouring it over Port's face.

He finally sat up, sputtering like a wet cat. I was the first to speak.

"They didn't mean to do it," I said apologetically.

He didn't hear me, still shaking off the water.

"They didn't mean to do it," I repeated, louder.

"Do what?" he asked gruffly.

I was beginning to regret what I had done, but it was too late to turn back now.

"They were drunk," I explained. "Otherwise they wouldn't have done it."

"Done what?" he demanded, looking around at the men, probably wondering why everyone had assembled around him.

"You told them to do it." I paused. "Even sharpened the razor yourself."

Nothing more needed to be said. Vigorously Port shook his head. The long strands of hair did not whip in front of his eyes as they should have. He froze, staring blankly into space. Very slowly, his left hand, which had been resting on his thigh, began to move toward his head.

What little color there had been in his face when the cold water brought him to his senses was gone now. He was as pale as death.

And his hand was shaking, very noticeably, as it continued to move toward the side of his head.

I was thinking that this wasn't such a good joke after all. In fact, it was a very bad one. I wanted to tell him it was only a trick, that all his hair was still on his head. But I couldn't. Things had already gone too far. By speaking now, I would only be hurrying up the wrath that was sure to come, and I didn't dare do that. The other men must have felt the same. No one said a word.

It seemed like an eternity before his fingertips finally reached the wet bladder. Port seemed in a death trance as the fingers touched the smooth surface. Then quickly he pulled his hand away.

The second time, the fingers stayed longer, this time pushing against the bladder, which gave way to his touch, the hair padding beneath offering little resistance.

Without warning, Port's trembling white hand turned into a steel claw and ripped the bladder from his head, waves of gray-brown hair falling about his shoulders.

Now Port was looking at the men, one face at a time. His left hand was still at his shoulder, gripping tightly a handful of hair. His right hand moved from his lap to the butt of the pistol on his belt.

Port seemed to be trying to read in the faces who was responsible for putting the bladder on his head. Some of the men returned his stare, but most looked away. Nobody said a word, not even Port. The suspense was unbearable.

Finally he looked at me. That's when he spoke.

"Storm," he said. "Did you put this thing on my head?"

I nodded, without hesitation. There was no percentage in trying to postpone the consequences of my ill-conceived practical joke. The other men were looking at me now.

Suddenly Port was laughing, a strong hearty laugh as the tension seemed to burst from his open mouth. He slapped his thighs with both hands, rolling on his side, laughing harder than ever. I was relieved to see his right hand move away from the gun. All of us were laughing now—more a laughter of relief than humor.

When Port finally got hold of himself, his now rosy cheeks

soaked with tears, he pointed his right forefinger at me, shaking it vigorously.

"Storm," he yelled. "If you ever do anything like that again, I'll kill you. I swear I'll kill you."

The other men laughed louder than ever. But not me. I was wondering if Port really meant what he was saying.

Chapter 10

The flat beside Poison Spider Creek had become a huge tent city, appearing to approach in size Great Salt Lake City, except that nothing was permanent. There were hundreds of tents and wagons in neat rows, thousands of mules and oxen on the nearby hills, dozens of smoky cookfires, and men everywhere, soldiers and teamsters, twenty-five hundred in all—an entire army moving across a vast wilderness to put the Mormons in their place.

It was almost dark as I rode down the hill toward the huge encampment. I could see no sign of sentries or guards anywhere, other than a few herdsmen with the livestock. Apparently General Harney didn't believe there was any danger of confronting Mormons this far away from Great Salt Lake City. He certainly wasn't aware that Porter Rockwell and his men were camped less than five miles away.

Before launching any full-scale harassment of the federal troops, Port wanted to gather some intelligence. That was my assignment as I rode toward the army camp. Port and some of the men were hidden in a draw a short distance behind me. Their plan was to raid the livestock during the night or at first light, as soon as I was through with the spying.

My disguise was that of a discouraged California gold miner heading home to Missouri. I had supposedly followed the southern route through the Utah Territory and had observed some of the preparations the Mormons were making to resist federal troops. It was expected that this item of information would get me an interview with the general himself, or at least with one of his top aides. Of course, my purpose in getting such an interview was to find out as much as I could about the army, its strength, and plans.

I'm not sure why Port selected me to infiltrate the enemy camp, unless it was his way of getting back at me for putting the pig bladder on his head. Maybe Port figured that anyone with enough grit to play a practical joke like that on the territory's most notorious gunfighter would probably have the composure and nerve to be a spy in a U.S. army camp. I was about to find out.

"What's for supper?" I asked as I pulled my horse and packhorse to a halt in front of the nearest cookfire. A big, heavyset man was leaning over the biggest fry pan I had ever seen, at least four feet across, piled high with big chunks of red beef. He was sprinkling salt on the huge pile of meat.

"You a Mormon?" asked the big man, looking me over carefully.

"Nope," I lied, "but I just passed through Mormon country. They's getting ready to put up a real fight when you men get there." I threw my cards on the table right away, wanting to get my meeting with Harney as soon as possible so I could get away from this place. I felt mighty uneasy.

"Good," said the big man. "Hope them Mormons fight like wildcats."

I didn't know what to say. I hadn't anticipated him saying something like that. I watched him as he put down the salt and began stirring the now sizzling meat with a big stick.

"All I hear around here is talk of killing, raping, burning, and looting," he said as he continued to stir the meat.

"Mormons got it coming," I said, hoping my comment would keep him talking. It did.

"Maybe old Brigham and the apostles got it coming. But not all of them other folks, even if they is polygamists," he said.

"All believe the same nonsense doctrine," I said. "Don't know how you can separate them out, the good ones from the rotten ones."

"Passed a bunch of Dutchmen a ways back," the man said, putting down the stick, looking me square in the eye. "Women and kids with them, old people, too. Pushing two-wheeled carts, all the way from Iowa City. Nothing in the carts other than blankets, tents, and food. Came all the way from the old country. Going to Utah to be Mormons. Tough going without horses and oxen."

He paused and I wondered why he was telling me about the handcart company.

"An ox got his foot run over just as we was passing them. Gave it to them and they was mighty grateful, first fresh meat for them in days."

"Why did you do that?"

"Because they needed it more than us," he said. "And because they weren't bad people. Simple, honest, poor folk trying to get to Utah. Uncle has no business sending troops against people like that."

"Then why are you here?" I asked. It was apparent he was not a soldier but a hired cook and teamster.

"Uncle pays me a dollar a day to cook this meat and drive that wagon. If I didn't do it, someone else would. Don't have to like the duty."

He stabbed a big chunk of half-cooked meat with his knife and handed it to me. I thanked him before biting off a mouthful. The meat was a pleasant change after all the greasy pork of the night before. When finished, I asked him if I could leave my horses tied to his wagon while I looked for the general.

"What do you want with old Harney?" he asked.

"Thought he might be interested in the condition of the trail up ahead. Gets pretty rough in places. Might be able to save you men some trouble."

"The stream'll lead you to Harney's tent," said the man. "You can leave your ponies here."

★ ★ ★

I followed the stream as the big man suggested, and it wasn't long until I found Harney's tent. It was easy to spot. Though there were no sentries on the nearby hills, there were two guarding the general's tent, plus a number of officers mingling in the vicinity.

I walked right up to one of the guards and told him I had just passed through Utah from California on my way to Missouri and had some information about the Mormons that might interest the general.

The guard disappeared into the tent, returning a few seconds later with the message that General Harney wanted to see me, but first I had to be checked for weapons. I wasn't carrying a gun, other than the rifle in the scabbard on my saddle. He took my knife, promising to return it after my interview with the general. I was taken to a waiting area, just inside the tent, where it seemed like I waited nearly an hour before the general was ready to see me.

General Harney was a gruff man. He didn't smile, shake my hand, or offer any kind of a greeting. He just began asking questions about who I was, where I came from, and where I was headed.

He looked almost fifty, a thin wiry man with square shoulders, steel-gray eyes, and thinning gray-brown hair, combed straight back.

He asked a lot of questions about California and Missouri, seeming intent on trapping me if I was not familiar with those places as I claimed. Fortunately I had spent sufficient time in both California and Missouri to be able to answer his questions satisfactorily, or so I thought.

"What are the Mormons doing?" he asked.

"Cleaning their guns," I said.

He reached into a box, pulled out a big brown cigar, and bit off one end, taking his time lighting it with a wooden match. Finally he offered me one. He seemed surprised when I declined his offer.

"What else besides cleaning their guns?" he asked.

"Mustering up the militia in every community."

"Nauvoo Legion, they call it. How many men would you guess?"

"I don't know. Maybe five thousand. Brigham's got little towns all over the territory."

"Any talk of coming east over the passes to fight me here?" asked the general.

I had to be careful how I answered that question. On the one hand I didn't want the general to think he had it too easy, that he could just march into the Utah Territory without opposition. But neither did I want him to feel threatened to the point where he would feel a need to call for reinforcements or make more out of the situation than it was with the Eastern news media. Brigham Young wanted the army stalled so it couldn't reach the valley before the passes filled with snow. By keeping the army out until the following spring, maybe a peaceful solution to the problem could be reached.

"All I saw was farmers and tradesmen, simple people preparing to protect their homes and farms from an invading army. They don't want to fight," I told him. "You leave them alone, and I think they'll leave you alone. I don't think they'll come out here to take on the U.S. Army, but if you invade their homeland, I think you'll have hell to pay."

"You really think they'll fight?" asked the general, puffing thoughtfully on his cigar.

"They were driven from Missouri in '38, then from Illinois in '46. They say they'll not be driven again, not without a fight."

"Sounds like the army needs better public relations," said the general.

"Sir?" I asked, not understanding what he was getting at.

"The U.S. Army has no intention of driving those poor people from their homes and farms."

"Why, then, are you going to Utah?" I asked, grateful that now I was the one asking the questions.

"Just to keep the peace. Build a fort to keep the peace and install a new governor."

"What about Brigham?" I asked.

"Now there's a problem. Don't know whether to hang him with or without a trial." He laughed.

I took advantage of an increasingly relaxed situation and asked another question.

"When do you think you'll reach Great Salt Lake City?"

"Week ago I'd have said by the end of September," responded the general. "Now it'll be later. Got new orders to take the cavalry down to Kansas to stop some Indian troubles. Wagons'll have to keep moving so as not to run out of grass. Hope we'll be back and caught up with them by the time they reach Fort Bridger."

All I wanted now was to get out of this place and get back to Port. I had some important information. With the general and the cavalry going to Kansas Territory, the seven-hundred-wagon supply train would be essentially unguarded, at our mercy. I wanted to ask the general how many men were in the cavalry that would be leaving with him, but I decided against pushing my luck. Besides, counting the men as they departed for Kansas would be a simple matter.

"Any more questions I can answer for you, General?" I asked, hoping he would dismiss me.

"Yes, I have another question. What are you wearing under that buckskin shirt?"

"Underwear," I said, after a brief moment of hesitation.

"Let's see," he said. "Take off the shirt."

I didn't move. I knew what he wanted to see—if my underwear carried the sacred markings worn on the underwear of all Mormons who had experienced the endowment ceremony prior to celestial marriage. My underwear carried those markings. What a foolish oversight. I should have taken them off before entering the enemy camp.

"Help this man off with his shirt," said General Harney to the guard who had remained in the room with us.

"That won't be necessary," I said, beginning to unbutton my buckskins, wondering if the general would believe me if I told him I had purchased the underwear in Salt Lake, that in Mormon country they were the only kind available.

"I am curious as to why a general in the U.S. Army is interested in looking at a man's underwear," I said. "Now if I were a woman, that I could understand, but a man, that's strange . . ."

"Shut up and get that shirt off," ordered the general. "Occurred to me you might be a Mormon spy. Just wanted to see if you're wearing those special markings on your long johns that I hear all good Mormons wear. Take the shirt off."

"Come on, General," I said, trying to sound calm while my heart was pounding furiously and the adrenaline was gushing into my veins, almost making me sick to my stomach. "You don't think a Mormon spy would be dumb enough to wear a garment that would so easily give away his identity, do you?"

"If you'll hurry and take that shirt off, we'll find out," said the general. I had stalled too long in taking off the shirt. He was becoming more confident in his suspicion that he had caught a spy. There was no way he would buy the story about me buying the underwear while passing through Salt Lake.

I was wondering if it would be best to let him put me in shackles or make a run for it while still unfettered. Suddenly a guard jerked back the tent flap and shouted, "Injuns! Running off the stock!"

The air filled with the noise of shouting, shooting, and the thunder of stampeding hooves. I guessed the guard was wrong about "Injuns" being the cause of the commotion. For some reason, unknown to me, Port had decided to go ahead with the raid on the livestock before I was finished with my spying.

"Damn," shouted the general as he charged outside.

The remaining guard looked at me, at the departing general, then followed the general outside.

"Get back in there and shackle that man," shouted the general when he discovered the guard's mistake. But by the time the guard reentered the general's office, I had taken advantage of the error and had dived under the back of the tent, crawling into the darkness.

Total confusion reigned. Men were running in every direction, shouting, shooting, and trying to saddle horses. I had no trouble making my way back to the wagon where my horses were tied. The fact that I was running attracted no undue attention. Everyone else was running too.

My horses were gone.

"Pulled away and joined some stampeding mules," said the big man from the other side of the wagon when he saw me. He was occupied trying to hang onto some horses that were rearing and snorting, wanting to join my horses and others that had stampeded off into the night.

"Take one of these," he said. "I'll tell the army it ran off with the others."

He handed me the lead rope to a big sorrel. I leaped upon the animal's back.

"You don't want to leave now, not with all the shooting," cautioned the big man. "Wait till morning and I'll outfit you with enough food to get to Fort Leavenworth. You can sleep under the wagon."

"Thanks," I said as I dug my heels into the horse's ribs, "but I don't think old Harney would take kindly to a Mormon spy spending the night in his camp."

Chapter 11

"Brother Brigham's got troubles of his own back home," said the scout, "with everybody trying to get ready to fight the U.S. Army, and a wagon train full of Mormon-hating Missourians right in the middle of everything . . ."

The man had just ridden in with the latest news from Salt Lake and fresh orders from President Young. In fact, he and I had arrived at the same time, him from the west, me from the east, where I had escaped from the army camp the night before. It was almost midday.

After the raid, Port had moved camp farther away from the army, and it had taken me this long to find them. The new camp looked different from the old one in that there were many more horses and mules. The raid had been successful, with Port and the men ending up with nineteen additional horses and over seventy mules. In addition, a fresh ox was roasting on a spit.

"Do they call themselves the Missouri Wildcats?" asked Port, referring to the wagon train that was causing the trouble. The scout nodded.

"Thought they'd be far out in the western desert by now," said Port. "Surprises me they're still around."

"They didn't go west," said the scout. "Got worried about early snow in the Sierras, this late in the season and all, so they—along with Fancher's party from Arkansas—decided to take the southern route, right through the middle of the Mormon settlements."

Suddenly there was a sick feeling in my stomach and a chill in the back of my neck as I remembered who was traveling with that wagon train. My old enemy Dick Boggs was heading south through American Fork. Certainly by now Boggs knew I was the man who had fought Seth Stevenson, and it would be a simple matter for him to find out I lived in American Fork. And if Boggs knew I was off scouting the U.S. Army, what kind of mischief would he stir up with Caroline and Sarah?

"Did General Harney have a message for Brother Brigham?" asked Port, turning to me, remembering he hadn't yet received my report on the previous night's spying.

"Sure did," I said, loud enough for all the men to hear. "Said his biggest problem was trying to decide whether or not to hold a trial before he strung up old Brigham."

"If you were headed back to the army camp," said Port coldly, "I'd ask you to tell the general that as far as his future is concerned, we've already held trial."

Port drew one of his pistols. "I'd have you tell him I've got a special bullet, all greased up with rancid pig fat, with his name on it."

"Got some good news, too," I said. "Harney's got a burr under his saddle over Uncle ordering him and his cavalry off to Kansas Territory to put down an Indian uprising. Could be gone up to a month."

"You're funning me!" exclaimed Port, a look of total disbelief on his face.

"That's what he told me," I assured him. "Far as I can figure, Harney and maybe a thousand mounted soldiers, though I'm not sure exactly how many, will be headed east right away—leaving those seven hundred wagons practically unguarded."

"I know, I know," exclaimed Port, rubbing his hands together like a hungry fox that had just discovered the hen house door left open.

"What are the new orders from Brother Brigham?" asked Port, turning again to the scout.

"You're going to have to hang onto that greasy bullet for a while," he said. "President Young says no killing, but he wants you to stop 'em. Harass the army so it can't get to Utah this year. But no killing. Them's his orders."

"Only Brother Brigham would ask his most loyal servant to fight a grizzly bear with a willow stick," said Port, his voice heavy with self-pity, "but with all them troops heading off to Kansas, I guess we'll manage."

"Do you think you can manage without me?" I asked.

Port looked surprised. I explained my concern over the news of the Missouri wagon train heading south instead of west, about my old enemy Dick Boggs, who was now going through American Fork, how I was certain he would not pass by without causing some kind of trouble for my wives, who would not anticipate or be prepared for that kind of trouble. I needed to be with them, now. And with Harney heading off to Kansas, Port and his men should have easy pickings without me around.

"If I said no," said Port, eyeing me carefully, "if I ordered you to stay here, would you?"

"No," I said.

"Then why did you ask for permission to go?"

"Seemed like the right thing. Still, I know what I've gotta do. My family needs me now."

"If a man knows what he's got to do, guess he better get on with doing it."

"Thanks," I said.

"This thing with the army could go on all winter," said Port. "After you get things worked out with this Boggs feller and can see your way back, I'd like to have you back."

"Thanks," I said again.

"Besides," said Port, suddenly grinning, "I need you back so I can repay you for putting that pig bladder on my head. Meanest thing anybody's ever done to me. I'll be paying you back in kind, one of these days."

"You already did, last night," I said, surprising him.

"What do you mean?"

"I was in the lion's den, spying on old Harney in his tent, and you came galloping up and drove off my getaway horse, leaving me on foot in the middle of twenty-five hundred enemy soldiers."

"How'd you get the new horse?" he asked.

"When a teamster saw mine driven off by you bandits, he felt sorry for me and gave me one of Uncle's horses."

Port had a good laugh, then asked if on my way back to Salt Lake I would help drive the stolen animals to Fort Supply.

"Yes," continued Port, "got to start moving them animals west because I plan to steal plenty more the next few weeks—oxen too. When Harney gets back, there won't be any animals to pull his wagons. He'll have to pull 'em himself, if he wants to get to Utah this year."

★ ★ ★

Port did launch some daring raids on the U.S. Army supply train after I left. But not all of them turned out like he wanted them to. Like the night when the army reached Pacific Springs at South Pass. Port and five other men galloped right through the middle of the sleeping camp, shouting, screaming, and shooting in the air, driving off every mule and horse in camp.

About three miles down the road, the delighted thieves at the head of the herd stopped the stampeding animals to assess the extent of the thieves' victory, take inventory, and let the stragglers catch up. When the herd, containing more than two thousand mules, came to a halt, Port and his companion who were bringing up the rear didn't really know what was going on, but welcoming the brief rest, dismounted to stretch their legs. For some unknown reason, the men in the front had dismounted too.

That's when Uncle's boys back in the army camp sounded the stable call on their bugles. The long-eared mules heard the bugling, and before Port and his men could get back on their horses, the mules were headed for breakfast back at the army camp. Port and his men were left on foot three miles down the road, their saddle horses having pulled free from the bushes where they were tied, to join the stampeding mules.

Port and his men headed down to hide in the mesquite along the Little Sandy until evening, when they hoped to steal their mounts back.

As they approached the army camp that night, they came across a dozen or so horses already saddled and tethered out to graze.

Accepting their good luck without question, they took the horses and returned to the Mormon camp. Upon arrival, they discovered the new horses they had stolen belonged to a Mormon raiding party, who were now left on foot in enemy territory.

Nevertheless, Port and his men, stealing livestock, burning feed, and destroying wagons, managed to delay the U.S. Army sufficiently so it did not get to Utah in 1857. The U.S. Army was stopped without a single man being killed.

Chapter 12

Caroline was surprised to hear a knock on the door. Sarah and the children never knocked. Even Indians, who came begging for food on occasion, usually called from the front gate. She was surprised one of the dogs hadn't barked, then remembered the boys had gone fishing down to the creek and the dogs had probably followed. Sarah and the girls had gone to town earlier in the wagon and weren't expected back until dark. The baby was sleeping in the crib.

Caroline felt a little uneasy, as if something was wrong, as if there was something to fear. How silly. She shouldn't feel that way just because Dan was off in Wyoming with Porter Rockwell. Dan was the one in danger, not her.

She was standing near the wood stove, stirring a steamy kettle of chokecherry preserves. Pushing the kettle to a cooler part of the stove, she wiped her hands on a moist towel.

"Is anyone home?" asked a distantly familiar voice as the knock sounded again. Caroline had heard that voice before, but she couldn't remember where. It was probably an old friend. Still, she resisted the temptation to just ask the visitor in. She put the towel down, making sure she completely covered a long butcher knife lying on the counter. She felt a little foolish about the uneasy feeling in her stomach that refused to go away.

As Caroline reached for the door latch, she took note of Dan's old .40 caliber Hawken rifle leaning against the jamb on the hinge side of the door. Dan usually kept that gun loaded, but she couldn't remember if it was loaded now.

Swinging the door wide, she was speechless, recognizing Dan's old Missouri enemy, a grinning Dick Boggs. His grease-stained hat was in his hand, a gesture of pretended politeness. The top of his mostly bald head was smooth and white like the belly of a fish.

Boggs's curly red beard was partly gray now, still flecked with specks of dried food—enough to make her wonder if he had washed it since their last meeting nearly nine years earlier. She noticed the chipped and dirty wooden leg stub—apparently the same one installed after losing his foot in Dan's bear trap.

The patch over Boggs's eye was new since she had last seen him. Caroline remembered Dan telling her how the big brown and white dog had grabbed Boggs by the head, penetrating the eye socket and shredding an ear. She assumed the eye patch was a result of the same injury, since there was a mangled ear on the same side.

Boggs's paunch was different too, not as large as before. The past few months on the trail had thinned him down, made him tougher and meaner-looking, if that were possible. There was a pistol on his hip. Beyond him, behind the gate, was a team of mules and a wagon.

★ ★ ★

"Aren't you going to invite an old friend in?" asked Boggs, a hint of mockery in his voice. Caroline didn't play along.

"You're not an old friend," she replied. "Now get off this place, right now." Caroline was surprised at how firm her voice sounded. Inside she was shaking.

"Is Dan around?" hissed Boggs without moving.

"Yes. In the fields," she lied. "You'll be sorry if he finds you here when he returns . . . and that could be any time now."

Boggs didn't appear to be alarmed by her threat.

"Must have an awful fast horse," said Boggs.

"What?"

"Last I saw old Storm, he was heading east to South Pass with Rockwell. Just a few days ago," said Boggs, seemingly delighted at catching her in her lie.

"What do you want?" demanded Caroline.

"First of all, like to git off this stub," he said, stepping forward through the doorway without waiting for her to invite him in. Caroline drew back, giving Boggs the space he needed. He pushed the door shut behind him.

Too late, she decided she should have slammed the door in his face. He seated himself on a stool next to the sleeping baby's crib, resting one of his grimy hands on the crib railing. As she looked at Boggs, Caroline was thinking about the rifle behind the door and the knife under the towel. If Boggs touched the child, she would go for one or the other.

"Storm's kid?" asked Boggs, nodding toward the sleeping infant.

Caroline didn't respond. Her heart was thundering in her chest, her palms were wet, her stomach was queasy. She was ready to defend the baby, with her life, if necessary.

Boggs seemed to sense her alarm, slowly removing his hand from the crib. A fast or sudden movement would have triggered an attack by Caroline.

"What do you want?" demanded Caroline.

"To make you sweat a little," chuckled Boggs.

"You've done that already."

"Guess I have, the way that dress is sticking to your body."

Caroline didn't look down. She decided that when the time arrived for action she would go for the knife.

"Maybe you ought to take it off, make yourself more comfortable," continued Boggs.

Again he sensed Caroline was about to do something and attempted to calm her. "Look," he said, an unfamiliar calmness to his voice, "it's been a long time, those fights between Storm and me. Hate grows stale."

He paused, carefully picking his words, maintaining what seemed to be a thoughtful mood.

"I figure Storm owes me something for this leg, this eye, and this ear. I'm on my way to California. Need supplies. How about helping me out?"

"What do you need?" asked Caroline, a glimmer of hope in her voice. Maybe, just maybe, Boggs could be satisfied with some supplies.

"Flour, bacon, beans, coffee, harness leather, the usual. A little whiskey wouldn't hurt."

Utah was under martial law, and Caroline knew an order had been issued by Daniel H. Wells not to sell supplies to emigrant trains. With the U.S. Army invading Utah, there might not be any crops the following year, and every available bit of food needed to be preserved. Still, she knew the authorities would understand why she had to give supplies to Boggs. Anything to get rid of him.

She turned and pulled a sack of flour out from under the counter, then the remains of a large sack of sugar.

"We don't have any beans," she said. "But after we put this stuff in your wagon I'll get some bacon and harness leather from the barn."

Boggs didn't move. He just sat there, continuing to stare at Caroline.

"Is there anything else?" she asked.

"Gets mighty lonely, a man traveling alone across the plains," he said. He stood up.

Caroline realized she had been foolish thinking Boggs would be satisfied with supplies only. She lunged for the knife, but Boggs was there first.

"Wondered why you kept looking at that towel," he said, backing away, slipping the knife into his belt. Then to her surprise he said, "Get me a cup of water and I'll load these supplies and be on my way." Maybe, Caroline thought, he really was going to leave without harming her or the baby.

She reached for the dipper and filled it with cool spring water from the bucket beneath the counter. Reaching out slowly, she handed it to Boggs.

Sipping slowly from the cup, he backed toward the door, never taking his eyes from her. When his back touched the door, he reached out and poured the rest of the water down the barrel of the old Hawken rifle. Loaded or not, the rifle was now useless.

Boggs started toward Caroline, his wooden stump thumping solidly on the plank floor. She backed up until she felt the warm stove on the back of her legs, then leaned back over the stove as he continued toward her.

Boggs stopped a step or two in front of her. "Better get out of that dress now," he hissed. Caroline didn't really think about what she was doing as she grabbed the big kettle of steaming chokecherry preserves and slid it across the stove top toward Boggs. Her intention was to gather enough momentum to enable her to sling the big pot into Boggs's belly. But he was too far away.

The heavy pot landed on the floor at Boggs's feet, the hot, sticky contents spilling over his black boot and around the wooden stub, which became a helpless support in the sea of slippery jam. Boggs was momentarily off balance, and when he tried to plant the wooden stub on a dry spot of floor, the stub was slippery and useless. He fell to the floor as Caroline lunged for the baby.

She had just picked up the baby and was headed for the door when the click of the cocking hammer on Boggs's pistol brought her to a halt.

"Stop or I'll shoot," ordered Boggs.

Caroline turned, wishing Dan had killed this man years ago.

"Who shall I shoot first, you or the kid?" laughed Boggs.

Suddenly the door burst open. "Injuns!" shouted Sarah's oldest son Pat as he charged into the cabin, almost falling over the fallen Boggs before catching himself.

"Git over by your ma," ordered Boggs. The boy was only eleven, but he understood the danger of the threatening pistol and obeyed.

"Now clean this slop up so I can get up," ordered Boggs, speaking to the boy. "Stay where you are," he said to Caroline.

The boy didn't move.

"Do what he says," said Caroline, beginning to give the boy instructions on how to clean up the jam.

"But Injuns is coming," protested the boy.

"Git to work. Injuns'll keep," said Boggs.

The boy had no sooner begun scooping the jam into an empty pail when a new voice was heard from the doorway.

"Betta put dat gun down, Massah Boggs," ordered a strong, masculine voice—but not an Indian voice.

Boggs twisted around in his jam wallow and looked up into the face of the biggest, blackest Indian he had ever seen, dressed in leggings, breechcloth, and moccasins—bare from the waist up—a broad, muscular man with short, curly black hair.

" 'Member me, Boss? Was yo' big buck, Ike," said the black man.

"Still are," said Boggs, swinging his pistol around and pointing it at the black Indian. "Got the papers in my wagon to prove it. You ran away and are going to pay hell for it."

Caroline was amazed at how fast Boggs could react. One instant he was getting ready to kill her and her baby. The next he was unleashing hate and venom on a former slave he hadn't seen for nearly ten years.

Ike, who was standing in the doorway, turned his head and said something in Indian to his companions mounted on ponies beyond the front gate. Then he turned back to Boggs.

"Tell them to get out of here," ordered Boggs.

"Already tol' 'em what to do," said Ike. "Somedin' happen to me or de missus and dey shoot dem mules, stake you out in de corral. Plenty flies dere. Den skin ol' Boggs, a inch at a time. Take a week. Dem Injuns doan understan' English. Do what I say. Me boss man."

"You're a dumb nigger!" screamed Boggs. "Now tell them Indians to get the . . ."

Ike's foot shot forward, faster than Boggs could react. Before Boggs could pull the trigger, the gun was flying across the room. Young Pat scampered after it, picking it up with both hands and pointing it back at Boggs.

"Shoot 'em, boy," said Ike.

"No!" shouted Caroline. Her intention was not to save Boggs's life but to protect the boy from the memory of having killed a man.

"Git in yo' wagon," ordered Ike.

"Can't get up," whimpered Boggs. "Floor's too slippery for my wooden leg."

Ike picked up the pail Pat had begun scraping the jam into and poured the sticky contents over Boggs's head.

"Crawl," ordered Ike, delivering a swift, firm kick to the belly to help Boggs off to a fast start. Ike's companions were at the door now, helping to hurry Boggs along as he crawled, cursing, to his wagon. They rolled him in the dust several times, a thick coat of dust caking the sticky jam. After returning the knife to Caroline, the Indians threw Boggs into the back of his wagon and whipped his mules into a gallop.

"Where's dat hay you wants cut and hauled?" asked Ike, finally turning to Caroline. That's when she remembered having sent for Ike to help with the hay as Dan had asked her to do. She was glad Ike had arrived when he had.

Chapter 13

Little Plume was tired, and the trail was hot and dusty as she approached her little patch of corn and tobacco in a flat meadow not far from the Corn Creek sloughs, about a hundred miles south of Salt Lake City.

She was in her late twenties, but wrinkles from years of exposure to sun and wind made her look older. Her body was thin, but still strong, and her black eyes were intense and piercing. Her straight black hair hung loosely about her shoulders, which were covered with a deerskin smock. Her feet were bare.

Little Plume was happy. Her man was Ike, war chief of the Gosiutes. Ike was a strange name for an Indian, but so was the color of his skin. He was black, like the horn of a buffalo, and had come from beyond the mountains nine years earlier.

Ike was bigger and stronger than any man Little Plume had ever seen, a great warrior. Almost single-handedly he had stopped the stealing of Gosiute children by the Utes and other tribes. He had obtained horses and taught her people how to use them to hunt buffalo. The people followed Ike. Because of him, their life was better.

Ike had planted the corn and tobacco in the spring and had brought Little Plume and her children from the main camp in the west to begin the harvest. Ike and some other Indians had journeyed on to Utah Valley to help Dan Storm get in a crop of hay.

Little Plume hoped to get most of the corn in before Ike's return so they could leave immediately for the main camp, where preparations had already begun for the fall buffalo hunt. She wasn't afraid of being left behind with her children. All the Indians in the area knew she was Ike's squaw and would not bother her.

In fact, Little Plume felt honored that Ike had brought her with him to harvest the corn and tobacco. He had other wives, four in all, two of whom were younger and prettier than Little Plume. But she was his first wife, the first to bear him a child. Plus he praised her frequently for being industrious and hard-working, someone he could depend on. And he had never beaten her. She was lucky to have his love and protection.

Little Plume carried her youngest child, a fat eleven-month-old male, on her hip. Her twin daughters, age four, were trailing dutifully behind, tired too from a day of harvesting corn and fishing in the sloughs.

Up ahead her eight-year-old son, Wolf Running, stalked quietly through the cedars, a string of fat trout in one hand, bow and arrow in the other. In the hand of an eight-year-old, the bow looked like a toy. But it was more than a toy; it was made of fine cedar and backed with deer sinew. A mature woman would find this bow hard to draw, but from years of daily practice the boy's arms were stronger than they looked. He was a good shot, too, bringing home an increasing number of rabbits and grouse for the family kettle.

Wolf Running was wearing a rabbit skin loincloth and a quiver full of razor-sharp, obsidian-tipped arrows, nothing more.

Even though the afternoon's fishing had been successful, the boy was hoping for a shot at an unwary rabbit before reaching camp. Wolf Running was an alert boy, thin and wiry. He was different from other boys his age in that his skin was blacker and his hair was bushy with curls. But that didn't bother him. He was the son of Ike, the great war chief, and he fully intended to be a great warrior too.

Wolf Running was the first to see the wagon. That didn't bother him. A train of many wagons had passed several days earlier. This one could be a straggler.

What bothered him were the two unhitched mules grazing in his family's corn patch. Apparently the driver of the wagon hadn't noticed the brush wickiup and two picketed ponies beyond the corn patch.

Listening, Wolf Running could hear the grumbling of a man he couldn't see. The man was probably in the draw beyond the wagon where the little stream ran through the meadow. Wolf Running waved to his mother to hurry forward and help evaluate the situation. It wouldn't take long for the mules to do substantial damage to the corn crop.

As soon as Little Plume saw the wagon and mules, she seated the baby on the ground in the shade of a piñon pine, giving Wolf Running strict orders to stay with his sisters and brother, keeping them quiet.

Picking up a dead limb at the foot of the tree, Little Plume forgot how tired she had felt a moment earlier and struck out across the meadow, determined to save the family harvest and get those mules out of the corn.

"Aye-eee," she yelled, hoping to startle the mules and get them moving.

A surprised Dick Boggs stumbled out of the creek bottom, thinking he was being attacked by Indians. He was bare from the waist up, his wide black suspenders and long-sleeved underwear hanging down over his trousers. He had been washing—not a regular habit with him, but necessary to get rid of the dried chokecherry jam and mud that had been attracting an unusual number of flies and wasps.

Boggs slowed to a comfortable saunter when he discovered the attacker was nothing more than a squaw with a stick, headed for his mules to chase them out of her corn.

"Hold it," he roared as he reached the wagon. "Leave them mules be."

★ ★ ★

Little Plume slowed her pace, looking at the man for the first time. She understood enough English to know what he was yelling. She noticed the man had a wooden leg. She was repulsed by the white flabbiness of his chest and belly. Compared to her powerful, muscular Ike, this man was nothing.

She changed directions, deciding to put the man in his place before chasing his mules out of her corn.

"Me Ike's squaw. That Ike's corn. You get mules," she shouted. Wherever she traveled, everyone knew her man. Using his name would get results. It didn't occur to her that a stranger passing through to California might not know of Ike. But that was not the case with this stranger, who had just been kicked in the belly and driven from Dan Storm's house by her man. Boggs grinned at his good fortune.

"You Ike's squaw?" he asked, just to make sure.

"Me Ike's squaw," she responded, thinking this ugly man would now be very cooperative.

"The big black man?"

She nodded.

"At Dan Storm's?" he asked, pointing to the north.

Again, she nodded.

"Got a present for you," grinned Boggs, reaching under the wagon seat.

Little Plume smiled. This white man respected Ike enough to want to give her a present. She was fortunate to be Ike's squaw. She turned and waved for the children to come forward.

As she turned back toward the stranger, the quiet of the little valley was shattered by the report of Boggs's big pistol. Little Plume was knocked backwards in the grass, blood spurting from a little hole in her chest and gushing from a bigger hole in her back. She rolled to her stomach and began to crawl toward her children. She didn't go far, maybe three or four feet, before rolling on her side, her eyes wide and empty in death.

"That'll teach the nigger to mess with me," grumbled Boggs as he placed the pistol back under the seat. That's when he first noticed the wailing of the children.

He turned toward the noise just in time to duck an arrow from Wolf Running's bow. Boggs grabbed the pistol, missing twice before the boy disappeared into the corn patch. The two little girls were standing next to the baby, all three wailing for their mother.

A few seconds later the mules emerged from the corn, charging toward the wagon. The first had one of Wolf Running's arrows in its left side, not far behind the shoulder. As it reached the open ground, the frightened animal reached back and grabbed the shaft in its teeth, breaking it off, then reached again for the remaining portion. Blood was rushing from its nose and mouth as its lungs filled with blood. Finally its knees buckled as it fell to the ground just a short distance from Little Plume's lifeless body. At first the mule tried to get up again, but soon rolled over on its side, resigned to the quickly approaching blackness.

Not bothering to put the mule out of its misery, or even waiting for it to die, Boggs grabbed the halter of the second mule and began hitching it to the wagon. There was no telling who might have heard the shooting. He could waste no time catching up with the wagon train. As he worked, he looked frequently over his shoulder toward the corn patch for any sign of the boy, who might attempt to shoot more arrows at him.

But the boy had left the far side of the corn patch, mounted his pony, and was galloping to the top of a nearby hill where he could look over the clearing at a safe distance and decide what to do next.

When the mule was hitched to the wagon, Boggs did not climb right up. Instead, he looked at the crying children, thoughtfully rubbing his chin.

"Slave girls might bring a good price in California," he mumbled. "Might want to keep them for breeding stock for my own herd."

He hurried to the children, sweeping up the sobbing girls, one under each arm. But the little boy was too young, would be too much trouble. He walked back to the wagon, leaving the baby beside the piñon pine.

Upon reaching the top of the hill, Wolf Running saw Boggs throw his two sisters into the back of the wagon. He assumed the baby was in the wagon too, being too far away to see his little brother in the shade of the tree.

Wolf Running turned his horse northward, digging his heels

into its ribs. Tears were streaming down his cheeks. His mother was dead, his sisters and brother were being kidnapped by a stranger, and he was helpless to do anything about it.

Wolf Running had been to the Storm ranch before. It would take all night and most of the next day to get there, maybe two nights, but he knew he could find the place again. His father, the great Gosiute warrior, was there. Ike would save the children and kill the man with the wooden leg.

At the edge of the clearing Boggs pulled his wagon to a halt. The woman he had just killed probably had friends and relatives. When they found her body, they would see the wagon tracks and want revenge.

He had an idea of what might slow them down. Stopping the wagon beside the dead mule, he reached into a box beneath the seat and retrieved a small brown bottle with a cork in the top. He got down from the wagon. Holding a dirty handkerchief over his nose and mouth, he removed the cork from the bottle and sprinkled fine white powder over the dead mule. Returning the cork to the bottle, he climbed back in the wagon and headed south.

Chapter 14

We had just arrived at the barn with another load of Timothy hay when Wolf Running arrived. He was hanging onto the horse's mane with both hands, humped over, head down, barely able to keep his eyes open. The animal was also weary, streaked with sweat, its head down and ears limp. It was apparent they had come a long way in a very short period of time.

I didn't recognize Wolf Running right off, but Ike did, pulling the boy down into his strong arms. The boy was talking rapidly, in Gosiute, making weak gestures with his hands. Though I couldn't understand the words, I could determine from Ike's alarmed attention that something was very wrong. Even before the boy was finished, Ike's two companions were racing toward the corral where their horses were kept.

"Me leave boy here?" were Ike's first words to me.

As we carried Wolf Running to the house, Ike explained the boy's message, that his mother had been shot by a man with a wooden leg who had taken the little girls and baby away in his wagon. Without saying the name, we both knew the man was Boggs. How he had ever stumbled onto Little Plume and her children we didn't know.

* * *

An hour later we were on the trail. Had it not been for the conflicts between me and Boggs I felt none of this would have happened. I felt partly responsible and intended to see the thing through to the end. The hay could wait; the little girls and baby could not.

Our saddlebags were full of dried beef, corn and apples, and plenty of ammunition. While Ike and I had saddles, the two Indians were riding bareback. They carried bows and arrows, while Ike and I had rifles.

The Indians were quiet, hard men, both thin and wiry, used to hardship on the trail, men who could handle pain and probably fierce fighters. Their names were Yellow Leg and Almost A Dog.

We didn't know how long we would be on the trail or what kind of trouble we would face. While we hoped to catch up with Boggs before he rejoined his wagon train, we figured that was unlikely. From his earlier confrontation with Caroline we knew he and his fellow Missouri Wildcats, as they called themselves, had joined with the Fancher party from Arkansas. All were headed for California. The boy said Boggs was heading south after shooting Little Plume. Now that he had murdered a woman and kidnapped her children, Boggs probably figured he needed the protection of his fellow Missourians.

We traveled in twos, following the wagon ruts, the horses moving at a fast trot. Galloping was smoother, but more tiring for the horses.

With no moon, we were forced to stop when it became too dark to see our way. We camped beside a tiny stream flowing westward from towering Mt. Nebo. After drinking deeply from the cold water, we stuffed ourselves with dried beef and apples, then tried to get some sleep.

But sleep wouldn't come. I suppose Ike was thinking about Little Plume, the bride of his youth, the mother of his children. Probably wondering if she were really dead, or possibly just wounded. And the children—how would Boggs abuse them, hurt them, neglect them?

I don't think it was midnight yet when we abandoned our futile attempt at rest and resumed our journey, leading the horses through the blackness. One of us stumbled occasionally, but even without any moonlight there was sufficient light from the distant stars to enable us to stay on the rutted wagon path. As soon as the stars began to fade in the gray dawn, we mounted the horses again, urging them into a fast trot.

It was midday when we reached Ike's little patch of corn and tobacco. When the little valley first came into view, we spotted grazing horses and smoke from a campfire. My first thought was to check the priming on my rifle, but Ike recognized the grazing horses as belonging to friends of his. We whipped our tired horses into a full gallop the last mile.

As we reined our horses to a halt in front of the brush wickiup, we were greeted by a crying Indian woman. She was carrying a baby in her arms. Ike was the first to dismount, taking the baby from her. It was his baby, the little boy. Wolf Running had been mistaken about Boggs taking the boy. Fortunately for the baby, this woman and her family had come along, heard his cries, and taken him in.

The woman belonged to Bear Head, one of Ike's followers. She pointed over to the little gully where the creek flowed beyond the corn patch, all the time saying things in Gosiute that I could not understand.

She pointed back into the wickiup where someone seemed to be writhing in pain, groaning and coughing. It was Bear Head, too sick to come out.

"Bear Head sick after skinning mule," said Ike.

I dismounted and walked over to the fresh hide rolled in a pile in front of the wickiup. Using a stout stick, I spread it out, flesh side up. It was dirty and bloodstained, but I noticed nothing unusual. There was nothing different about the smell, either. When I turned it over, however, I spotted a patch of hair dusted with white powder. My first thought was to touch the powder with a wet finger to see how it tasted, but I didn't know enough about poison to know if it should be bitter, sweet, or have no taste at all. I figured it was probably cyanide or arsenic, but I decided against any further testing. The Indian had probably inhaled the powder while skinning the mule.

"Boggs might have sprinkled it with poison," I said. "Better check out Bear Head."

The Indian's face was swollen and red. He was delirious with pain, holding his stomach and writhing about. We didn't know what to do for him.

Ike asked Yellow Leg to stay behind and help care for Bear Head. He also asked the woman to continue caring for the baby. Yellow Leg was asked to return to the main camp as soon as Bear Head was well enough to travel, if he were fortunate enough to recover. Ike gave them strict orders not to touch the mule hide or eat any of the meat. We gave them half our food, then resumed our journey after exchanging our spent horses for Bear Head's fresh ones.

Just beyond the corn patch, at the place where the woman had been pointing when we first arrived, Ike dismounted and walked over to the little creek where fresh dirt had been pushed down from the bank, the spot where Bear Head had buried Little Plume.

There had been no attempt to mark the grave for fear unfriendly Indians or white men might dig it up for plunder or to scalp Little Plume.

Ike didn't disturb the grave. He didn't cry, either. Turning to me he said, "To Little Plume, Ike a great warrior. No nigger slave. We get the boss man who kill her."

He leaped upon his horse without the use of a stirrup. The animal needed no coaxing to break into a fast trot, heading south. Almost A Dog and I followed. Boggs's wagon tracks were easy to follow.

Chapter 15

Susannah Stevenson couldn't understand the strange Indian tongue. Still, she loved the two little girls. According to Dick Boggs, their mother had been killed by Indians from another tribe, and he had taken them in to save their lives. Boggs said the same Indians who had killed the girls' mother had also killed his mule. He said he had sprinkled the dead animal with poison just in case the hostile Indians returned to skin or eat it.

It didn't bother Susannah that the children were black and, according to Boggs, the future breeding stock of the California slave population. She couldn't see them anyway. To her they were two four-year-old girls who had lost their mother and needed mothering from someone else.

And Boggs was perfectly willing to let Susannah take in the girls. His only interest in them was keeping them alive until they were old enough to become his breeding stock. Until then, Susannah could save him a lot of bother—as long as she didn't put any ideas in their heads about not wanting to be slaves. But there was no danger of that now. The little girls could neither understand nor speak English.

Ever since Susannah had first volunteered to take care of the girls, they had followed her about more closely than if they were her own. They chattered back and forth to each other in their strange Indian language.

At first they seemed very unhappy, certainly the result of being uprooted from their family and experiencing the death of their mother. When they cried, they usually did it together, Susannah holding them close in her arms. If there was anything they really liked, it was being held by Susannah.

If there was anything they didn't like, it was Dick Boggs. At first Susannah thought the terror she felt in their little bodies when Boggs came around was a result of the rough treatment they had received at his hands before she began caring for them. When he had brought them to Susannah, ragged and dirty, they had had leather collars around their necks. Boggs had used the collars to tie them up at night or when he was away from the wagon. He had tethered them, like dogs.

As time passed and the children's terror of Boggs did not diminish, Susannah began to think that perhaps Boggs had lied, or at least not told the entire story about where the girls had come from and how their mother had died. Perhaps Boggs was at least partly responsible. That would explain the terror the girls had of him.

Susannah had a lot of questions about the girls. Why were they black? Who was their father? If they belonged to an Indian tribe, shouldn't they be returned to that tribe? Perhaps they had relatives who would want to raise them. Wasn't Boggs breaking the law by taking the girls out of the territory? After all, Deseret or Utah was not a slave territory. What was better for the girls—growing up as slaves to white people or living among the savages? Why did none of the other people in the company seem concerned about Boggs taking the girls? Perhaps the fact that every one in the company was from Missouri or Arkansas, both slave states, had something to do with it. Both girls had strong Negro features.

Susannah mourned her blindness. It inhibited her ability to find answers. If only she could see the girls, watch them, seek out other people to talk to, go into nearby towns by herself or talk to strangers. Being blind made it difficult just to stay beside her own wagon. If only she could see, things would be different.

Still, Susannah wanted to care for the girls. Having them around helped her forget the bitterness and emptiness she felt at not having children of her own. They filled a need, and she loved them. She really did.

And the children responded. They trusted this beautiful white woman who couldn't see. Not only did she make sure they were washed, fed, and kept warm—but she tried to comfort them when they cried, and most of all, she held them close when the man with the wooden leg came around, the man who had killed their mother.

The girls responded to Susannah's love, helping where they could—gathering firewood, watching the grazing oxen, helping tend the fire, cleaning up after supper, rolling out the night's bedding.

Susannah's husband, Seth, didn't object to having the girls around. He welcomed the dollar a week Boggs paid Susannah for taking care of them.

Susannah was a beautiful woman, and Seth savored the comments of envy and appreciation from other men in the company. Still, being married to a blind woman while crossing a vast wilderness was a chore. There were so many things she could not do. The dollar a week from Boggs compensated, at least in part, for some of those things.

Chapter 16

Susannah named the little girls Ruth and Lucy. At first she couldn't tell them apart, except for the marks on their necks where Boggs's leather collars had been. Ruth's neck had more bruises and scabs. Susannah, of course, couldn't see the bruises, but she could feel the scabs. Ruth had fought the collar with a lot more intensity than Lucy had.

Gradually Susannah began to notice other differences. Lucy was more affectionate and seemed to crave being held. Lucy talked more, too. She even seemed more helpful when it came to fetching items to help prepare supper. Ruth helped too, but not as eagerly. Her mind was often elsewhere.

Susannah longed to talk with the girls. Even though they were learning words like *food, horse, wagon,* and *gun,* it would be some time before they would know enough English to carry on the kind of conversations Susannah longed for.

But the big difference between the two girls was the way they behaved when Dick Boggs came around. While Lucy scrambled into Susannah's lap, hiding her face against Susannah's breast, Ruth would stand at her side, facing Boggs. When Susannah put her arm around Ruth, she could feel the taut muscles and the trembling, deep inside. A touch to the cheek revealed an uplifted face, looking directly at Boggs.

At first Susannah thought little Ruth was consumed by fear, but touching one of the little clenched fists and the set jaw told Susannah that it was defiance, not fear, that consumed the little girl. A defiance spawned by hate, perhaps. If only the girls could speak English.

Susannah wondered at so much defiance in one so little, so young. How could this little girl become a slave, especially to a man like Boggs? How would he try to break her spirit? How would she fight back? How long before she would succumb to the submissive role demanded of slave girls and women?

It wasn't until the Fancher Company reached the outskirts of the little town of Parowan that Susannah began to wonder if Boggs or anyone else would ever break Ruth's defiant spirit.

It was early afternoon when the wagons halted prematurely because the gates to the town had been closed to the Fancher wagon train. The main road led through town, and with the road now blocked, they would have to break trail around the town.

There was a lot of heated discussion throughout the company. It had been bad enough having the Mormons refuse to sell them badly needed supplies like dairy products, produce, honey, and, most of all, fresh meat. The hunting had been very poor near the Mormon settlements. But now the Mormons were even blocking the road, causing unnecessary delay and hardship. The mood was ugly.

Furthermore, one of the Missouri men in the company had shot an Indian about a week earlier, back near Corn Creek. The company had stopped at what seemed a friendly Indian camp to attempt some trading. When the Missourian asked to see a brave's bow and arrows, the Indian refused. The settler persisted until the Indian expressed his annoyance by jabbing the man in the ribs with one of the arrows. The settler drew his pistol and shot the Indian dead.

Add to that Boggs's bragging about sprinkling poison over the dead mule, and you had a group of settlers constantly looking over their shoulders for hostile Indians. In fact, several braves had been seen on distant ridges, watching the progress of the wagon train. There was an urgency to get out of this country as quickly as possible, and now the road was blocked.

A delegation of five men approached the town in an effort to negotiate safe passage. To their surprise, the Mormon populace was friendlier than at earlier settlements. The bishop, the man in charge, expressed regret that his people could not sell supplies to the settlers. Deseret, as he called the Utah Territory, was at war with the United States. It was therefore forbidden to sell supplies to U.S. citizens, especially since those supplies would be desperately needed by the Mormons when the U.S. Army invaded.

As for the closed gates, the bishop stunned the settlers by telling them a large number of Indians were assembling to attack the wagon train. Their worst fears were suddenly reality. The bishop knew about the Indian who had been shot with the revolver. He also knew about the poisoned mule. News traveled fast, even on the frontier.

The bishop explained that the balance between peace and war with the Indians in this part of the territory was very delicate, especially with the Indians outnumbering the whites four to one. Allowing settlers, who had already alienated the Indians, to enter and enjoy the safety of their town could upset that balance, and the bishop simply could not endanger the lives of the people under his care by allowing the settlers to come into the town.

The bishop promised the settlers that after they passed he would order a beef cow killed in an effort to slow the Indians, who were always hungry for fresh beef. He said the Indians were indeed serious about attacking the settlers, and if the Missourians didn't get out of the country very quickly, they would probably find themselves under attack. He said he regretted not being able to do more for them.

When the five men returned and reported what the bishop had told them, a hush fell over the company. The ugly boisterousness that had existed for weeks, blaming the Mormons for everything that went wrong, suddenly gave way to cold, silent fear. For the first time, the people of the Fancher Company realized they were in deep trouble with nowhere to turn. Some regretted the nasty comments they had made about Brigham Young and other Church leaders when passing through Mormon settlements. Some had second thoughts about the threats they had made that upon arriving in California they would urge Californians to send another army to Utah from that direction.

There was no more talk about Mormon leaders and the order not to sell supplies to settlers. The items of discussion in the camp outside Parowan that night concerned the number of Indians following them. How many guns did they have? When might the Indians attack? How far away was the U.S. Army? Might there be any hope of Mormons helping the settlers fight the savages?

Later that evening while cleaning up after the evening meal, Susannah noticed the girls gathering close about her legs. Someone was coming.

The uneven shuffle of a single boot across the rocky soil told her the approaching person was Dick Boggs. Unusual. He had paid her the weekly tending fee just the day before. He couldn't be coming by for that.

"Going to take one of the girls," said Boggs without any preliminary conversation.

"No," responded Susannah. "You can't do that. They have lost their mother. They need each other."

"Too bad," said Boggs coldly. "But I sold one of them to Luke Jenkins. Got to make delivery."

Susannah knew Luke Jenkins, another of the Missouri Wildcats, a large filthy man with a foul mouth. He didn't have a wife to help care for a little girl.

Susannah noticed the girls clinging closer, especially Lucy, as if they sensed what Boggs was up to. What she didn't see was the leash and collar in Boggs's hand. But the little girls saw it and knew what it was. Without understanding English, they knew why Boggs had come.

"I have come to take my property—half, that is," said Boggs calmly, reaching out and grabbing Lucy by the arm. She began to cry as Boggs pulled her toward him. She was still holding onto Susannah's outstretched hands as Boggs began to fasten the collar.

"Please, Mr. Boggs," pleaded Susannah, "tell Luke I'll take care of the child for him."

"Naw, he wants the girl delivered, and that I aim to do."

"No!" screamed Ruth, surprising Susannah, Boggs, and even Lucy.

"No!" she screamed a second time.

Susannah reached out to touch Ruth, who was standing a little to the side and forward a foot or so. The shoulder was taut, the little muscles much harder than one would expect in a child so small. The child did not respond to the touch. Perhaps she didn't notice it. It was as if she felt no need for the protection of an adult, not even in confronting a strong and cruel man like Dick Boggs.

"No!" she screamed a third time.

"She's mine and I'm going to take her," said Boggs, his voice less gruff than before.

"No!" screamed Ruth, louder this time. But it wasn't the volume of the voice that sent the chills up and down Susannah's spine. There was an intensity in the voice, a force that was more than loudness. Had the girl been whispering, Susannah felt the effect would have been the same. The voice was more than a voice, more like an arm, or an extension of an unseen power, a power that could not be ignored, denied, or swept aside.

Susannah wondered what effect this strange child was having on the hardened Dick Boggs. How would he respond to a challenge from a helpless child? Would he strike her? Would he draw his pistol and shoot her? Susannah had never seen Boggs back down to anyone, not men with guns, not painted Indians. How could this child be so foolish?

Ruth remained still. Boggs was silent for what seemed a long time. Susannah's ears told her that neither Boggs nor the girl had moved since the beginning of the confrontation. She assumed both were looking into each other's eyes.

Boggs was the first to speak and he spoke to Susannah, not Ruth. "I'll tell Luke about your offer. If he wants the little hellcat, he can come and fetch her hisself." He let go of Lucy, turned, and shuffled away.

Lucy flew into Susannah's arms.

As Susannah began to loosen the collar, she wondered if she had experienced a miracle. Who was this little Ruth? How had this child whipped the cruel, strong Dick Boggs?

Chapter 17

The Fancher Company halted a few miles outside Cedar City—the last Mormon settlement of any significant size, the last chance to purchase critically needed supplies. There were several Mormon communities beyond Cedar City, like Pinto and Santa Clara, but there were no stores or trading posts of any size in these tiny outposts. If supplies were going to be obtained before the long trek across the barren desert, they would have to be obtained at Cedar City. The company needed grease for wagon axles; leather for worn-out harnesses and shoes; iron shoes for horses and oxen; powder and lead for guns; coffee, sugar, grain, and dozens of other items. Getting more lead and powder was especially important now that it was known the company was being followed by a growing band of hostile Indians.

Since the stop was temporary, the wagons didn't pull into a circle, but remained strung out along the road, the horses and oxen standing quietly in their harnesses and yokes. The women stayed near their wagons, while the men gathered beside one of the middle wagons to discuss how supplies might be obtained at Cedar City. Some of the older boys were watching the herd of grazing cattle and horses, the animals not hitched to wagons.

The discussion was heated. The men divided into two general groups. Most of the Arkansas men favored the humble approach, a desperate plea from weary travelers whose only goal was to get to

California and leave the Mormons alone. They wanted to show the people in Cedar City how badly they needed supplies by having the women wear their most worn-out shoes and having the children beg for food. Surely the hearts of the Mormons would be touched, causing them to sell some desperately needed supplies.

The other group, those mostly from Missouri, those who called themselves the Wildcats, felt differently. Give the stubborn Mormons one more chance to sell them supplies, they said. If they refused, a band of men would return to Cedar City under cover of darkness and steal the critical supplies.

Dick Boggs offered another alternative.

The gathering was by his wagon, and while the rest of the men were on the ground, Boggs was high on the wagon seat. "I know how we can git all the supplies we wants, clear out the Injuns, and never fire a shot," he said. As the men looked up to hear what he had to say, Boggs spat out a brown wad of tobacco and cleared his throat.

"When we get to town, let's tell them we want to be baptized Mormons."

A roar of disapproval and laughter erupted spontaneously from the group of men. Nobody liked Boggs's idea.

"Think about it," he said calmly. "If we was Mormons there wouldn't be any laws against selling us supplies. We could buy everything we wanted. If we was Mormons the Injuns would also have to back off, we being allies instead of enemies. Being Mormons would change everything. Worth a dip in the horse trough, if you ask me."

"I'd rather fight Injuns than have some damn Mormon praying over me while he dunked me in a ditch," said Seth Stevenson.

"Not me," countered Boggs. "I want to see California without my hair being lifted."

"Me, too," said one of the other men. As absurd and impossible as Boggs's suggestion had seemed at first, some of the men were beginning to give it more serious consideration. Every alternative had to be considered. The situation was desperate.

"How would you get 'em to believe we were sincere?" asked an older Arkansas man.

"Yeah," shouted another. "Mormons is stupid, but not stupid enough to swallow a line like that, not after all the fights and differences of the past few weeks. They'd laugh us out of town."

"Oh, I don't know," said Boggs. "Suppose we tell 'em we went into the woods to pray to God for protection from the Injuns, when suddenly we see'd a light come down from the sky, brighter than the sun, but we looks at it anyway, and there's a man standing in the middle of it, all dressed in white clothes and full of bullet holes . . ."

"Angels don't have bullet holes," objected one of the listeners.

"This one does," said Boggs. "Got 'em at Carthage Jail. His name is Joe Smith, come back from the dead to tell us somethin'."

"What does he tell us?" asked one of the men.

"That the Injuns'll kill us all and we'll burn in hell forever and ever if we don't repent and become baptized Mormons. So we tell the fanatics in Cedar City that's why we want to be baptized. Even promise to send old Brigham a double tithing as soon as we get to California."

"They'll never buy it," said one man.

"I don't know," said another.

"Let's have a vote," said Seth Stevenson.

Charles Fancher presented the three alternatives. Boggs was the only one who voted that they request to be baptized. The rest of the votes were divided between humbly pleading for help and stealing what they needed.

"Let's do 'em both," suggested Seth. "We try the humble pleadings and if that don't work, we'll come back at night and take what we need."

There was a general murmur of agreement.

As the men began returning to their wagons, the quiet of the afternoon was shattered by the report of a rifle. Then another shot, from the direction of the grazing livestock. An Indian tumbled out of a tall cedar tree.

"We got him," shouted two young men standing beneath the tree, smoking rifles in their hands.

"Make a circle," shouted Fancher, anticipating a possible Indian attack. Men raced to their wagons. As whips cracked and men shouted, the wagons lurched forward, filling the air with dust as the circle was formed. Women and children scampered behind crates and boxes. Men checked the priming on their weapons and made sure powder and balls were on hand.

Then silence. Fingers on triggers, eyes on the nearby hillsides. Listening, for any abnormal sound—the snapping of a twig, a loose rock rolling down a ledge, the stomping of an impatient hoof. Nothing.

Maybe the Indian was alone. A scout, perhaps. Cautiously, two men left the circle of wagons and approached the dead Indian. Each took hold of a foot and began dragging him back to the safety of the wagons. He was a large Indian and didn't drag easily across the rough ground.

Once inside the circle, the men dropped the feet. Others gathered around to take a closer look. No one thought to ask the boys why they had shot the Indian. No weapon had fallen out of the tree with him.

The Indian was broad and muscular, with a wide forehead, bushy eyebrows, and large, clear eyes.

"Looks like a Mormon missionary I once heard preach back home," said one of the Arkansas men.

"Parley P. Pratt," said another. "Looks a lot like him, 'cept his eyes is black."

"Sure does," said another, who had also heard the fiery Mormon apostle preach in Arkansas.

"Both look alike, both die the same year. Interesting coincidence," said the first, referring to Pratt's murder the previous April.

"Hector McLean shot him, and if a Mormon preacher ran off with my woman I'd do the same," said the second.

"You men go hide the body," ordered Fancher. "Got to get these wagons rolling."

Seth and another man grabbed the Indian's feet and were dragging him toward the closest patch of sagebrush when Boggs approached them.

"When old Parley there gets to stinking, the Injuns'll find him and be madder than ever," said Boggs.

"Don't aim to bury him," said Seth. "Take too long, and besides, the Injuns would find the fresh dirt and dig him up."

"Take old Parley to my wagon and slip him in the big barrel in the back," said Boggs.

"What?" asked an astonished Seth. "You got to be fooling."

"Just do it," said Boggs.

"Why?"

"Got a big surprise for them folks in Cedar City," answered Boggs as he began shuffling toward his wagon.

Chapter 18

There was a feeling of relief in Cedar City after the Fancher Company moved out of sight. Had the settlers from Arkansas and Missouri been contentious and threatening—as they had been in communities farther north—refusing to sell them supplies would have been easy. But this time the Missourians were begging, pointing to squeaky axles, shoeless horses and oxen, the worn-out shoes of their women and children. Some of their children were even begging for food. Many people were moved to offer help.

Still, Utah Territory was at war and an invading United States Army was at the border. Utah was in a state of martial law, and the strict orders not to sell supplies to outsiders had to be obeyed. No supplies were sold to the Fancher Company as it passed through Cedar City.

"At least sell us some powder and lead so we can protect ourselves from the Indians," pleaded Charles Fancher as his wagons began moving out of town.

"How much powder and lead did you sell us to protect ourselves at Haun's Mill and Carthage?" demanded a nearby Mormon.

⋆ ⋆ ⋆

Just when it looked like the Fancher Company was gone from Mormon country forever, a single wagon that had apparently fallen behind the others pulled up and stopped in the alley behind Allen's Dry Goods Mercantile on Center Street.

Dick Boggs slipped down from the wagon seat and after tying his mules' lead rope to a brass ring on a hitching post, shuffled to the back door, where he knocked softly.

A young man wearing a brown apron opened the door. Politely, Boggs asked to see Brother Allen, proprietor of the store.

The young man disappeared and a moment later an older man, also wearing a brown apron, appeared in the doorway. His face was round and plump, with pink cheeks and a deeply wrinkled forehead. His hair was thick and white, like a lamb's tail. A pair of gold-rimmed bifocals hung low on his nose.

"If you're part of that Arkansas company I can't sell you anything," said the store owner without any preliminary greetings.

"Didn't come to buy," said Boggs.

"Then what can I do for you?"

"Ever hear of Parley Pratt?"

"Apostle of the Lord. Murdered in Arkansas last spring by a man named Hector McLean. You bet I've heard of Parley P. Heard him preach a time or two."

"What happened to the body after McLean shot him?" asked Boggs.

"Some say McLean chopped him up and fed him to the alligators, but nobody seems to know for sure. Body just disappeared."

"I know what happened to it," said Boggs, inching closer to the store owner and talking more softly.

"What?" asked Allen, taking a step back, not sure why Boggs was telling him all this.

"We was passing through when it happened," said Boggs. "Saw the body right in the middle of the road, all shot full of holes, nobody wanting to give it a proper burial because Pratt was a Mormon. Dogs was waitin' on the sides of the road to start chewing on it as soon as we passed by."

Boggs paused, pulling a brown twist of tobacco from his pocket and gnawing off a wad with his yellow teeth.

"Please continue," said Allen.

"I couldn't see just leaving a man to rot in the middle of the road, even if he was a Mormon who stole another man's wife," said

Boggs. "Had a couple of men throw him in the back of my wagon, figuring I'd give him to the first Mormons I met, possibly in the next town."

Boggs looked closely at Allen, who was now listening carefully to every word. Confident the store owner was believing his story, Boggs continued.

"There was no Mormons in the next town, or the next. And it was so warm, the body was beginning to stink . . ."

"Why didn't you bury him?" asked Allen.

"That's just what I was gonna do," said Boggs. "Then I got to thinkin' that old Parley probably had a lot of wives and kids out in Utah who'd like to bury him proper and put flowers on his grave."

"You certainly didn't contemplate bringing a body almost two thousand miles in summer weather. It would rot before you were halfway," said Allen.

"That's why I put him in a big barrel and covered him with a brine of salt, lye, and vinegar," said Boggs.

"You're not serious," said the astonished store owner.

"Got him in the back of this here wagon," boasted Boggs. "Wanna see 'im?"

"But if you brought him all the way to Utah, why didn't you give him to the Church authorities in Salt Lake?" asked the astonished storekeeper, shaking his head to decline the invitation.

"That's what I was gonna do," said Boggs, "but there was so much fighting between us and the Mormons in Salt Lake that I was afraid if I showed 'em Parley they'd think I had somethin' to do with killing him. Figured I'd just dump him off at the next town where things was more peaceable. But it got worse at every town—more fighting, more harsh words between us and the Mormons. Didn't want to get blamed for killing him. Didn't know the Mormons knew Hector McLean was the killer."

"Why are you bringing the body to me?" asked Allen, appearing to believe Boggs's incredible story.

"This is the last Mormon town," said Boggs, a hint of desperation in his voice. "If I don't get rid of him here, I'll have to dump him out in the desert somewhere—and all my troubles to get him home will be wasted."

"What do you want me to do?" asked Allen.

"Just take him off my hands," said Boggs, "and when I'm gone send him to his family. They'll be grateful to you and so will President Young. Maybe he'll send you a letter, a reward, make you bishop, or something like that."

"Let me see the body," said Allen.

"No problem," said Boggs, shuffling toward the wagon.

Both men climbed up into the back of the wagon, where Boggs removed the lid from the big barrel.

Allen stared at the submerged body, while Boggs stared at Allen.

"Looks like Parley P. Pratt, all right," said Allen. "But why is the skin so dark, almost like an Indian?"

"Too much vinegar in the brine" was Boggs's quick reaction. "Put him in a lye brine for a couple of days and his skin will be as white as a baby's."

Allen continued to stare at the body.

"Reach in," said Boggs, "you can feel the bullet holes in his chest."

"No thanks," said Allen, quickly jumping to the ground. Boggs returned the wooden lid to the top of the barrel.

Boggs backed the wagon up to the back door of the store, and with the help of the young clerk, the three men maneuvered the big barrel into the back room of the store.

"What's your name?" asked Allen when the barrel was in its place.

"Boggs, Dick Boggs."

"On behalf of the Church and the Pratt family, I'd like to thank you for this noble effort," he said.

"Glad to do it," said Boggs. "Where do you want me to dump him?"

"What?" asked the astonished Allen.

"That's the only barrel I got," said Boggs. "A poor man like me just can't leave valuable stuff behind. I brung the body two thousand miles. That's enough. I want my barrel back. Need it for water, now we're heading into the desert."

"I'll gladly pay you for the barrel," said Allen.

"You will?" said Boggs, appearing surprised.

"How much would be fair?"

"I don't want any money," said Boggs with pretended pride.

"What would you like?"

* * *

Ten minutes later Boggs's wagon was hurrying down the road to Pinto in an effort to catch up with the Fancher Company. Boggs was laughing out loud. Under his wagon seat was a brand new five-gallon keg of axle grease, a bar of lead, a can of black powder, and a side of bacon wrapped in brown paper.

"Bet that Injun never guessed he'd get buried on Temple Square in Great Salt Lake City," he shouted to his mules.

Chapter 19

Mountain Meadows was a beautiful place, a long green valley straddling the divide at the southern edge of the Great Basin. The fresh waters of a cool spring trickled to the north where the Fancher Company entered the valley. Eight miles farther south another spring bubbled from the ground, running south toward the Colorado River.

Mountain Meadows was a last oasis before the land dropped off into hot, barren desert. On both sides of the divide the grass was lush and thick, watered by numerous seeps. Both sides of the valley were bordered with sage and low brush, spotted with gnarled and scattered junipers on the tops of the low rolling hills. In the draws and washes the scrub oak was already turning red and orange with the first fall frosts.

Mountain Meadows was a welcome sight to the people in the Fancher Company. The last major Mormon town, Cedar City, was thirty-five miles behind. The last Mormon outpost, the stone fort of Santa Clara, with a dozen families, was only twenty miles ahead. From there the company would head into the barren desert, leaving the unfriendly Mormon fanatics and the hostile Indians behind.

The desert, however, with its scarce feed and infrequent watering places, would make for difficult travel. The stock needed several days of rest and grazing at lush Mountain Meadows before venturing into the harsh desert.

The Fancher Company picked an ideal place for the Mountain Meadows camp, just west of the spring that flowed to the south. There was plenty of cold, clean water, with grass up to the cattle's bellies. The brushy hillsides were far enough away to decrease the possibility of a surprise attack by Indians; plus the brush on the hillsides was too sparse to give any kind of security to attacking Indians. The Indians would not dare attack there, or so the Fancher Company thought.

No Indians had been spotted in several days, and most people thought they had given up the chase, probably out of respect for the Missouri riflemen in the company. More and more thoughts were turning to the California paradise beyond the stark desert.

Since the confrontation at Parowan, Boggs had pretty much left Susannah and the little girls alone. Luke Jenkins, however, had been around to inspect his property, but Susannah had been able to convince him the two girls should stay together.

Susannah knew it was time for her to make a major decision concerning the future of the two girls. If she did nothing, it appeared the girls would be California slaves. If she succeeded in returning them to their people, they would become Utah savages. She wasn't sure which, if either, of the two alternatives was better.

She considered other possibilities too. She remembered the Storm family—Caroline, Sarah, and their husband, Dan—whom she had met in Salt Lake after the fight. They seemed to be good people who could give two little girls a decent upbringing. Perhaps she should try to give the girls to a Mormon family.

It also occurred to Susannah that slavery might not be allowed in California, making it possible for her to keep the girls and raise them herself. That she would like. She was growing fonder of them every day as—in spite of her blindness—she increased in her confidence to care for them. These were the children she had always longed for. She didn't care if they were half-black and half-Indian. She only knew what she felt in her heart, that she would do anything to protect and care for these helpless little girls, though she had doubts about how helpless little Ruth was after what the girl had done to Boggs. Still, Ruth was a child needing a mother's care, nurturing, and protection if that unusual spirit within her were to reach its full potential.

Susannah had figured out what to do if she decided to leave the girls behind. She would hide them in some bushes outside Santa Clara, with instructions to enter the town when the wagon train was gone. They would be carrying a handwritten note explaining who they were and where their family could probably be found. But Susannah had doubts. How could she be sure the girls would understand her instructions to go into the settlement? How could she be sure the Mormons who found them would treat them right and try to return them to their families? What would stop Boggs and Jenkins from returning to Santa Clara and claiming the girls after they discovered them missing?

Susannah welcomed the stop at Mountain Meadows; it gave her more time to think over a very difficult decision, more time to spend with the girls before possibly having to give them up. She prayed fervently for God to help her make the right decision. There were so many things, possible consequences, she just couldn't foresee. God would have to guide her.

She knew she would get no help from Seth. Though he put up with the girls, to him they were merely slave girls, the property of Dick Boggs and Luke Jenkins.

Chapter 20

It was Sunday evening but still light when Ike and I reached Cedar City. Almost A Dog was following about half a mile behind. We were pushing our horses hard, determined to catch up with Boggs and the Fancher Company before they headed out into the desert. We knew we were less than two days behind them and had half-expected to catch them at Cedar City, but that was not the case.

It didn't take long to discover that all of the men were gathered at the church, and not for religious services. Seems there had been a number of burglaries the previous night, stores broken into and items missing, the kinds of things the people in the Fancher Company were wanting to buy two days earlier—harness leather, horseshoes and nails, all kinds of nonperishable foodstuffs, powder and lead. Everyone believed men from the Fancher Company were responsible for the burglaries.

The church assembly room was filled with men. Not just Mormons in their Sunday meeting clothes, though they were the majority, but other men in work clothes, some in buckskins.

Behind the podium and addressing the group was Isaac C. Haight, the local Mormon stake president and second in command under William Dame of the Iron Military District. Behind Haight, seated on a wooden chair, was a burly, red-bearded man with a star on his vest, whom I assumed to be the local sheriff.

President Haight was speaking. "The Missourians drove us out to starve. When we pled for mercy, Haun's Mill was our answer, and when we asked for bread they gave us stones.

"We left the confines of civilization and came far into the wilderness where we could worship God according to the dictates of our own consciences without annoyance to our neighbors. We resolved that if they would leave us alone we would never trouble them.

"But the gentiles will not leave us alone. They have followed us and hounded us. They came among us asking us to trade with them, and in the name of humanity to feed them. All of these we have done and now they are sending an army to exterminate us.

"So far as I am concerned I have been driven from my home for the last time. I am prepared to feed to the gentiles the same bread they fed to us. God being my helper I will give my last ounce of strength and if need be my last drop of blood in defense of Zion."

President Haight then turned and looked at the sheriff behind him, as if waiting for the sheriff to say something. The sheriff remained silent, so the president turned and resumed speaking.

"The immediate problem, however, is how to deal with this Fancher Company. As you know, several of our stores were burglarized last night with almost two hundred dollars' worth of goods stolen—the kind of goods needed by the Fancher Company to complete their journey to California.

"The sheriff reports that when he rode out to their camp at Mountain Meadows this morning, the Missourians would not let him look for stolen property, nor would they cooperate in any way. The sheriff wants us to call up the militia to go back out there tomorrow, not only to help him look for stolen property, but to arrest and bring back anyone found to possess such property."

President Haight turned and looked back a second time at the sheriff, who was nodding his agreement to what had been said. The sheriff looked tired and irritable, a result undoubtedly of many hours in the saddle that day.

"What about the trick with the dead Indian?" shouted Tom Allen, the store owner who had taken the dead Indian from Dick

Boggs. "That Boggs needs to be punished for engaging in such a distasteful trick."

"And what about the poisoned mule and springs up by Nephi?" shouted another. "Are we going to let them get away with killing Piedes, our allies against the United States?"

"Most of us here have made some sacred covenants," said Haight, still standing at the podium. "We have vowed to avenge the murders of Joseph and Hyrum at Carthage Jail in Illinois. As you know, some of the Missourians in this company claimed to have been in the mob that stormed Carthage Jail. One of them even claims to have a pistol from which bullets were fired into our beloved Joseph."

He paused, the emotion welling up inside.

"Brethren, our vows are not to be taken lightly."

"Ah-men," said one man loudly—and before he was finished, many others joined in.

"Since the Fancher Company did not cooperate with the sheriff today," began Haight, "it appears our first item of business should be to decide whether or not we are going to do something about this situation or just let this company slip away and go to California—that is, if the Indians will let them.

"All in favor of doing something to handle the situation now, show by the raise of the right hand," said Haight. It appeared every hand in the room went up.

"All opposed, or any favoring letting the company go without any attempt to right the wrongs that have been committed, please raise the right hand," he continued. No hands went up.

"Now that it has been decided to handle the situation, the question remains as to how to do that. Is there any discussion?" he asked.

Suddenly the room became noisy as nearly everyone tried to speak at once.

"Silence!" boomed the voice of President Haight. He waited for the room to become quiet again, then said, "All who wish to speak get in line behind the pulpit. Everyone wishing to speak will get his turn."

Men, perhaps a fourth of those in the room, scrambled for the pulpit.

The first man suggested a list be made of all the charges against the men in the Fancher Company, that the militia go with the sheriff to arrest and bring back to Cedar City those who had charges against them, and that the ones found guilty be sentenced to at least six months in jail.

"If we do that," shouted a man out of turn, "nearly every one of them will be in jail. Then who will have to feed their families?"

Haight ordered this man to get in line if he wished to speak. The next man at the pulpit was in his Sunday best, a young man with neatly trimmed sideburns and beard. Probably a member of a local bishopric, or perhaps a youthful high councilman, he spoke with confidence. "We all agree we're at war with the United States. Right now an army of twenty-five hundred U.S. troops with the biggest supply train in the history of American warfare is marching across Wyoming to invade Utah. We're at war!" Everyone was listening to the dynamic young man, and everyone agreed with what he had said thus far.

"Now, how do you win a war?" he asked. He paused, letting his words sink in, giving every man a chance to think how he would go about winning a war.

"By whipping the enemy!" shouted the young man. There was a roar of approval from the audience. Haight let the young man continue.

"We know Johnston's Army is the enemy. Anybody can see that. But what about these folks in the Fancher Company? Are they the enemy too?" He held out the palm of his hand, commanding silence so he could continue.

"They have insulted us in every conceivable way, calling our women whores, naming their oxen after our leaders, poisoning some of our waterways, killing our Indian friends, even stealing from us right here in Cedar City. They say that when they get to California they will make sure an army is raised there to come against Utah, killing our leaders, and spreading us to the four winds.

"Now let me ask you," he continued, his voice getting louder, his face redder, his fist striking harder at the podium, "whose side are these people on? Are they on our side? Heavens, no. They are on the side of the United States. They are our enemies!

"I say let the war begin here. I say we go out to Mountain Meadows tomorrow, join up with our Indian allies, whip our enemies, and give President Young his first victory in the Utah war!"

The room erupted in loud cheering. When additional attempts were made to speak from the pulpit, the speaker could not be heard. Excited talk of war filled the room. The men would not be silenced.

But the feeling was not unanimous. Several individuals were arguing vigorously against an attack on the Fancher Company, saying it was not a military body. Already on their way to California, they posed no direct threat. And there were women and children in the company. Waging war on women and children was not right.

Ike and I stood near the back door and listened, absorbing the feeling of the place. The excitement was contagious, tempered by the reality of what was happening. A half-hour must have passed before President Haight finally took control of the meeting again.

"Brethren!" he boomed. The noise subsided until there was silence.

"I think what we are contemplating is too momentous and far-reaching to be decided here. I propose we send a messenger to President Young tonight, asking for his advice. James Haslem has volunteered to leave immediately. All who will support me in this please show by raising the right hand."

Most of the hands went up.

Before he could ask for a show of hands by those opposed to his proposition, one of the Indians said, "Injuns no wait for Chief Brigham to send message. Mericats go into desert. Injuns fight now."

Haight reacted quickly. "I also propose that we send for John D. Lee, official farmer to the Piedes, that he be sent to Mountain Meadows to persuade the Indians to postpone their attack until we receive word from President Young. All in favor raise the right hand."

Most of the hands went up again. Jacob Hamblin might have

been a better choice as a peacemaker with the Indians, but Hamblin was still in Salt Lake, following his recent meeting with President Young and numerous Indian chiefs. Rumor had it Hamblin would be slow coming home because he was honeymooning with a new plural wife.

James Haslem marched out of the room, a grim look on his face. He would be in the saddle almost nonstop for the next six or seven days. I didn't envy him. Another man marched out of the room, on his way, I figured, to fetch John D. Lee, who was at Harmony, not more than a few hours away.

Ike and I decided to spend the night at Cedar City, then head for Mountain Meadows the next morning. We still didn't know how we would get his girls away from Boggs.

Chapter 21

After finding a farmer near the edge of town who was willing to turn our horses into his pasture for the night, we made our way to the town's abandoned iron works. The sky was threatening rain, and we welcomed the thought of having a roof over our heads for the night.

Behind one of the support walls Ike and I found a pile of fairly clean straw and made our beds there for the night. We were exhausted after many long days on the trail, so after gulping down some water and eating some jerky, I was soon fast asleep.

The next thing I remember was a big hand over my mouth and someone shaking me very gently. It was Ike, trying to wake me up without me making any noise. Someone else had picked the iron works as a quiet, out-of-the-way place to spend the night. I could hear voices on the other side of the support wall.

Coming to my senses, I quickly recognized one of the voices as that of Isaac C. Haight, the man who had been in control of the meeting just a few hours earlier. My first question was why he would come to the iron works when he had a comfortable home just a few blocks away. It had something to do with the Fancher Company, for sure, something very secret, so secret he didn't want to risk being overheard, not even by a member of his own family.

When the other man said something about coming as quickly as possible from Harmony, I figured he was John D. Lee, farmer to the

Piedes, whom a messenger had been sent to fetch at the conclusion of the meeting.

My first thought was to speak up and let them know their meeting was not as private as they thought. But on second thought, I chose to be silent and listen. Ike and I had come south to rescue two little Indian girls. Haight and Lee were considering more weighty matters concerning a people at war and upcoming secret plans for a possible battle. Maybe by overhearing their conversation Ike and I would obtain information that would aid us in freeing the little girls without interfering in the bigger plans concerning the war—plans we would probably remain ignorant of if we missed this conversation.

Haight was doing most of the talking, rehearsing the activities of the emigrant train while traveling through Utah—its insulting Mormon women, poisoning waters, killing Indians, destroying fences and crops, threatening to help hang Brigham Young and other Church leaders, and promising to send an army from California to help Johnston's Army fight the Mormons.

He explained how members of the Fancher Company had violated the ordinances of Cedar City by stealing goods from stores and using fence rails for firewood, allowing livestock to ruin some local crops. And how when the sheriff went to their camp to arrest the guilty parties, he was turned back at gunpoint.

Haight said Chief Konosh and some of the other local chiefs were following the emigrants with a large band of Indians who wanted to avenge the crimes against their people by attacking the company.

Haight described the public meeting earlier in the day, the meeting Ike and I had attended, plus a secret council meeting that was apparently held after the public meeting. He mentioned James Haslem, who was already on his way to Great Salt Lake City to get the prophet's counsel on the matter.

In the meantime, the council had decided to offer additional provisions, arms, and ammunition to the Indians and encourage them to give the emigrants a brush. If they killed some of them, so much the better. No Mormons were to be involved in the attack.

Haight emphasized that the emigrants were common enemies of the Indians and the Mormons, that they had no written pass allowing them to go through the country. Because Utah was at war with the United States, written passes were required of all non-Mormon, non-Indian travelers in the territory.

When Lee questioned Haight on the wisdom of encouraging the Indians to attack a company of white settlers, Haight assured Lee that all the leaders were in agreement on this matter, especially in light of the future threat posed by the settlers once they reached California and helped raise armies to come against Utah. It was the consensus feeling that the more the emigrants could be weakened and reduced in numbers by Indian attack, the less threat they would pose in California.

Haight instructed Lee to return to Harmony and send his son-in-law and Indian interpreter, Carl Shirts, to the tribes to the south, inviting them to join the other Indians at the meadows. Haight said Nephi Johnson, another interpreter, was also going out to invite local tribes to join in the fight. All the Indians were needed if the plan were to succeed. No whites would be involved.

Haight and Lee discussed the matter most of the night, and it wasn't until the stars were beginning to fade that they finally left.

A short time later we hurried to the pasture where we had left our horses. We had to get to Mountain Meadows and rescue the girls before the Indians attacked. We had one, maybe two days in which to get the job done.

Chapter 22

It was early Monday morning, just starting to get light when Susannah heard the first shot. She sat up in her wagon bed, automatically touching the sleeping girls on either side of her to make sure they were all right. Since taking in the two little girls Seth had been sleeping under the wagon, at least most of the time.

Hearing shooting early in the morning wasn't unusual; perhaps someone was trying to get a deer or rabbit, butcher a beef cow, or just shoot at a target. But this shot was different, louder, sharper, because the gun was pointed toward the wagons instead of away.

Before Susannah could sort out in her sleepy mind why the shot sounded different, there were three more reports, then some shrill yells.

"Injuns!" shouted a male voice from one of the nearby wagons.

Now there were more shots than could be counted, dozens, perhaps hundreds, followed by yelling and screaming everywhere. Fire was being returned from the cover of nearby wagons.

Holding the now crying girls in her arms, Susannah pushed them into a narrow space between a large chest and the inside wagon wall, covering them with her body, waiting, listening.

Though she felt helpless in her blindness, Susannah did not cry out for help. From the many sounds coming to her ears, she knew what was happening. The company was being attacked by Indians, lots of them, some on horseback, some on foot. The men of the company were fighting back, apparently with success. There were times when the fire from the Indians seemed to grow farther away. Susannah knew the men in the company, especially the Missourians and her husband, Seth, were excellent shots.

She heard the report of Seth's rifle from beneath the wagon, then the banging of his ramrod against the wagon box as he shoved another ball into place.

"Seth," she called out, "do you want me to get you more balls or powder?"

"No, stay down," he shouted back. Seth fired several more times. Then she could hear him scrambling out from under the wagon.

"Stay down," he yelled again. "Injuns are gettin' too close on the other side. Goin' over there." Before Susannah could beg him to be careful, he was gone.

She crouched closer to the girls, at the same time reaching into the box of cooking utensils and pulling out a sharp butcher knife. Being blind there was no way she could react if an Indian decided to shoot her, but if someone laid a hand on her or the girls she would be ready to fight.

Susannah wondered if she were more afraid than the women who could see. She didn't think the men were afraid—they were too busy fighting and didn't have time to contemplate the possibilities. But for the women and children huddled in wagon boxes, there was nothing else to do but contemplate the horrible things that might happen. She wondered if the women who could see the painted faces and the bleeding wounds were more afraid than she. They shouldn't be, she thought. At least they could do something about their fears, perhaps dodge arrows and bullets, pick up the gun of a man who had been wounded or killed and shoot back. At least they could run from an approaching enemy. Susannah could do none of these, only hold tightly to the knife and wait for someone to grab her.

Beginning to cry, she repeated the prayer she had said a thousand times before, asking God for the return of her eyesight, a prayer that had never been answered, and she didn't know why.

★ ★ ★

The fighting ended almost as quickly as it had begun, the Indians retreating under the intense and accurate fire of the Missourians. As the dust settled, seven Missouri and Arkansas men were dead and three severely wounded. Some Indians had also been killed, but no one knew for sure how many.

Though the actual attack was over, the Indians continued firing from the safety of distant cover, continuing to kill livestock scattered in the attack. Dead and dying cattle, mules, and horses seemed to be everywhere inside and outside the circle of wagons.

The first item of business following the attack was to push the wagons closer together, making a tighter circle, chaining the wheels together so the circle could not be broken. Susannah and the girls crawled down from the wagon to help push their wagon into place. Susannah called for Seth, and when he did not answer she assumed he was helping somewhere else.

As she pushed against the heavy wheel, she could feel a growing lump in her throat as she fought desperately against wondering if perhaps Seth had been shot or killed. A growing panic to find out was tempered by her keen sense of not wanting to interrupt those occupied in preserving the lives of those around her.

"Seth!" screamed Susannah, unable to hold back any longer. If he was anywhere in the circle of wagons he could answer her without leaving whatever he was doing. Then at least she would know he was alive.

There was no answer.

Chapter 23

It was almost noon when Ike, Almost A Dog, and I reached Mountain Meadows. We were still more than a mile away when we realized there was trouble. We didn't hear any shooting, but we could hear shouting and yelling. And we could see hundreds of Indians moving about, here and there, on foot and on horseback, like hornets in a hornet's nest. Most of the men were painted for battle.

When they spotted us, half a dozen braves galloped out to meet us. While their greeting to me was cool, they were delighted to see Ike, whose reputation as war chief of the Gosiutes had spread far and wide, at least among the Utah tribes.

We were escorted to a large brush wickiup where the chiefs were gathered, arguing furiously with each other, one of them trying to sketch possible attack plans in the dust. On the way to the wickiup we saw several wounded braves and one dead man, his companions wailing his death.

I recognized some of the chiefs. There was Walker's brother Ammon leading a band of Piedes from Beaver, Moquetas, and Big Bill from the Cedar City area, and Konosh from the Sevier River valley. Konosh was the one who had led the successful attack on Captain John Gunnison's survey party in '53. There was a Tonaquint chief from the Santa Clara area whose name I didn't remember, and Chief Toshob leading the lower Virgin and Muddy tribes.

He seemed to be more in charge than anyone else. When he saw Ike he puckered up his mouth until it looked like the rear end of a cat, and howled like a timber wolf, right in our faces.

Apparently Toshob knew one of Ike's wives had been killed by the Missourians and figured Ike would be an eager ally in attacking the wagon train. Ike had a reputation among the Indians as a fearless fighter.

It seemed all the Indians were talking at once, in four or five different languages, as far as I could tell. But most of the actual communication seemed to be taking place in sign language. We soon learned about the unsuccessful attack on the Mericats that morning in which three Indians were killed and five wounded.

The chiefs were gathered now in council to decide what to do next. Some of the chiefs were angry, some enthusiastic, some very disheartened. All were very excited. They seemed totally taken aback by the fact that their force consisting of hundreds of Indians had been turned back by fifty or sixty white men.

After listening to them for a while, three different courses of action seemed to be distilling out of all the talk and sign language. Toshob and those siding with him were arguing for another attack, immediately, before the settlers had a chance to dig in or perhaps send for help. Ammon and those with him were arguing for a long siege, where the enemy would be weakened with time, forcing the Mericats to use up their supplies and ammunition until they were too weak to resist another attack. Included in this plan was a nighttime maneuver to poison the spring just below the circle of wagons. Without good water the enemy would weaken quickly.

Moquetas and Big Bill were arguing that since the settlers were enemies of the Mormons too, the Indians should seek reinforcements from the Mormons. The Mormons had lots of guns and were at war with the United States. Big Bill reminded the chiefs that the big chief of the Mormons and the Indians had recently made a pact to help each other in defending against the American invasion. The Mormons were obligated to help.

When it became apparent the Indians weren't going to reach any quick decisions, Ike and I withdrew from the powwow to discuss what, if anything, we could do to save his little girls.

There was a cookfire not far from the wickiup where a leg of beef was lying on the ground at the edge and partly into the smoldering ashes. We seated ourselves on the ground, slicing off half-cooked pieces of meat, talking as we chewed.

"Me sneak in there tonight," said Ike. "Get girls."

"Too risky," I said. "They'll have a close guard, probably kill you."

"Dey's my little girls," was his simple reply as he continued to chew on the beef.

We continued to eat, me thinking there had to be a better way. Finally I said, "What if I went in there with a white flag, in broad daylight?"

"Too risky," Ike responded, repeating my exact words. "Dey have a close guard, prob'ly kill you.

"Dey's my girls, not yours," Ike reminded me. "If a body gets killed, it be Ike, not Dan."

"But nobody needs to get killed," I said. "I'd guess those people are pretty worried about now, and would welcome a chance to talk with a white man carrying a white flag."

"But why dey give up girls?"

"I'll tell them those girls are one of the reasons they are under attack, that by letting them go, they may soften the hearts of some of their attackers."

"Dat's not true," said Ike. "Lettin' girls go won't make Injuns go 'way."

"If they let your girls go," I asked, "won't you feel more inclined to let these people go?"

Ike nodded.

"Then there's one black Indian whose heart will be softened for sure. Maybe there's more. Those folks just might give up the girls. They have so much to lose. Got to try anything and everything that might help save their skins."

We got to our feet and walked to the edge of the trees to get a better look at the distant circle of wagons. The canvas tops were flapping gently in a light afternoon breeze. The view would have been peaceful if it weren't for the dead horses and cattle scattered around the outside of the circle. The carcasses were already beginning to bloat, and a dozen or so eagles and hawks were circling overhead. By the next day the place would be filled with the stench of rotting flesh. There was no longer any doubt in my mind but what these white people would be eager to talk with a man carrying a white flag.

"When you go?" asked Ike.

"Soon as we tell the chiefs what we're doing, and as soon as I can borrow a white shirt for a flag," I said. We turned and walked toward the wickiup.

Chapter 24

Only when I started walking out across the meadow toward the circle of wagons did I begin to realize the extent of my danger. Not only was there the worry that one of the settlers might think my white flag some kind of trick and decide to put a bullet in me, but also the worry that my actions might be misinterpreted by an Indian, who might shoot me in the back. The Indians were in a state of frustration and confusion after their unsuccessful attack that morning, and if any suspected that because I was white I was doing something to help the Mericats, there was no telling what might happen. Then there was always the chance that Dick Boggs would recognize me and shoot me on sight. As far as I was concerned, for me to be unarmed around Boggs was about as safe as a rabbit in a snake pit. Nevertheless, leaving my rifle behind and waving a piece of white horse blanket on a long stick high over my head, I set out across the meadow.

"Halt," commanded a male voice when I had covered about three-fourths the distance to the wagons. "Who are you? Explain your business."

I told them who I was and that I was coming in peace with a plan that might help save some lives.

"Any tricks and you're dead," returned the voice.

"No tricks," I shouted, resuming my walk toward the wagons.

Chains were removed from two of the wagons and a small

opening was created, just big enough for me to squeeze through. As I entered the circle I was bombarded with questions and hostile accusations; apparently many of the people believed I had participated in the morning attack.

"Who's in charge here?" I demanded, without answering any of the questions. Then I saw him, my old enemy, Dick Boggs, not more than ten feet away.

In ten years he had hardly changed at all except for the patch over his eye and the shredded ear where my dog Port had chewed on him at our last encounter. Boggs was still fat, still filthy, with grease-stained clothing. His red beard was still clotted with old food and stained with brown tobacco juice, which matched the color of his broken teeth.

His sweat-stained hat was pulled low over his brow, making his eyes hard to see, but I could feel his glare, the hatred. Then I noticed his wooden leg and remembered him stepping into my bear trap and being dragged off into the night behind the runaway wagon. Still, I had no sympathy for the man, not after what he had done, then and now—attempting to hurt Caroline, killing Ike's squaw, kidnapping the little girls.

"Quiet," ordered a firm, gruff voice, the same voice that had addressed me in the meadow.

The tall, wiry man with a bushy black mustache introduced himself as Charles Fancher. We shook hands. The rest of the men, including Boggs, stayed close but quiet now, allowing Fancher to do the talking.

"How many Indians are out there?" he asked.

"Hundreds," I said, "from all over the territory, and more are coming."

"Did we get many this morning?"

I told them I had only been in the valley a short time but that it appeared two or three Indians had been killed and a handful wounded.

"We lost seven men this morning," he said very soberly, "and three more are seriously wounded. They'll probably die if we can't get them to a doctor."

"Closest doc is at Cedar City," I said.

"Are they planning another attack?" he asked.

"Some want to right away," I said. "Others want to wait you out, force you to use up supplies and ammo before launching another attack. Don't know which side will get its way."

"Are there Mormons with the Indians?" asked Fancher, catching me by surprise. With all the problems these people had at the Mormon settlements, I could see why they would think that maybe the Mormons were after them too.

"No," I said, "didn't see anything but Indians when I rode through their camp. Think I was the only white man out there."

I told them I had come to Mountain Meadows with Ike, war chief of the Gosiutes, to retrieve his two little girls.

"We don't have any Indian children here," said Fancher.

"Their father is a former slave, a black man," I explained. "The little girls would probably look more Negro than Indian."

"Boggs!" yelled Fancher. "Come here." A grumbling Boggs pushed forward through the crowd.

"He's the one who stole 'em," I said, pointing at Boggs.

"Just a couple of homeless orphans," shrugged Boggs. "Would have starved. I saved their lives. Picked 'em up after their old lady went to the happy hunting grounds."

"After you shot her," I said coldly.

"Is that true?" Fancher asked Boggs.

"Storm here don't know what he's talkin' about," said Boggs. Fancher turned to me for an explanation.

"The girls' older brother saw him shoot their mother and carry off the girls. The boy rode to my place to find his father. The boy had no reason to lie about that. Boggs did it, all right."

"The grimy squaw pulled a knife on me, had to shoot her in self-defense," said Boggs, finally admitting to the killing.

'The girls are here," said Fancher. "They've been well taken care of, not harmed in any way."

"Can I take them back with me?" I asked.

"Will the Indians withdraw if I give you the girls?" asked Fancher.

"You know I can't guarantee that," I said.

"Then why should I turn them over to you?" he asked.

"So I can return them to their father."

"Then knowing his girls are safely out of the way," said Fancher, "he'll be free to join his savage friends in attacking us."

"No," I said. "He'll take his girls and go, maybe take some others with him."

"Hope you don't believe that nonsense," interrupted Boggs.

"Shut up," ordered Fancher. "Seems like keeping the girls may be a chip on our side of the table. I don't imagine Indians like shooting up their own children. Keeping the girls here may discourage the Indians from attacking again."

"Yeah," said Boggs. "Tell yer Injun pals next time they come at us, I'll hold one of them little girls up by the heels and slit her throat."

"Shut up!" ordered Fancher, louder than before.

"Look," I said, realizing my chances of getting the girls were rapidly evaporating. "You folks don't realize the trouble you're in. There are hundreds of mad Indians out there, just aching to tear you apart, scalp every one of you. They mean business."

"We found that out this morning," said Fancher, "but I still don't see where giving up two hostages will make a difference."

"How would you people feel," I began, loud enough for all the men to hear, "if an Indian killed one of your women and ran off with two of her kids? Would you go after him? Would you want to kill him? Sure you would, and that's how those Indians out there feel. Boggs killed one of their women and ran off with her kids. They want those kids back, and they want Boggs."

They were finally listening to me, so I decided to push my luck.

"Let me take the girls back with me, and Boggs too," I said.

"You're crazy!" shouted Boggs.

"Shut up!" ordered Fancher a third time. Turning to me he asked, "Do you really think that would back the Indians off?"

"I don't know about that," I said honestly. "But I am pretty sure they would be so busy with Boggs for a day or two that they probably wouldn't get around to launching another attack. Maybe by then they'd cool off and peace could be made. Perhaps by then the Mormons could get their militia over here to put an end to this thing."

"What would they do to Boggs?" asked Fancher. Everyone was waiting eagerly for my answer, even Boggs.

"Probably start off by castrating him," I said. "Then burn his eyes out, then begin skinning him, very slowly, using lots of salt to keep the flies away. Not an Indian in the bunch would miss that show. Good chance for you folks to slip away, at least send some men out for help. Give me the girls and Boggs."

Suddenly order was gone. Everyone seemed to be talking at once, arguing for and against giving up Boggs.

★ ★ ★

It was Fancher who finally established order, commanding two of the men to escort me to the far side of the circle, and two more to escort Boggs to his wagon. The rest remained with Fancher to help determine the fate of their traveling companion, Dick Boggs.

While waiting for them to make a decision, I spotted the two little girls. They were sitting on the ground, their backs against a wagon wheel. Beside them was a pretty young woman who had a very familiar look. Yes, the blind woman was Susannah Stevenson, whose husband had fought me in the streets of Salt Lake. The girls looked content and happy, considering the circumstances.

"Can I see the children?" I asked the two men who were guarding me. They said I couldn't, that the children couldn't speak English anyway. I persisted, but they wouldn't give in.

Finally Fancher signaled for me and Boggs to return to the main group.

"Boggs may have killed the mother," he said, "but killing an Indian isn't the same as killing a real person. Can't give up a man to die for something like that. Civilized people have to stick together against the savages."

"What about the girls?" I asked.

"Tell the Indians that if they'll let us go, we'll leave the girls unharmed at Las Vegas. They can get them there. Tell them if they attack us again, the little girls will be in very great danger. You are free to go."

"Is that all?" I asked. "Maybe we should talk some more."

"There's nothing more to say, Mr. Storm, but if you are a Christian man, you will do everything in your power to talk peace to those savages, and go to Cedar City and ask the Mormons to help us."

"I'll do what I can," I said. Thinking maybe I shouldn't have been so specific as to how the Indians would treat Boggs, I picked up the white flag and started back to the Indian camp.

Chapter 25

Upon reaching the wickiup I realized something had happened while I was gone. Only Ike was waiting to greet me. The rest of the Indians had departed.

I told Ike what had happened, about Fancher's refusal to give up the girls, and how he had refused to turn Boggs over to me too. I told Ike I had seen the girls, that they appeared to have been well cared for. Somewhat hesitatingly I told him about the warning of probable harm coming to the girls if another attack was attempted. Then I asked him where all the Indians were.

★ ★ ★

He said some white men had arrived with a wagonload of supplies for the Indians. They had gone to the wagon to divide things up.

As Ike and I walked through the trees toward the road where the Indians were gathered around the wagon, I asked him if he had any ideas on how we might get the girls out.

"If dey leave da girls in Las Vegas, we get 'em dere."

"If we can get the Indians to let the wagons go."

I was glad Ike had given up on the idea of trying to sneak into the circle of wagons to rescue the girls. I was sure such an attempt would be suicide, and it appeared Ike now agreed with me on that point. I knew he was not afraid to do whatever it took to save his girls, but in attempting to get into the highly fortified circle of wagons he would not only be risking his own life, but possibly the lives of the girls as well.

"Will they leave the girls at Las Vegas as they promised?" he asked.

"I don't know," I said. "Boggs would be against it, but I don't know how strong Fancher is, or if he will keep his word. I guess we'll have to wait and see, assuming the company can get away from here, and I'm not sure how they are going to accomplish that."

About a hundred Indians were gathered around the supply wagon, eagerly receiving powder, balls, guns, and various food supplies including beans, flour, bacon, and apples.

I recognized the white man on top of the wagon, dispersing most of the supplies as the young man with the neatly trimmed beard who had given the fiery sermon in Cedar City, calling for the Saints to give President Young his first victory in the Utah War.

"And there's plenty more where this came from," I heard him say as the last of the supplies disappeared into the hands of the eager Indians.

The mood of the Indians changed quickly. They were not out of supplies or low on ammunition before the wagon arrived. Still, there was something about the arrival of the supply wagon that unified the Indians and got them all in the mood for another attack on the Fancher Company.

It was spontaneous, without any visible direction. Once the supplies were dispersed, Toshob and the chiefs began in earnest to plan their next attack. The rest of the Indians busied themselves applying new war paint, sharpening arrow and spear tips, checking ammunition and firearms, even praying and dancing in small groups, getting up their courage for battle.

I'm still not sure how it all came about, except maybe after all the talk about how the Mormons and Indians had to stick together against the Americans, this wagonload of supplies was the first concrete sign that the Mormons were really serious about having a battle alliance with their red brothers. This outward sign of support from the Mormons was just what the Indians needed to turn their indecision to commitment to accomplish a great victory.

Ike and I were the only dissenters now, and Ike didn't wait long to let his feelings be known. He waded right into the middle of the chiefs, who were sketching an elaborate battle plan in the dirt. After messing up their plan with his feet to get their attention, Ike told them they could not attack until he got his little girls out.

They tried to reassure Ike that the braves would not shoot Indian children, only white people. But Ike had been in enough battles to know that no one in the circle of wagons would be safe once the shooting started.

The chiefs told Ike he should ride with them and avenge the death of his wife. Ike shook his head, insisting that first he must save his girls.

Finally the chiefs became angry with Ike and ordered him to leave. Reluctantly, he obeyed.

After discussing the situation we decided to get on our horses and ride through the Indian ranks, urging them to be on the look-out for the two little girls and to be careful where they shot their bullets and arrows. We didn't know if our urgings would do any good, but we had to try.

Then we headed for the road where the wagon had been unloaded. Our intent was to position ourselves on the hill above the road, where we could have a good view of the battle as it developed and at the same time be in position to respond quickly should a situation present itself for riding in to rescue the girls.

When we reached the road the wagon was still there, but turned around, the team facing Cedar City. The bearded young man was holding the reins. Another white man was seated beside him, and two more nearby were on horseback.

"Thought you men would be on your way out of here by now," I said as we crossed the road.

"Not on your life," said the young man with the beard. "Been waiting too long to see the Missourians get the short end of a fight. Wouldn't miss this for anything."

"Going in with the Indians?" I asked.

"Nope," he responded. "That'd be against orders, but no orders against just watching."

"Lots of women and kids in that circle of wagons," I said, irritated by the man's cavalier attitude. I didn't like the sound of his voice, like he was all excited about getting to watch a dog or rooster fight.

"Lots of women and kids at Haun's Mill," he said, suddenly getting very serious. "My father was killed at Haun's Mill. I was only seven. Been waiting twenty years to see them Missourians get some of their own medicine. Hope the women and children can be spared."

Ike and I rode on to the top of the hill and turned to face the circle of wagons below. It was a quiet scene, the canvas flapping gently in the afternoon breeze, cattle and horses grazing both in and outside the circle, the smoke of two or three cookfires dancing upward through the warm air, eventually disappearing against a blue sky. If it weren't for the dead cattle and horses scattered about the meadow, it would have been hard to believe that another battle was about to take place.

Chapter 26

The Indians' plan of attack was simple. The main group of mounted warriors was to begin the attack from the bottom of the meadow, from the north. Hopefully, the assault would be sufficiently strong to draw the defenders to the north side of the wagon circle. As soon as that was accomplished, as determined by one of the chiefs watching with a glass from the top of a high hill, a signal would be given for the second group to attack from the south, forcing a good number of Missourians to abandon their newfound positions on the north to defend the south side. As the Missourians were running back and forth, some of the Indians would hopefully create a break in the circle to allow mounted warriors inside. As soon as that was accomplished, the battle would be over quickly, or so they thought.

Some of the Indians were carrying ropes, which they hoped would be useful in pulling wagons apart to make a break in the circle. Others were carrying burning torches to be thrown onto the canvas-topped wagons. The circle of wagons was about fifty yards from the spring, so it was hoped that in the event the Indians failed to overcome the whites, at least the fires would force the Mericats to use up their precious water supplies prematurely.

But plans don't always work the way they are supposed to, even with the Indians outnumbering the whites five, or six to one. As soon as the first group of Indians began their attack from the north, they began falling from their horses. The Missourians, resting their Kentucky long rifles on oak wagon spokes and mounds of dirt, just didn't miss very often, even at two hundred yards. The Missourians were excellent marksmen, and with their lives on the line, they were making sure every shot counted.

The Indian attack began to falter before it had hardly begun; groups of angry braves gathered around their wounded companions and helped them back to the safety of the trees.

In frustration, the chief on the hill who was watching the attack in his glass waved for the Indians to the south to launch their attack, even though the defenders on the south side of the circle had not yet been drawn from their positions.

Again the fire from the Kentucky long rifles was accurate and deadly; Indians began to fall from their horses as soon as they came in sight of the wagons. On the other hand, the Indian return fire from the backs of galloping ponies was wild and random, doing little harm to the Mericats. Several brave warriors, however, did get close enough to toss burning torches onto some of the wagons. The fires were quickly doused with buckets of water.

Twenty minutes after the first shot was fired, the Indians regrouped at the north end of the meadow to assess the damages. Two more Indians had been killed and about a dozen wounded. Those not caring for the dead or wounded, still mounted on their ponies, were arguing with each other and their leaders, casting blame in every direction.

Suddenly all of the Indians in the gathering, about a hundred of them, began galloping toward the road, toward the supply wagon from Cedar City and the four Mormons who had been watching the battle. Ike and I hurried down the hill from the other direction, thinking the Indians might need to be stopped from harming their allies.

When we arrived at the wagon it was surrounded by angry Indians, shouting threats and pointing weapons at the frightened white men. Some of the warriors seemed determined to have white man's blood regardless of where it came from.

Toshob brought order to the situation. Mounted on a big gray gelding, he fired several shots into the air, demanding silence so he could speak. The silence was finally granted, as much as could be expected with excited horses milling about.

Toshob rode up beside the wagon and spoke directly to the young man with the beard, the one who told me his father had been killed at Haun's Mill. Toshob spoke loud enough, not only for the white men to hear him, but also for all the Indians too, and I think most of them understood enough English to get an idea of what he was saying.

In fairly good English Toshob told the four Mormons to get themselves back to Cedar City and tell their leaders that Toshob and the other Indians at the meadows expected a reinforcement of Mormon troops to join them by noon the next day. The Indians and Mormons were both at war with the United States, and it wasn't right that the Mormons sat back in their safe, comfortable homes while the Indians did all the fighting and dying.

Then Toshob surprised everyone, including the Indians, with an ultimatum. He said that if the Mormons didn't come to help, he would consider the alliance between the Mormons and Indians broken and would lead his braves against the Mormons as well as the Mericats. The Indians outnumbered the whites four to one in southern Utah, and the white communities were scattered and poorly fortified. Everyone knew the Mormons would be in big trouble if the Indians turned against them.

It had been a long time since an Indian had been so openly defiant of the Mormons. Still, Toshob's comments were well-received by the Indians, and some of the other chiefs acknowledged their support of Toshob's stand.

When Toshob finished and he was sure the Mormons had understood his message, the young man with the beard and his three companions were sent galloping down the road toward Cedar City.

Ike and I looked at each other, neither of us speaking. Both of us were wondering what this would lead to. Would the Mormons really come and help the Indians? If they didn't, would the Indians attack the Mormon settlements? What would happen to the Fancher Company and Ike's little girls?

We looked back in the direction of the wagons. The sun was down, but the evening was not too dark to prevent us from seeing four or five men with buckets, running toward the spring to replenish their water supply. Water would not be a problem for the Fancher Company. Under cover of darkness, getting water from the spring would be easy and fairly safe.

Ike and I set up camp between two cedar trees on the side of the hill where we had been watching the battle. Sleep didn't come easily, as I wondered what Tuesday would bring. I figured the Indians and the people in the Fancher Company, and even the Mormon leaders in Cedar City, weren't sleeping very well either.

Chapter 27

At first light Ike and I could see two or three gray forms retreating from the spring to the circle of wagons. It appeared the Fancher Company had the day's supply of water stored up, plus some extra in case the Indians fired more flaming arrows into their wagons.

Directly below us, the Indian camp was still quiet. There was not even the smoke from a cookfire yet.

"How far dis Hamblin's cabin?" asked Ike.

He was referring to Jacob Hamblin's ranch, which was supposed to be a little ways farther up the valley.

"Shouldn't be more than a couple of miles beyond the wagons," I said, "but Hamblin's off to Salt Lake."

"Probably some kids or Injuns around. I be going up dere," he said, picking up his saddle and bridle and walking over to where his horse was tethered.

"What you got in mind?" I asked.

He didn't respond until he had thrown the blanket and saddle across the animal's back. Then he asked, "You got any money?"

"A ten-dollar gold piece," I said.

He led his horse over to me, took the coin, and slipped it in his pocket.

"Doan think the Mormons'll have an army here today," he said. "Injuns won't be in a hurry to attack again neither."

I nodded my agreement to both his statements. I knew the last thing in the world the Mormons wanted to do was turn the Indians against them. On the other hand, I didn't see them sending an army up to join the Indians based on a single threat. They'd probably want to talk about it for a while before they made that big decision.

"What's on your mind?" I asked.

"If nothin' happen today, maybe get girls out in da mornin'," he said as he swung into the saddle without using the stirrup. Ike turned the horse uphill and began galloping to the top of the ridge that would take him south past the wagons to Hamblin's ranch.

★ ★ ★

During the course of the morning, several new groups of Indians arrived, a total of about thirty new warriors. But there was little enthusiasm for a renewed attack. The Missourians were too firmly entrenched and too accurate with the Kentucky long rifles. There seemed to be no way to successfully overcome the Fancher Company without giving up a lot of lives, and the Indians weren't willing to do that.

With the wagons close to the spring, enabling the white men to sneak down to the water's edge under cover of darkness to fill buckets, the wagon fortress could be maintained for months. None of the Indians wanted to maintain a siege that long. The only reasonable alternative seemed to be the one Toshob demanded of the white men the previous evening—to get help from the Mormons—though no one seemed to know how additional Mormon troops would make an attack less risky.

It was about noon when word spread through the camp that the Mormon reinforcements were coming. A few minutes later six white men rode into the camp, a group hardly numerous enough to be called reinforcements.

Leading the group was John D. Lee, one of the first colonizers of southern Utah, Brigham Young's adopted son, the man who had met secretly with Isaac Haight in Cedar City the night Ike and I had slept in the old iron works. The only other one in the group I recognized was the young man with the neatly trimmed beard, the one who had been driving the wagon the day before.

Lee was a formidable-looking man, his face strong with wide

cheekbones angling down to a strong mouth. His eyes were clear and intense, under a firm, straight brow. Both his eyes and mouth were turned down at the corners, giving the impression that here was a man who meant business, who got things done. Although in his mid-forties, he had a full head of hair with a natural waviness and no wrinkles on his forehead. He didn't appear to be a man inclined to worry about things, but rather a man who when confronted with a problem merely rolled up his sleeves and worked his way out of it.

John D. Lee's exploits were well known among the Mormons. When the Saints were driven from Nauvoo in the spring of 1846, critically short of provisions because they had been mostly unable to sell their homes and farms, it was John D. Lee who performed what many considered a miracle near Grand River, Iowa Territory.

As purchasing agent for the ill-equipped Mormon companies pushing across Iowa, Lee entered a small community called Miller's to trade some horses and harnesses for oxen and cows. He was leading seventeen empty wagons when he entered the town. After the stock was turned out to graze, the owner of the store, a Mr. Clancy, invited Lee home with him for dinner.

Upon entering the home, Lee met Clancy's partner, an Irishman by the name of Patrick Dorsey, who was very ill. Dorsey had been tormented with pain in his eyes, insomuch that he had not been able to sleep day or night, and he was losing his eyesight.

Lee found out Dorsey was a Catholic, Lee's religion before joining the Mormons, then asked the sick man if he wanted a blessing.

Dorsey asked Lee if he was a minister, to which the Mormon replied he was. But he did not mention which church, afraid the word *Mormon* would cause the man to change his mind, since there was so much anti-Mormon sentiment in Iowa at the time.

Lee laid his hands on the man's head, asking the Father in the name of the Son and by virtue of the holy priesthood to stay his sufferings and heal him.

The pain left the man instantly. Dorsey got up from his bed, put on his hat, and walked with Lee to Miller's house, where everyone was astonished to see the man without pain. They asked Dorsey what had happened.

"I was in distress," he answered. "A stranger laid hands on my head and prayed and made me whole, but who he is or whence he came, I know not. But this I know, that I was almost blind and now I see. I was sick, but am well."

This incident created much excitement in the settlement, and Lee was asked to preach the next evening, which he did. A collection was made and Lee was given five dollars, plus the people agreed to fill one of his wagons with provisions.

Lee was asked to preach again the following night, and though he said he was not much in the mood, he spoke for an hour and a half, this time receiving ten dollars and an offer to fill another of his wagons with flour, bacon, and potatoes.

The people in this little community were so pleased with Lee's preaching that they tried to talk him into settling there, taking up a farm, preaching and starting up a church. They promised him their full support, if he would stay with them. He told them he couldn't, that he was bound for the Rocky Mountains.

Lee stayed a week at Miller's, and when he finally returned to Brigham Young and the main Mormon camp at Grand River, he was leading his seventeen wagons plus three more, fully loaded with bacon, flour, meal, soap, powder, lead, blankets, thirty rifles, knives, tobacco, calico, spades, hoes, plows, harrows, and twelve feather beds. Behind the wagons were twelve new yokes of oxen and twenty-five cows. For all this, Lee had given the people at Miller's deeds to Nauvoo real estate, valued at twenty-five cents on the dollar, real estate the Mormons had been unable to sell in their hurry to leave Nauvoo. Some of the people from Miller's had already left for Nauvoo to take possession of their new property.

President Young was so pleased with Lee's performance that the following winter, when someone was needed to go through hostile Indian country all the way to Santa Fe to receive and bring back the wages of the five hundred Mormon Battalion volunteers, Lee was given the assignment. In spite of bad weather, ornery mules, dishonest white men, and hostile Indians, Lee brought the gold safely home to Winter Quarters.

When the first companies of Mormon settlers crossed the

Missouri River the following summer, heading for the Rocky Mountains, Lee was left behind at what some called Summer Quarters, to grow crops for the Mormons still there and still coming from the East. He was successful in this assignment, too, producing a bumper harvest.

Upon arriving in the Salt Lake Valley a year later, Lee began to establish himself in the Salt Lake area, only to be ordered a short time later to take his families and settle southern Utah. This he did in a grand manner.

Lee was a man with a reputation for prospering, no matter where he went. In 1849 when thousands were rushing to the California gold fields, Lee headed east from Salt Lake City on what he called a picking up expedition. In their hurry to get to California the travelers had discarded a fortune in goods along the trail. Eight days after leaving Salt Lake, Lee turned his empty wagon around, and with the help of his wife Rachel, began loading the wagon with kegs of powder, new stoves, lead, cooking utensils, nails, tools, bacon, sugar, clothing, trunks, boot legs, axes, harnesses, and numerous other items. Later he said this one journey earned him the equivalent of two years' wages and was the foundation of what he accumulated later.

At the time of the Mountain Meadows incident, Lee had about a dozen wives scattered about southern Utah on farms and other properties he owned.

I had heard a lot about John D. Lee over the years, but the first time I met him face-to-face and shook his hand was on the Tuesday afternoon when he rode into the Indian camp at Mountain Meadows.

Toshob and the rest of the Indians weren't very happy when Lee told them he and the men with him were not reinforcements and would not be joining them in the fight. He gave them several reasons that I would call excuses, like how the Mormon militia was being readied to fight the U.S. Army and men couldn't be spared for this particular fight. A messenger, however, had been sent to President Young, and if it was the president's wish that the Mormons send reinforcements to the meadows, it would be done.

Lee told the Indians that if they needed any supplies, food, horses, or powder in the meantime, he would send a man back to Cedar City to get what was needed. While he said he was sorry he could not bring reinforcements, he emphasized several times the importance of the Indians and Mormons getting along with each other. If they used up their resources and men fighting each other, he said, it would not be possible to keep the U.S. Army out of Utah, which would result in Indians and Mormons being driven from their homes.

While the Indians weren't happy with Lee's message, they seemed resigned to the fact that they were not going to get Mormon reinforcements.

While the chiefs resumed their arguing about what to do next, Lee asked me to show him the battlefield. We mounted our horses and rode up the hill where Ike and I had camped the previous night. From there we had an excellent view of both the circle of wagons and the main Indian camp. I say "main" Indian camp because the Indians were not organized like a white man's army might be. They arrived in generally small groups and that's the way they camped, picking whatever place suited their fancy. The biggest sign of organization and leadership was the placement of armed lookouts around the meadows. They wanted to be sure none of the Fancher people got away.

We seated ourselves on a fallen cedar log, and I proceeded to describe the events of the last two days, especially what I had heard about the first attack Monday morning and the second attack that I had personally witnessed early Monday evening. I told about going in under a white flag to request the release of Ike's little girls and how they had turned me down.

"They said seven were killed and three wounded in the first attack. But they were caught by surprise," I said. "I doubt they had any hit the second time."

"I've never seen wagons chained together like that," said Lee. "A lot of men will die before this wagon fortress falls, unless they run out of ball and powder. Did you see anything that would indicate they were low on ammunition?"

I said I hadn't.

"I wonder what Joseph would have done in a situation like this," he said thoughtfully, after a brief pause. I assumed he was referring to Joseph Smith.

"I don't know," I said.

"Remember once in Nauvoo, at the fourth of July celebration in '43," began Lee. "I was there. The brethren were making toasts. Getting everyone's attention, Joseph raised a glass of water high above his head and said he wished all the mobocrats of the nineteenth century were in the middle of the sea in a stone canoe with an iron paddle. That a shark might swallow the canoe, and the shark be thrust into the nethermost pit of hell, the door locked, the key lost, and a blind man hunting for it."

"Mobs have given us a lot of trouble over the years," I said.

"And today we're on the side of the mob. Seems almost hypocritical."

"Shoe's on the other foot, all right," I said. "Those Missouri Wildcats are the ones wondering if they'll see another sunrise. But I suppose they asked for it, killing Indians, destroying property, threatening to send armies from California against Utah."

"How many women and children are in there?" asked Lee.

"Maybe thirty or forty."

"Sure feel uneasy about this whole thing."

"Me too."

"After all the mobs have done to us, it's like we're the mob now, or at least helping the mob."

"Maybe we shouldn't be giving the Indians supplies."

"Got to," he said. "Can't risk them turning on us. They've got us outnumbered four to one in southern Utah. Got Mormon families scattered all over. The Indians turn on us and hundreds of innocent people would die overnight. Got to help the Indians. Got to do everything we can to keep them from turning on us.

"Still," he continued, looking toward the wagons, "those folks down there are not an invading army, just a bunch of settlers on the way to California. In their stupidity they've killed a few Indians and insulted the Mormons a hundred times, but that's not cause for all of them to die."

"If they were let go, they'd just move on to California," I said. "Can't see where they pose any real danger."

"Wish I could go back to Harmony and forget the whole thing," said Lee.

We sat quietly for a while, deep in our own thoughts, watching the Indian camp and the wagon circle. Lee was the first to hear the clacking of horseshoes on rocks behind us. We turned around and saw Ike working his way down the ridge, balancing something heavy across his saddle horn. As he came closer I could see he was bringing back a small bear trap.

Chapter 28

Ike announced he was going to catch himself a hostage. That's why he had spent my ten-dollar gold piece buying the old bear trap from an Indian who seemed to be in charge at Hamblin's ranch.

Ike spent the rest of the afternoon riding among the Indians, telling them of his plan so they wouldn't get trigger-happy if they started hearing a lot of noise in the middle of the night. He told them if they heard a bunch of screaming, then saw a horse coming out of the meadow, to be sure not to shoot because it would be him bringing out his hostage. While circulating among the Indians, Ike borrowed four or five ropes, which he promised to return the next day. The big black warrior didn't ask for my help or anyone else's. He knew exactly what he was doing.

As soon as it was dark, Ike disappeared into the meadow, leading his horse, which was carrying the ropes and the bear trap.

Ike's plan was simple. Picketing his horse about fifty yards below the spring, he heaved the ropes over his shoulder, removed the heavy trap from the saddle, and crept quietly and cautiously to the upper shore of the spring, the exact spot where he had seen the Missourians dipping out water early that morning.

Quietly he set the trap, carefully covering it with loose dirt and dry grass. After tying one of the ropes to the ring at the end of the trap chain, he began backtracking to where his horse was picketed, quietly uncoiling the rope as he did so. When he came to the end of the first rope, he tied on the second rope and continued toward his horse.

Upon reaching the horse, Ike first made sure the cinch on his saddle was tight, then seated himself in the grass, holding the horse's reins in one hand, the end of the long rope attached to the bear trap in the other. Patiently the big black man waited for the Missourians to come to the spring for water. He was prepared to sit all night if necessary.

But an all-night vigil was not necessary. About midnight, he heard a quiet clank, barely noticeable. But the scream that followed, accompanied by cries for help, left no doubt in Ike's mind as to what had happened.

Ike threw the reins over his horse's neck, leaped into the saddle, made two quick loops around the saddle horn with the free end of the rope, turned the horse's head toward the Indian camp, then dug his heels into the horse's ribs.

There was another scream, louder than the first, then a bunch of splashing sounds as the man was dragged from the grassy bank into the water. A few seconds later the coughing, sputtering victim plowed from the water and across the damp grass, and continued to gain speed. By now the man was holding on to the chain with both hands in a desperate effort to save his foot. Before his companions could react, the poor Missourian had disappeared into the night.

When Ike's horse finally appeared in the firelight by the big wickiup, the animal had slowed to a fast walk. Ike was twisted sideways in the saddle, allowing the tight rope to pull straight back without hurting his thigh. Ike was looking behind him into the darkness where an angry victim was cursing, swearing, and crying, all at the same time.

Ike's horse passed the fire and kept on going. A few seconds later the victim appeared, sliding along the ground, still hanging onto the chain, swearing with all his might. Indians were rushing in from every direction, howling their delight.

When the Missourian was within a few feet of the fire, Ike

turned his horse around and headed back, urging the animal into a full gallop, because already four or five Indians had piled onto the victim and one had a knife out to remove the poor man's scalp.

Ike leaped from his horse before it had even come to a stop and waded into the Indians, throwing them right and left like a wild man tossing bundles of straw. Ike's steel-hard muscles glistened in the firelight. None of the Indians fought back. None wanted any more of Ike's wrath. None wanted to fight the great Gosiute war chief.

"Him belong to me," shouted Ike, pointing first to the victim, then to himself. "Anybody who kill him, Ike kill dem. No touch. No hurt."

Ike glared into the eyes of all who were looking on, making sure they understood he meant business. The Indians backed off, grumbling and disappointed over the fun they were going to miss with this captive, but they respected Ike's right to do as he pleased with the hostage he had caught without anyone's help.

After tying the man's hands behind his back, Ike began to remove the bear trap. The man was lucky to have been wearing heavy cowhide boots instead of moccasins or lighter shoes. While his foot was badly bruised, it didn't appear to be broken. All the time Ike was removing the trap, the man was calling him a stupid buck nigger, language which Ike seemed to be ignoring. As the man persisted in his abusive language I figured it was just a matter of time before Ike flattened the man's nose.

"You be quiet," was Ike's first response after the trap had been removed and set to one side. The man responded by again calling Ike a stupid buck nigger. I thought surely Ike would strike the man. Instead the big black warrior calmly rose to his full stature, walked to the edge of the firelight, picked up something from the ground, and returned to the cursing hostage.

Taking the man's jaw in his powerful hand, Ike's thumb and forefinger tightened like a vise on each side of the jaw, forcing the man to open his mouth. Then Ike's other hand came quickly forward, forcing two day-old horse apples into the open mouth.

The man got the message and stopped the swearing and name-calling. But he was engaged in a considerable amount of spitting for the next half hour.

"What do you aim to do with him?" I asked Ike.

"Come morning I trade him back to wagon master for little girls."

Chapter 29

Tuesday morning a brief funeral was held for the seven men of the Fancher Company, including Seth Stevenson, who had been killed the previous day. It was not an early funeral, there being many fearful of another Indian attack in the early hours of the day. But when the attack didn't come, a hole was dug near the center of the circle, and the seven men were laid to rest, wrapped in blankets. As the dirt was shoveled over them, the preacher recited the Lord's Prayer.

Susannah didn't cry as the dirt was shoveled over Seth. It wasn't that she hadn't loved her husband. She had. Though Seth had been loud and boisterous with a quick temper, he had been very patient with her blindness. He had not pampered her, often leaving her alone while he was off hunting, fishing, fighting, or drinking with his friends, but he had never been cruel to her.

Now he was gone, shot by Indians, buried in a common grave with six other men. Susannah thought that under relatively normal conditions she would have cried over Seth's passing, but under the present circumstances, she couldn't allow herself that luxury. She couldn't let go of herself, even for a moment. She had a wagon, oxen, horses, and two little Indian girls who couldn't speak English. Even if the present crisis passed, how would she manage to get to California? And what would she do when she got there? Susannah had too much weighing on her mind and heart to allow her to fall apart at Seth's death.

★ ★ ★

It was early afternoon when Charles Fancher stopped by to see Susannah. She was in the back of the wagon, going through the food supplies, trying to figure out what could be prepared without cooking. The firewood was nearly gone, and word had gone around the camp that by the next day there would be no cookfires.

"Mrs. Stevenson, I'm sorry about Seth," began Fancher.

"Me too," she said, knowing Fancher hadn't come by to console her. He had hardly spoken to her since the trip began back in Arkansas. That's why he still called her Mrs. Stevenson. She had sensed that he didn't like the idea of having a blind woman in his wagon train, that in times of crisis, like they were in now, she would be too much of a burden. She climbed down from the wagon.

"Do you believe we'll get out of here alive?" she asked.

"If the ammunition holds out I think we will," he said. "Used almost half in the first two attacks. They come at us a couple more times and we'll be at the end of our rope."

"And if the ammunition holds out?" she asked.

"Winter's coming. The Indians will get tired of waiting, will want to get back to their families. Then we'll just drive out of here. We'll have less supplies, taking away what we've used up here, but the desert will be cooler the longer we wait. If only the ammunition holds out."

"Do you think there are some men or boys who would help me with my stock once we get moving again?" she asked.

"That's what I came to talk to you about," Fancher said, a note of hesitation in his voice. She wondered why.

"You don't need much help taking care of your livestock," he said.

"What are you saying?"

"All your oxen and all but one of your horses have been run off or killed. You only have one horse left."

"One horse can't pull a wagon," she said.

"That's right," he responded.

"Is there a family, perhaps, that would take me and the girls in?" Susannah asked. "We wouldn't be a burden and would do our share of the work."

"That was my first thought," he said, "but the preacher's against it."

"The preacher! Why would he be against a family taking in a desperate blind woman and two little girls?"

"Mrs. Stevenson, you may be blind, but you are still a very beautiful woman."

"What are you getting at?" she demanded, not feeling even a little bit flattered by his comment about her looks.

"Living in wagons brings people in close contact with one another," he said, his voice faltering.

"And," she said, "please continue." Susannah felt the blood rising in her neck, a surge of anger swelling in her breast.

"The preacher thinks if you moved in with one of the families you might be the cause of an adulterous relationship."

"That's ridiculous," stammered Susannah. She didn't know whether to strike the man or cry. She felt like doing both. "I'm not that kind of woman."

"I know," said Fancher, "but the preacher insists . . ."

"Maybe he'd rather have me move in with some of the single men," she said.

"Oh no," said Fancher, taking her seriously. "That would be even worse."

"Then why don't you just turn me out to be raped by three hundred savages?" said Susannah without thinking. She was losing control. Tears began to well up in her eyes.

"Please try to get ahold of yourself," said Fancher, putting his big hand on her shoulder. She pushed it away, letting anger stop the flow of tears.

"What do you want me to do?" she demanded, holding her face up though she could not see him.

"I know your Seth is barely cold in the ground," he began, "and I know it is customary for a widow to wait six months or a year before remarrying, but considering the circumstances, I think it would be entirely appropriate if you remarried right away—like in the next few days."

Susannah was stunned, but responded quickly and spontaneously.

"Seth has been covered over about three hours now," she said, "and I can't recall anyone proposing marriage yet."

"Look, young lady," said Fancher, getting angry too, "in your present state without eyesight or a husband, you are a big burden to a lot of people who are in a struggle for their very lives. You need to make yourself less of a burden as quickly as possible, and you can do that by remarrying. If, when you get to California, you think you made a mistake, you can have the marriage annulled."

"It is not customary for men to fall over themselves to marry blind women," she said coldly. "What makes you think there's anyone in this company who will have me?"

"I've already brought up the subject among the men," said Fancher, "and two have expressed a willingness to marry you. It is up to you now to choose."

"That's wonderful," said Susannah, trying unsuccessfully to hide the sarcasm in her voice. "Don't you find it strange that they would tell you of their desires to marry me before they would tell me?"

"Not under the circumstances," he said, "but they will be by shortly to talk to you."

"We can have a funeral and a wedding feast on the same day," said Susannah.

"I just want you to remember what a burden you are to this company in your unmarried state," said Fancher. "And I hope you will see the wisdom in correcting that situation very soon." He turned and started walking away.

"Wait a minute," called Susannah. "Who are they?" Fancher turned to face her.

"Henry Dunlap is one—said he would be mighty glad to assume Seth's husbandly duties."

Susannah knew Henry Dunlap all too well. He was one of Seth's drinking companions. Loved whiskey, gambling, and whoring. Got Seth into a lot of trouble. Susannah had never liked Henry or his foul mouth. Seemed he was always swearing, even in the company of women.

"Who's the other one?" she asked.

"Dick Boggs," said Fancher, turning and walking away.

As Susannah climbed back into the wagon she felt a tightness in her chest, so tight she could hardly breathe. She felt trapped. Oh, why did Seth have to go? Why couldn't she have been killed with him? Why did she have to be blind? For the first time since Seth's death, she was unable to hold back the huge sobs of grief that welled up in her chest.

Chapter 30

Henry Dunlap was the first to visit Susannah. He was thin and wiry, like Seth, but shorter. In his late twenties, he was a fierce fighter and an excellent shot, but had a reputation for being irresponsible. Henry was always broke, it seemed. Susannah figured that's why he frequently invited Seth to go drinking with him, so Seth could pay the bill. Susannah guessed Henry was probably a handsome man, having nearly been killed on several occasions for fooling around with other men's wives.

"Sorry about Seth," said Henry, the same sentiment Susannah had been hearing all day.

"Me too," she answered, then waited to hear what he had to say next. She had no intention of making this easy for him.

"Did Charles Fancher stop by to talk to you?" he asked.

"Yes," was her only response, followed by a long pause.

"What'd he have to say?" asked Henry.

"Something about you wanting to assume Seth's husbandly duties," she said matter-of-factly.

"He said it that way?"

"More or less." Again there was a long silence.

"Seth and me was good friends," he began, looking at his feet as he kicked up a pile of dust. "Least I can do is look after his woman, I figure."

"And assume all his husbandly duties," added Susannah.

"On one condition," he said, his confidence growing.

"And what is that?" she asked.

"That I don't have to make a bunch of promises I won't keep anyway."

"Like what?" asked Susannah.

"Like giving up cussing and drinking, like going to church, working all the time, or getting a steady job—those kinds of things."

"Doesn't my being blind bother you?" asked Susannah.

"Won't at night when it's dark," he laughed, supposing he had said something clever. Susannah didn't laugh.

"What about the girls?" she asked.

"The little nigger-Injuns belong to Boggs. Guess you'll have to give 'em back."

"You won't let me keep them, even if Boggs pays?"

"If he pays, that might change things. Let me think about it."

"Henry, you'd better think hard," she said, "because there'll be no wedding if the girls are not included. We're a package deal, all or nothing."

"I said I'd think about it," said Henry, starting to get mad, too, not wanting to be pushed. He turned and walked away.

Less than an hour passed before Boggs dropped by. Susannah was expecting him and already knew what she was going to say to the man who admitted to killing Ruth and Lucy's mother. Boggs was a master deceiver, the one who tried to get everyone to pretend conversion to Mormonism so they could buy goods in Cedar City, the one who passed off a dead Indian as the body of Parley Pratt to a merchant, a man without principle or morals, and a confessed murderer to boot.

"Sorry about Seth," said Boggs as he shuffled up.

"Mr. Boggs, I am not going to marry you," she said, figuring there was no reason to beat around the bush. There was a pause as Boggs shifted his thinking from a situation of anticipated game-playing to direct talk.

"Thought you loved them little girls," he said.

"I do."

"Thought you wanted to raise them."

"I do."

"Have you talked to Charles Fancher?"

"I have."

"Then I don't understand what you are saying," he said.

"I am not going to marry you," she repeated.

"Then you'll never get near those little girls again when we leave this place."

"They are not yours to take away," she said coldly. "You're a murderer and a kidnapper."

"And you think you, a blind woman, can stop me from taking what's mine?"

"Yes," she said firmly, having no idea how she might do it.

"Let me know if you change your mind," he said gruffly, turning and shuffling away.

Susannah crawled back into the wagon, where the girls were waiting for her. Her strength was gone and she felt frightened and alone, even with her arms around the little girls.

She began to ask some questions of herself that she had never asked before. Could Susannah Stevenson survive the future events of her life? What changes might improve her chances of survival? Should she back off on some of her principles and become more like Henry Dunlap? Should she become more deceitful like Dick Boggs? Would such changes, no matter how distasteful, increase her chances of survival and her ability to care for the girls? Her world was changing for the worse. Did she have to become that way too in order to survive?

If she refused to marry Henry Dunlap or Dick Boggs, how could she continue? If she refused, would she really be too much of a burden on the others as Charles Fancher had said? If she married Boggs, would he really let her raise the girls? Or would she be better off with the irresponsible Henry Dunlap?

Susannah was still wide awake when she heard the screaming down by the spring. A minute later she heard the news that poor Henry Dunlap had been dragged off by Indians.

Chapter 31

Wednesday morning at first light I was walking through the wet grass toward the circle of wagons, holding high the white flag I had made two days earlier. I had convinced Ike I was the one who should negotiate for the release of his two little girls. The people in the Fancher Company had talked to me before, and I figured there would be less chance of having problems if I went out to propose the trade.

The Indians had been notified ahead of time that I would be going out under the white flag, so I didn't anticipate any surprises from them. New Indians had arrived the previous day, so I figured well over three hundred redskins were watching me as I approached the wagons.

"What do you want?" shouted Fancher when I was about fifty yards off.

"Want to talk," I yelled back.

"Put your hands over your head and proceed slowly."

A few minutes later I was standing up against two wagon wheels that were still chained together. This time the company did not make an opening for me to enter the circle, which was fine with me. Fancher and his men were less than eight feet away, so there was no trouble hearing each other.

"What's happened to Henry Dunlap?" asked Fancher.

"Except for a bruised foot, he's fine," I said.

"I find it hard to believe he's not scalped and skinned by now," said Fancher.

I explained that Dunlap hadn't been captured by Indians, but by Ike, the black father of the two little girls.

"Niggers ain't smart enough or brave enough to pull off something like that," said a man next to Fancher.

"This one is," I said. "And if he doesn't get his girls back, there's no telling what else he will do."

"What do you want?" said Fancher.

"Ike wants to return Henry Dunlap, unharmed, in exchange for the two little girls."

"And if we refuse?" asked Fancher.

"I'd guess Ike will try to strengthen his hand by catching somebody else tonight, or he might just give Dunlap to the Indians."

"I got a better idea," shouted a familiar voice from the back of the gathering. It was Dick Boggs, and he was pushing his way to the front.

"Tell that buck," he continued, "that if Dunlap isn't back within the hour, I'll personally hang one of them little girls from the back of my wagon and skin her alive. Tell him that." Some of the men grunted their support for what Boggs had said. They figured Boggs had Ike over a barrel.

Then Fancher said, "If this Ike is more committed to saving his girls than we are to saving Dunlap, he doesn't have a very strong bargaining position, does he?"

"Tell him," said another man, "that if Dunlap isn't carrying a barrel of powder and a couple of bars of lead when he returns, Boggs'll skin both girls."

"Shut up," ordered Fancher, realizing I had just been made aware of their shortage of ammunition.

"Can I say something?" I asked.

Fancher ordered the men to be silent while I spoke.

"It appears you people don't really understand what's going on with those Indians out there. There's over three hundred of them and more are arriving every day, even as I speak. Do you know why you folks are still alive?"

"Because we are crack shots," answered one of the men. Fancher hissed him to silence.

"I'll tell you why," I continued. "Because those Indians aren't totally dedicated to the cause. They want your scalps, all right, and your horses and wagons and clothing and supplies—but they don't want to get shot up in the process. Getting shot up is too high a price to pay."

They were all listening now, so I continued.

"Weren't you surprised how easy you turned them back those two times they attacked?" Some of the men nodded their agreement. "As soon as you shot some of them out of their saddles, they turned tail. Sure, they hate you people and want to kill you, but they aren't willing to die doing it."

"So what's going to happen?" asked Fancher.

"If you folks can hang on, if you have enough supplies and ammunition, they'll get tired of waiting and begin to leave. Some bad weather will hurry things up.

"Unless," I said, raising my voice, then pausing, making sure I had everyone's attention. "Unless something happens to stir them up, increase their willingness to risk their lives and even die, if necessary, to get you people.

"And let me tell you what would do that. Just let Boggs start cutting one of those little girls with his knife. You might as well walk into an old barn and swat three hundred hornet nests with a stick.

"Hurting those girls will change things. You'll have three hundred Indians charging in here, not caring if half of them get shot. It'll be all over for you folks, your women and kids, too. Don't let Boggs start swatting the hornet nests. Let's make a trade, sit this thing out, and eventually the Indians will give up and head for home. Then you can go to California."

"How would you propose making the switch?" asked Fancher, giving me hope that maybe I was getting through to them.

"I'll go back and get Dunlap, then return with him to the middle of the meadow, meeting one of your people there with the two little girls."

"Give us a few minutes to discuss it and vote," said Fancher, turning to talk to the men. I took a few steps back and waited.

I knew the decision was leaning in my direction when Boggs yelled, "I ain't going out there unarmed with Storm. Git somebody else. And who's going to pay for taking my property?"

A minute later, Fancher turned to me, saying, "Go get Dunlap. We'll meet you halfway, like you said. No tricks, or you'll have thirty Kentucky long rifles firing balls straight for your heart."

"No tricks," I said, turning and heading back to camp, holding the white flag high over my head.

Chapter 32

"Watch where you step when you go for water tonight," laughed Ike as I pushed Henry Dunlap ahead of me into the meadow. His hands were still tied behind his back with a lead rope coming back to me and allowing me to stop his progress at any time if I wished to do so. He was limping rather noticeably.

I was carrying the white flag, and except for a knife in my belt, was unarmed. I hoped there would be no trickery, especially once the little girls were in the meadow.

As we proceeded toward the halfway point, I became increasingly concerned that Boggs, and perhaps Fancher, might be up to something that was not part of the original agreement. I reminded Dunlap that Ike and some of the Indians had rifles aimed at him just in case he tried something funny.

"Don't try anything foolish and get yourself shot," I warned.

"I wouldn't try anything unless I thought it would get you and that big nigger shot," he hissed.

When we arrived at the halfway point, the predetermined meeting place, the girls had still not appeared from the wagon circle. I couldn't imagine what the trouble might be. I hoped Fancher hadn't changed his mind.

"We'll wait here," I told Dunlap. "I don't plan on getting any closer to those Kentucky long rifles."

"Can I sit down?" he asked.

"Sure," I said, "but do it slowly."

As he lowered himself to the ground, I did the same, being careful to keep him between me and the wagons. I had no intention of presenting an easy target to the Missouri Wildcats.

We waited nearly half an hour, and I was considering immobilizing Dunlap by tying his feet to his hands and going ahead with the white flag to ask what was holding them up, when I spotted three people crawling out from under one of the wagons. It was the two little girls and a woman, whom I recognized as Susannah. The girls had taken her hands and were helping to lead her along.

"That's Susannah Stevenson," I told Henry as I thought back on my fight with Seth Stevenson in Salt Lake and how his blind wife jumped me from behind, nearly tearing my head off and clawing at my face. He nodded.

"I may git a chance to wrassle with her tonight," he said, then explained how Seth had been killed in the Monday morning battle and how Fancher wanted one of the single men to marry Susannah right away so she wouldn't be a burden to the others.

"Before the nigger caught me in the bear trap, I was first in line for the job," he said.

"Poor, unfortunate woman," I added, not intending any humor.

"Why don't you join them Injuns in their next attack?" said Henry. "I'd sure like to plant a bullet in your guts."

I didn't respond but just watched Susannah and the little girls work their way across the meadow, Susannah leaning back, taking careful, deliberate steps, the two little girls eagerly pulling at her hands to hurry her along.

Susannah was holding her face high, an early morning breeze from the north pushing her long, dark hair behind her. She was still as beautiful as I remembered. I felt sorry for her, a beautiful blind woman in the middle of a wilderness, surrounded by hostile Indians, mourning the recent death of her husband, and being pressured to marry an idiot.

"Yep, no doubt about her choosing me over Boggs," said Dunlap, "especially now that the girls are gone and he can't hold that over her head."

"Did you say Boggs?" I asked.

"He's the other one who wants to marry her," explained Dunlap. "An old goat with a wooden leg and a patch over his eye. She's got to pick one of us." Susannah was worse off than I had imagined.

A minute later Susannah and the two little girls were standing in front of us.

"Hello," I said. "I'm Dan Storm, the man you and Seth got in the fight with in Salt Lake."

"I remember," she said. "How are Caroline and Sarah?"

"Very fine," I said, pleased she remembered my wives. "They have returned to the ranch in American Fork."

"Don't trust this man," warned Dunlap. "He's in with the Injuns that attacked us."

"Some of them are my friends," I said. "But I was not involved in the attacks on your wagons."

"Can I go now?" asked Dunlap.

"No," I said, "First let me see if the girls will come to me."

I dropped to one knee and held my arms out, trying to get them to come. Instead they just clung more tightly to Susannah's skirts.

When I said their father's name, they looked up at Susannah's face. She smiled to show her trust for me, and pushed them gently toward me. Timidly, they took my hands.

"Take ahold of my arm," said Dunlap to Susannah. "I'll guide you back to the wagons."

I noticed there were some tears running down her cheeks as she stepped toward him.

"I'll miss them," she said as she reached out to take his arm.

"Wait a minute," I said to Susannah. "I'd like to talk to you."

"That wasn't part of the deal," whined Dunlap. "We're going back to the wagons right now."

"What do you want to talk about?" asked Susannah, stopping.

"About you," I said. "I know about Seth and how they are pushing you to remarry right away."

"Keep out of this, Storm," snarled Dunlap.

"You're welcome to ride north with Ike and me and the girls," I said, trying to ignore Dunlap. "You can stay at my ranch with

Caroline and Sarah until you've decided what you want to do. If you want to return to Arkansas, we'll help you."

"Don't believe him for one minute," said Dunlap. "He just wants to turn you over to the Injuns, and you know what Injuns do to white women."

"That's not true," I said.

"What about the Indians?" asked Susannah.

"They won't harm you if you are with Ike and me, taking care of the girls."

"This isn't part of the deal," screamed Dunlap. "You're trying to take three hostages instead of two."

"Susannah's not a hostage," I said. "She only comes if she wants to. She's free to do what she wants."

It was quiet for a minute while Susannah thought over my offer.

"What about the Fancher Company?" she asked.

"If they don't do anything to further provoke the Indians, they might be able to pull out of here in a week or two, I think. I don't need to tell you the situation is very serious."

"Mr. Storm," said Susannah, her voice firm and confident, "I think I'll accept your kind offer."

"Dunlap," I said, "I have a feeling there's a couple of Indians about ready to race into the meadow to lift your scalp. You'd better git while you can."

Without another word to Susannah or me, Dunlap began racing toward the wagons, his hands still tied behind his back, the loose rope flopping through the grass behind him.

"Henry," called Susannah after him, "be sure and tell Mr. Boggs how sorry I am to have to miss the wedding."

We had covered about half the distance back to camp when Dunlap disappeared under the closest wagon. Suddenly gunfire erupted from the hills around us. Pushing Susannah and the girls to the ground, I looked back at the wagons to see what was happening. Three of Fancher's men had just galloped through an opening on the far side of the wagons and were racing south in an effort to get outside the circle of Indians, many of whom were firing from the hillsides. Some of the Indians were already on their horses, racing down through the scattered trees and brush to cut off the escaping white men.

Chapter 33

The Indians were intent on watching me exchange Henry for the girls when the three riders emerged from the circle of wagons. The Indians began firing at the riders immediately, but only one was hit before the other two galloped out of sight.

The wounded man fell from his horse, which galloped away after the others. But the man wasn't dead. Getting to his feet, holding a blood-stained shoulder, he began stumbling back toward the wagons.

★ ★ ★

Suddenly a rider emerged from the closest stand of oak brush, his horse racing at a full gallop to intercept the wounded man. To my amazement the rider was not an Indian, but the young man with the neatly trimmed beard whose father had been killed at Haun's Mill.

I still didn't know the man's name, but he was very brave. The Missourians inside the circle of wagons began to fire at him, but he didn't waver from his objective. Carrying a rifle in his right hand, the young man quickly closed in on the wounded runner. Then, bringing the rifle to his shoulder with one hand, he shot the wounded man a second time. This time the Missourian didn't get up.

As the bearded man turned his horse back toward the stand of oak brush, the animal's front legs buckled and it rolled to its side and lay still, apparently killed by one of the bullets fired from the circle of wagons.

The bearded man rolled ahead of the horse, dropping his rifle, quickly gaining his footing, then racing to the cover of the brush. The dirt was kicked up around his heels a few times as balls hit close, but he appeared uninjured as he disappeared into the oak brush. The shooting stopped almost as quickly as it had begun, except for some distant rifle reports from over the hill where Indians were still chasing the two men that had gotten away.

There had been no fire in our direction, so Susannah and the girls jumped to their feet and we hurried to cover. Ike hadn't come out to join us in the fear he might draw fire from the wagons, but he was waiting where we entered the trees. Dropping to his knees he swept the girls into his arms, squeezing them close in his muscular arms, big tears running down his cheeks.

After a minute he looked up, giving Susannah a questioning look.

"This is Susannah, the blind lady I told you about," I said, "the one who nearly beat me up in Salt Lake a few months back."

"What she doin' here?" he asked.

"She's been taking care of the girls ever since Boggs joined up with the train. Her husband was killed in the Monday morning attack. Offered to let her come back with us and stay at my place until she can decide what she wants to do."

Ike pushed his girls back just enough to give him room to look them over. There were no visible injuries or bruises. The bruises and scabs where Boggs's collars had rubbed against their necks were all healed by now. Both of them appeared well-fed, and there was plenty of sparkle in their eyes and smiles on their faces.

"Thank you," he said to Susannah, who nodded an acknowledgment.

"Storm!" shouted Lee as he came crashing into camp, followed by some Indians and white men, "What are those Missourians up to?"

"Can you tell us?" I asked Susannah. "What was their thinking in sending those three men out?"

"They hoped that while everyone was watching the exchange with the little girls, those men could break away and get back to Cedar City to get help from the Mormons. The company's worried about running out of ammunition."

"Stupid people," said Lee. "Things were just quieting down to where I figured some of the Indians would start going home. Now everything's stirred up again."

"I got one, I got one," shouted the young man with the beard as he came running up to Lee. Without warning, Lee turned to face the young man, at the same time striking him squarely in the nose with his fist and knocking him on his back as blood gushed.

"What'd you do that for?" cried the startled young man.

"You ought to be shot," snarled Lee.

"What for?"

"You had orders not to get involved in this fight."

"But they were trying to get away."

"And what's so bad about that? Now it's too late."

Lee's fists were clenched. His face was red. The veins were bulging out on his neck, as though he were straining to lift a horse. His jaw muscles were tight and quivering. I'd never seen a man whose life was not in immediate danger look so distraught.

Lee turned to me and said, "Better take the woman and girls and get out of here." Ike was already talking to the Indians about Susannah, making sure she wouldn't be harmed.

"What do you mean when you say it's too late?" I asked Lee.

"I wanted the Indians to let them go," he said.

"Maybe they still will," I said.

"But can we?" he asked, his voice almost a whisper.

"What do you mean?" I asked.

"Everyone in that company just saw a Mormon gallop out of cover and kill one of their men. When those people leave Mountain Meadows, they will tell the world how they were attacked by Indians and Mormons."

I was beginning to see what he was getting at.

"The mob persecutions in Missouri and Illinois were picnics," he continued, "compared to what will happen in Utah when word gets out that Mormons are attacking emigrant wagon trains. Everything we've worked so hard to establish here will be laid to waste. Johnston's Army is just the beginning."

The bearded man was beginning to get to his feet, but Lee shoved him down again, then turned and smashed his fist against the nearest tree.

Suddenly the Indians were shouting and pointing toward the circle of wagons. One of the Mericats was walking toward us, carrying a white flag.

All along they had assumed they were under attack by Indians only. According to Susannah the three men attempting to escape were headed for Cedar City, apparently believing the Mormons would help them in their fight against the savages. Now they were probably thinking the Mormons were equally responsible with the Indians for the attack and siege. Up to now they had been afraid to send out the white flag to Indians who would probably kill the man carrying it. But with the discovery that Mormons were involved, they probably felt they could conduct some civilized negotiations under the protection of a white flag.

I walked over to where I had leaned my white flag against a tree, picked it up, and handed it to Lee.

"You're the head white man here," I said. "Guess you'd better go out and talk to that fellow."

Lee took the flag and looked at the man walking across the meadow.

"No," he said finally. "I won't talk to him."

"Why not?" I asked.

"I've sent Higbee to Cedar City to tell President Haight of the new development. Until he returns with word on what the leaders want to do, I'm not in a position to negotiate anything. Go out and tell the fellow to return to the wagons, that it will be tomorrow night or Friday before any negotiations can take place." He handed back the white flag.

Holding it high over my head, I began walking toward the man, who was now stopped in the middle of the meadow, waiting for someone to meet him halfway. It was not Charles Fancher or anyone I knew by name. He was a big man with a gray beard. As I got close, it appeared his eyes were red with anger.

When I was within speaking distance, I gave him Lee's message.

"You Mormons sure had us fooled," he growled. "Making us think only Injuns was behind this. But now we know, and when we get out of here there'll be hell to pay for what you done here."

"I know," I said, as he turned and started back to the wagons.

Chapter 34

Lee wanted Ike and me to take Susannah and the girls and leave, but Ike refused. The man who had murdered Little Plume, the girls' mother, was in that circle of wagons, and Ike wasn't going to take any chances that Dick Boggs might get away, not as long as he could do anything about it.

I could have gone ahead with Susannah and the girls, but feeling partly responsible for Little Plume's death, having asked Ike to leave his family and come to my place, I decided to stay with Ike until everything was over. Susannah and the girls made themselves comfortable in the hillside camp Ike and I had set up Monday evening.

Thursday morning, groups of white men began arriving from the nearby Mormon communities, particularly Cedar City. They said they were responding to orders from Colonel Dame and Lieutenant Colonel Haight to report to Major Lee. Captain Higbee had still not arrived with any official orders.

Another group of Indians arrived too from the south, along the ridge above our camp. There were six of them, and they were shouting and whooping. It turned out they were not new recruits, but the ones who had gone after the two men who had escaped the previous afternoon.

The first two Indians were carrying scalps, evidence their chase had been successful.

About mid-morning Lee asked me to join him in walking

around the perimeter. As riled as the Indians were, the white men were told to stay in groups, not to get alone among the Indians. There was no telling what they might do.

I suppose Lee asked me, instead of one of his own men, to go with him because of the respect the Indians seemed to have for me, a result of my close friendship with Ike and the fact that I had once lived among the Utes.

Lee said he wanted to get an accurate assessment of the Indian strength and readiness, plus a detailed look at the terrain surrounding the meadows.

"Why?" I asked. "What's going to happen?"

"Haven't received any orders yet," he said, "but I can just about assure you, the way all these men are arriving, that we'll be ordered to help the Indians finish this thing off."

"How can you be so sure?"

"What else is there?"

"Try to get the Indians to let them go."

"Up until yesterday, that seemed the best way out. Now I don't know how we can let them go out and tell the world Mormons are attacking emigrant trains. How many Mormons will die as a result of that? Besides, you've been here long enough to know the Indians aren't about to walk away from this."

"With time, I think they would."

"Maybe," said Lee. "I would give anything, even an arm or a leg, to be able to walk away from this."

"That might turn out to be a bargain," I said, "considering how straight those Missourians can shoot."

"Some of us and a lot of Indians might die," he said. "Storm, do you know what bothers me about dying?"

"What?"

"Not the pain, the uncertainty, whether or not you'll get to the highest degree of heaven. Those kinds of things don't bother me."

"What does?"

"The unfinished business I'd be leaving behind, like broken fences that haven't been mended yet."

I wasn't sure what he was talking about. He certainly couldn't be concerned about fences at a time like this. "Do you mean real fences?" I asked.

"Not really," he said. "I have been a proud man, and in my younger days I thought I was perfection. In those days I expected perfection in all women. I know now that I was foolish in looking for that in anybody." He paused, his jaw muscles twitching. He looked away at the sky as he continued.

"I have for slight offenses turned away well-meaning young women who had been sealed to me, refused to hear their excuses, and sent them away heartbroken. In this I did wrong and have regretted it for many years."

"Who were they?" I asked.

"Emeline Woolsey and Polly Ann Workman. They were young and in their prime of life when I sent them from me."

"What happened to them?"

"They have since remarried and are the mothers of families. But they still have warm hearts toward me, in spite of my conduct toward them. They send me letters sometimes, saying only the kindest things, but their memory serves only to add to my self-reproach for my cruel treatment of them. I banished them from me for lesser offenses than I myself have been guilty of.

"If I were to die out in that meadow today or tomorrow, my last wish would be for God to pardon me for the wrong I did them when I drove them from me, poor young girls as they were."

I liked John D. Lee. I didn't think many men with a dozen or so wives and all that property could be so concerned for the feelings of women they hadn't seen for many years.

When we were four or five hundred yards above the circle of wagons, we decided to cross from one side of the valley to the other. We couldn't do so without being seen from the wagons, so we ran to avoid any possible bullets that might come our way.

Once inside the protective cover of the oak brush, Lee sat on a fallen log to catch his breath and assess that portion of the battlefield, while I climbed to the top of the nearest hill.

As soon as I got to the top and looked back, I spotted something very unusual out in the meadow, coming our way.

Two little boys, maybe seven or eight years old, were carrying a white flag and running to the spot where Lee and I had disappeared into the brush. It appeared the Fancher people were getting desperate. Lee had refused to talk to their adult emissary, so now they were sending out kids, figuring we would listen to them and have pity on them.

As I looked straight down, I could see Lee standing. He had seen the boys too. To my surprise, when the boys got close, Lee crawled into some bushes and hid himself. Until he had his orders, he didn't want to talk to anyone, not even to the children. Especially not the children.

The boys ran here and there in the oak brush for what seemed ten or fifteen minutes, looking for Lee. They didn't know I had gone to the top of the hill. Lee remained hidden until the boys finally gave up and returned to the wagons.

Lee finally came out of hiding and climbed to the top of the hill. Without speaking, we worked our way back to the camp at the bottom of the meadow, where John Higbee was waiting for us. Looking as sober as death, Higbee handed Lee a sealed envelope. Without a word Lee went off by himself to see what the leaders had decided to do.

Chapter 35

It took Lee a long time to read his orders from Cedar City. When he finally returned, he didn't say anything, and the paper was folded inside his shirt.

When some of the men began asking him what was going to happen, he told them they would find out soon enough. His eyes were evasive, as though he didn't want to look anyone square in the face. That was unusual for Lee.

"Bateman, Higbee, Klingonsmith, MacFarlane, Knight, Allen, McMurdy, White, Willis," he said, "and all you chiefs. There will be a council here in this clearing in one hour. All I will tell you now is that the time of waiting and wondering is over. A lot of things are going to happen in the next twenty-four hours which will involve all of you."

As he spoke, recently arrived Nephi Johnson was interpreting to the Indians, who let out some whoops and cheers at what they thought was good news.

"Storm, come with me," said Lee as he turned his back and started walking away through the cedar trees. I quickly caught up with him.

As I looked over at Lee, I was amazed to see tears running down his cheeks.

"What's happening?" I asked.

"Haight and Dame say to kill them all," he said without looking over at me.

"Even the women and children?" I asked.

"Everyone except those too little to tell what happened here."

We walked along in silence for a minute.

"Are you going to do it?" I asked.

"Those are my orders."

"Can you do it?" I asked. He stopped and looked at me.

"Don't know," he said. "Never killed anyone before. Have you?"

"Yes, but not like this."

"What was it like?" he asked.

"They were Indians, trying to kill me. Didn't have time to think about it. Just did it to save my skin. This is different."

"There's over a hundred people out there," he said, turning to walk again.

"How can they justify giving such an order?" I asked.

"I suppose they think it's better that one small company of emigrants perish than a whole nation of Mormons be killed and scattered by mobs."

"But a whole wagon train can't just disappear off the face of the earth without a lot of questions being asked. Surely Haight and Dame realize that someone will have to explain what happened to these people."

"The blame will be laid on the Indians."

"So the backlash will come against the Indians instead of the Mormons—assuming none of those three hundred Indians out there will tell what really happened."

"Look," said Lee. "I didn't issue these orders. I'm just the donkey that has to carry them out."

"What about Susannah?" I asked.

"The orders say everyone except the little children. Haight and Dame are Church leaders as well as military leaders. I'll do what they say."

"Even if you think they're making a mistake?"

"Did you ever hear how President Young sent me from Winter Quarters to Santa Fe to collect the Mormon Battalion wages?" he asked. I nodded.

"While I was in St. Louis getting outfitted," he continued, "I ran into Luke Johnson, one of the witnesses to the Book of Mormon. He had seen the gold plates and an angel of God and had still fallen away from the Church. I asked him to tell me about it.

"We took a walk on the river bank. I asked if he had really seen the plates and the angel as the document said—the one in the front of the Book of Mormon which Johnson and others had signed. He said the statement was true.

"I asked him how he could leave the Church after witnessing those things, especially since he had also been one of the original twelve apostles when the Church was founded. He admitted he was one of the original twelve apostles, and said he had never denied the truth of the Book of Mormon.

"He said that he and several others, including Oliver Cowdery, William Smith, and Sidney Rigdon got involved in a messy business deal that went sour. Some investment capital was lost. A Church court was held to deal with those involved. Since Sidney Rigdon was a member of the First Presidency, and William Smith was a brother to the Prophet, charges against these two men were dropped.

"Luke Johnson and Oliver Cowdery, however, were told to make a public confession, drawing all the blame upon themselves. If they refused to do so they would be dropped from the Church. Luke Johnson said he would make a public confession only if Sidney Rigdon would do so too. The leaders wouldn't go along with that, so Johnson left the Church, rather than accept a punishment he thought was unfair and unjust.

"As we walked along the river bank that day, he told me he wished he had done what the leaders wanted him to do, even though he felt it was wrong. He had been the one to suffer from not following counsel. He said the Lord knows what's in a man's heart, and somehow tends to render just rewards, at least in the end. Rigdon has since gone on to destruction, and William Smith isn't much better off. Johnson told me he was getting ready to return to the Saints and ask to be readmitted into the Church. Whether or not he actually did that, I don't know.

"At that time," concluded Lee, "I decided I would never go

against the counsel of Church leaders, even if I thought that counsel to be wrong."

"Then what about Susannah?" I asked.

"You want to know if I am going to kill her. Do you have anything to say in her defense?"

"Yes," I responded quickly. "First, at the time you received that order, this afternoon, she was no longer a member of the Fancher Company. Therefore the order does not apply to her. And second, even if it did, if you'll look at the reasoning behind the order—that no living witnesses be left to tell what they saw—she is again left out because she has not seen anything to tell. She is blind."

Lee thought a minute, then said, "I'll buy that, but keep her quiet and out of sight. If she were to get talking to the wrong reporters, there could be a lot of trouble."

"As I said, she hasn't seen anything. There won't be any trouble from Susannah."

Suddenly Lee held out his left hand, as if to engage with me in some kind of unusual handshake.

"What are you doing?" I asked.

"Thought maybe you were a Danite," he said.

I had heard of the Danites in Missouri and Nauvoo, but I didn't know they were still functioning in Utah Territory. When the mobs began attacking Mormons and burning their homes in Missouri, some of the Mormon men organized themselves into a secret order or group to fight back against the mobs. They had secret handshakes and oaths and were very secretive about what they did. The mobs raided and pillaged at night, and the Danites answered in kind. Having spent most of those early years out west, I never had the occasion to get involved with the Danites and had assumed the organization had been dissolved with the move to the Rocky Mountains. From Lee's actions, it appeared I was wrong, at least in southern Utah.

"All the white men here have taken blood oaths of secrecy," said Lee, his voice low and deadly serious. "I want your word that you will do the same."

"You have my word," I said, "that I will not be the one to let the world know what has or will happen here." I reached out and shook his hand.

"You may not want to stick around," he said.

"I'd be gone already," I said, "if it weren't for Ike and his desire to avenge his wife's death. Got to make sure Dick Boggs doesn't slip away."

"Would you like to join me in prayer?" asked Lee, catching me totally by surprise.

I could hardly believe my ears. This man was getting ready to take charge of the massacre of over a hundred people and he wanted to pray about it. A leader of soldiers, about to engage in a very dirty task—first he cries, then he wants to pray. An amazing man, this John D. Lee.

I had heard about the Spanish Inquisition, the Salem witch hunts, and other atrocities carried out by so-called religious people. I had always wondered how people so well trained, supposedly, in religious Christian principles could justify cold-blooded murder.

But Lee was not like the religious leaders I had read about in Salem and Spain. There was nothing cold-blooded about Lee. He was weeping, praying. From his comments, I don't even think he hated the people in the Fancher Company. Yet as much as he disliked the order and wasn't totally convinced it was the right thing to do, he seemed determined to do his duty, to follow the orders of his leaders, no matter what the consequences.

We knelt down behind a cedar tree, where I listened to John D. Lee pour out his soul to his God. After thanking the Lord for this land, he and his people had received for their inheritance, he asked that the heavens be opened to let him and his brethren know the will of the Lord in the things they were about to do. He begged for guidance, inspiration, assurance, even forgiveness for the things they were going to do.

Lee talked with his God like a man talks to a good friend, with respect and a certain amount of familiarity. He talked as if God were up in that cedar tree listening to every word.

I opened my eyes and looked at Lee. His head was not bowed, but facing straight ahead, his eyes closed tightly. His fists were clenched. His voice was low, but strong with emotion. I had never witnessed a more earnest prayer.

When we were finished, he asked if I wanted to pray, too. I said I didn't, that I thought he pretty much covered what needed to be said.

We got back on our feet, brushing the pine needles and dirt from our pant legs.

"Guess we'd better get back to camp," he said, "and see how the men feel about it, and how they want to carry it out."

Chapter 36

Lee's council meeting was late getting started. Some of the chiefs had wandered, and it took longer than expected to round them up.

When everyone was finally together, Lee's first item of business was for Nephi Johnson to tell the Indians that the Mormons had finally decided to join them in their attack on the Fancher Company. Immediately there was a lot of whooping and yelling among the Indians. Several of the chiefs were so excited they leaped on their horses and would have galloped off to round up their braves had not the others stopped them. The noise and confusion lasted for several minutes before Lee again had everyone's attention.

He expressed his concern over a conventional attack. The Mericats, as the Indians called them, were too well fortified. And even though there was strong evidence they were running out of ammunition, there was no way of estimating the number of men that would die before that happened. The Missourians were crack shots and not many bullets would miss the intended targets, especially if the Missourians knew they were low on ammunition. They would make every shot count. Many Indians and Mormons would die before the defenses crumbled.

There was no voiced opposition to the points Lee was making. Though outnumbering the white men almost five to one, the Indians had been easily driven back in their first two attacks. Nobody, not even the new Mormon allies, wanted to ride head-on against the Missouri sharpshooters.

"There's more than one way to skin a cat," said Lee. "Now if you'll hold your comments until I've finished, I'll lay out a plan wherein none of us will die."

Everyone was listening. Lee proceeded slowly, giving Nephi Johnson sufficient time to interpret for the chiefs who could not understand English. Lee did not say if the plan was his own or part of the written instructions he had received from Cedar City.

He began by mentioning the apparent eagerness on the part of the Missourians to negotiate under a white flag. They did not want any further fighting, if it could be avoided. Seven of them had been killed in the first attack, and three more seriously wounded. Perhaps more had been killed or wounded in the second attack. The Fancher Company was ready to talk.

Lee had considerable difficulty getting out the next part. His voice was breaking, and it was easy to see he was fighting back tears as he explained how one of the Mormons would approach the Mericats the next morning under a white flag, offering safe passage for everyone in the company back to Cedar City under Mormon guard, if they would agree to leave their livestock and wagons behind to appease the Indians. Once outside the circle of wagons, the Mericats would be vulnerable to attack.

There was quiet for a minute or two as the impact of Lee's words sunk in. As a whole the chiefs seemed pleased with what they thought was a clever plan. Victory would be easy once the Mericats had abandoned their wagon fortress. Lee told the chiefs to go and let their braves know what was going to happen the next morning. He told them he would have more details at first light. Excited over the prospects of an easy victory, the chiefs hurried off to give the news to their braves.

The looks on the faces of some of the white men showed serious misgivings.

"You mean," said one of the men, after the Indians had left, "that we're going to promise those people safe passage to Cedar City—then as soon as they leave the safety of their wagons, we'll go back on our promise and slaughter them?"

"That's the recommended plan," said Lee, so choked up he could barely talk.

"I don't like it," said the man. "It's not honorable. A victory gained by lies and deceit loses its savor."

"Would you rather gallop head-on into the sights of their rifles?" shouted one of the other men.

"They're going to die anyway," said another. "Wouldn't it be better if it were done in a way where none of us had to die, too? We'll need every man we can get when Johnston's Army invades Utah."

"By luring them out like that," said another, "we'll be able to separate out and save the little kids, many of whom would otherwise be killed."

"I still don't like it," said the first man. "Promising a man safe conduct to get his gun, then shooting him in the back, isn't my idea of a fair fight. I'd have trouble sleeping at night if I done that."

"Who says it has to be a fair fight?" responded one of the others. "Anything's fair in war. The idea is to win with as few casualties as possible, and Lee's plan seems well-suited for that."

"Well, I ain't going to shoot anybody who thinks I'm taking him to safety in Cedar City," said the man who didn't like the plan.

"You won't have to," said Lee. "There'll be plenty of Indians to do it for you."

"What about their guns?" asked one of the others, referring to the Mericats.

"They'll be told up front that giving up their arms is part of the deal," said Lee, "that the Indians won't stand to see them march out of here armed. There's no agreement if they don't give up their arms."

"And if they won't do it?" asked another.

"Then we'll just wait until they will," said Lee. "Maybe harass them some to get them to use up more ammunition. Eventually they'll have to go along with the plan."

"How about the women?" someone asked. "And the older children, those old enough to talk, but still children? I couldn't gun down an eight-year-old kid or a defenseless woman."

"What do the scriptures say about the shedding of innocent blood?" asked the man who was against the plan. "You've all heard of the unpardonable sin. I strongly suspect some of those women and children are innocent of sin. I don't want their blood on my hands." There was a murmur of agreement among the men.

"None of you will have to shed innocent blood," sobbed Lee. He explained more details of the plan, how the small children would be taken ahead in a wagon, where they would not be harmed. Following would come the women and the older children, and last the men. When the time came for the attack, the Mormons would help kill the men, but only Indians would kill the women and older children. Only Indians would be guilty of shedding innocent blood, if indeed there was innocent blood among the people of the Fancher Company.

I suddenly became ill and quickly turned away into the nearby brush to lose my noonday meal.

When I returned, Lee was seated on the ground, openly weeping. Some of the chiefs had returned and were staring with amazement at the soft-hearted white men. One of the white men asked them to leave. Reluctantly they did so, mumbling among themselves the word *Yauguts,* which I later learned meant "crying man." The chiefs had given Lee a new name, one that would spread far and wide among the Utes and Piedes, a name Lee would carry to the grave.

The mood among the white men had changed, even among those who earlier had seemed most eager to do battle. I think it was the final details of Lee's plan that did it. The idea of shooting unarmed people like fish in a barrel, and realizing they were going to be doing it the next morning, was too much to stomach, even for the toughest frontiersmen.

Some of the men tried to change the focus of the discussion, talk about the big picture, the invasion of Johnston's Army, the projected reality of what might happen if the people in the Fancher Company were allowed to go to California and tell how they had been attacked by Mormons, and the slaughter of Mormons that would follow. The same ideas were discussed again and again.

The murder of Mormons and the destruction of their property by Missouri mobs was discussed, as was the murder of Parley P. Pratt in Arkansas earlier that year. Men talked about sacred vows they had taken to avenge the murders of Joseph and Hyrum Smith. Nothing was left unsaid. It had been dark a long time, but no one was hungry or sleepy.

"Why aren't Haight and Dame here?" one of the men asked Lee.

"I don't know," he said.

"Seems the ones that give the orders should help carry them out," said the same man.

"It's one thing to sit back in Cedar City or Parowan and play general," said another, "but another thing to point the barrel of your gun at a man who's begging for mercy, then pull the trigger."

"And what'll it be like when the Injuns wade into the women and children?" demanded another.

Lee was still sitting on the ground, tears streaming down his cheeks.

"Maybe we should send a message to Haight and Dame that we won't do it unless they come," suggested one of the men.

"Maybe we should send them a message that we refuse to obey their order," suggested another.

"I hope you all understand the seriousness of disobeying a direct order in wartime," cautioned Lee. He repeated what he had said to me earlier, that if a mistake was made, the sin would be on the head of those who gave the orders, not on those who carried them out.

"Maybe we ought to pray about it," suggested the first man.

A moment later, everyone present was kneeling in a tight circle, heads bowed, eyes closed. Lee offered the first prayer, expressing sentiments similar to what he said when he and I had prayed earlier in the day. When Lee finished, one of the others offered a prayer, then another, until most of the men had poured out their concerns to God.

I joined them in the circle, even though I was not a member of their militia. My eyes were closed, too, and as each man prayed, I tried to keep my mind clear and open, listening, sensing, trying to hear or feel anything that God was trying to tell this sad bunch of men. There was nothing, nothing at all.

When we finished I felt as bad as when we had begun, and I don't think the prayers helped anyone else either, because no one went off to sleep. The heart-tearing discussion and weeping continued until the stars began to fade in the gray dawn.

Chapter 37

When the night was blackest, while Lee and his men were discussing their plan, the people in the circle of wagons were also holding sober counsel. With ammunition critically low and Lee refusing to talk with those sent out under the white flag, there was much heated discussion about what to do.

Some felt the safest thing was just to hang on, making sure every bullet brought down one of the enemy, hoping the Indians would run out of fight before the Fancher Company ran out of balls and powder.

Others were in favor of sending out more messengers in the hope one might eventually get away and find help, though there was considerable discussion as to where help might be found, short of a three-hundred-mile ride to California.

Then there were others who thought a peace could be negotiated, perhaps by paying off their attackers with cattle and horses. They knew their wagon fortress seemed impenetrable to the enemy, so they figured they had a strong bargaining position. The big question was how to begin the negotiations, since Lee had repeatedly refused to talk to those going out under the white flag.

"Maybe they're afraid of the Indians, too," suggested Dick Boggs. "Every time we send a man out with a white flag, there's hundreds of Injuns looking on. Maybe the Mormons are afraid to be friendly in front of the Injuns, fearing the redskins might turn on them, too. There's enough Injuns out there to kill them and us."

What Boggs said sounded reasonable. At this point, anything that offered the slightest hope was given serious consideration.

"Are you suggesting," asked Fancher, "that if we could get a messenger to the Mormons without the Indians knowing about it, they might be willing to talk to us and maybe work out something?"

"Might be worth a try," said Boggs.

"Anybody got any ideas on how we might do that?" asked Fancher. No one stepped forward. No one seemed to have an answer, not even a guess about something that might work. Boggs was the next to speak.

"If a man could get to Lee or Storm in the dark, the Injuns wouldn't know about it," he said. "Of course, going out in the night, a man's taking a chance of stepping on some sleeping Injuns before he finds the whites—then it's all over for that man."

"Maybe it's worth a try," said Fancher. "Anybody want to go out there in the dark to find Lee or Storm and ask them what can be done to get us out of here? Anybody want to volunteer for that?"

Nobody rushed forward to accept the risky assignment. The chances of stumbling onto one of two white men in a camp of three hundred Indians didn't seem very likely. As before, Boggs was the first to speak.

"Seeing as how I helped get us in this mess, shooting the squaw and taking the nigger's little girls, passing off a pickled Injun as the dead Pratt and all—maybe I should go. I'll give it a try."

Boggs was the last man anyone expected to step forward. Four months on the trail and you get to know a man pretty well—and whenever there was dirty or dangerous work to do, Boggs always seemed to be absent. He wasn't a man to volunteer for this kind of assignment, especially since he had killed a squaw and kidnapped Indian children. If they caught him, there would be no mercy. Stumbling through the dark with a wooden leg would certainly increase his chances of being heard and caught. Yet Boggs had stepped forward and volunteered.

The people of the Fancher Company found new respect for Dick Boggs. Adversity sometimes does good things to people, they decided. With his back against the wall, Boggs was abandoning his cowardly ways, or so they thought.

The men, and some of the women, patted Boggs on the back, offering him congratulations and encouragement as he tied a white flag to the barrel of his rifle. When that was finished, the one-legged Missourian asked Henry Dunlap to tell him everything he could remember about the location of Storm's camp. When Dunlap was finished, Boggs slipped between two wagon wheels where the chains had been removed, and disappeared into the night.

Even an open meadow is not easy to cross with a wooden leg, especially in the darkness. Of biggest concern were prairie dog and badger holes. Boggs moved slowly, carefully picking each step.

After covering about two hundred yards, Boggs stopped and listened. He could hear male voices behind him and in front of him. He tried to tell if the voices in front were those of Indians or white men, but they were too far away, and the sounds were too muffled by the rustle of grass and trees in the night breeze. Figuring he had reached the midpoint between the two camps, he seated himself on the ground and waited, thinking about his observations of the past several days.

Boggs had been carefully watching the rising smoke from enemy cookfires. Most of the smoke was in the north, near the bottom of the meadow. There was more smoke to the south, near the top of the meadow. In the early morning hours, he had spotted the smoke of several fires on the ridge to the west. But he had never seen the smoke of a single fire on the rugged, more thickly wooded ridges to the east. That got him thinking, and he had come up with a plan, the one he was now attempting to carry out.

Boggs waited almost an hour, eventually getting back on his feet but not moving more than a foot or two in any direction. Finally he began working his way back to the circle of wagons.

"Who's there?" challenged a guard when he was just a short distance away.

"It's me," hissed Boggs. "Take off the chains and let me in."

"Damn Mormons," growled Boggs as he shuffled between the wagons. "If every one of 'em don't burn in hell, there ain't no God. Bunch of no-good maggotheads."

When everyone was gathered around, Boggs told how he had found himself right in the middle of the enemy camp, surrounded by sleeping Indians, how he had managed to slip out without any of them awakening, and how eventually he had found the sleeping Lee.

"He couldn't believe I'd got past the Injuns without getting found out," said Boggs, "but once he realized I had, he was eager to talk." The men were gathered close, hanging on every word.

"We was right about one thing," continued Boggs. "Lee said he couldn't talk to our men with the white flags because he was afraid the Injuns would turn on him and his men for being friendly with us.

"I asked him if he could help us get out of this fix. He said it was too dangerous. I said we could make it worth his while, maybe give him some cattle or horses, or some wagons. Should have seen the grubber sit up and take a real interest.

"He asked if we had any gold. I told him we were poor emigrants and didn't have much money. He asked me how much we had. I said I didn't know.

"Then he said if we can get him two or three thousand dollars in gold tonight, he'll figure out a way to get us out of here tomorrow. He said some of the chiefs can be bought off with gold, but it would needs be done in secret, so none of the others would know about it. Said it would be very dangerous. Damn, greedy Mormons. Should of knowed all they wanted was our money."

Some of the other men began cussing the Mormons too.

"What do you think we should do?" asked Fancher, after telling the others to be silent.

"Don't know," said Boggs. "All I know is what I told you, that Lee said he could buy off some of the chiefs and get us out of here tomorrow if we gave him our gold. There ain't much dark left if we aim to do it tonight."

"I've heard about Lee," offered one of the men. "He's been

with the Mormons a long time, has a reputation of being an honest, hard-working businessman. Not dirt like most of them. Has a reputation of doing what he says he'll do."

A vote was taken and it was decided to send the gold out to Lee immediately. After about fifteen minutes of scrambling through wagon boxes, a leather pouch containing $1,920 in gold coins was handed over to Boggs.

"Would you rather have someone else take it?" asked Fancher.

"Nobody else knows where Lee is sleeping," answered Boggs.

"Would you like someone to go with you?"

"Two people make more noise than one," responded Boggs. "Don't worry. If I leave right now, I shouldn't have any trouble humping it back by daylight."

A minute later Boggs disappeared into the darkness for the second time that night. He had gone maybe a hundred yards when he made a sharp right turn and headed east toward the rocky brush-covered ridge, the ridge where he had been unable to spot any campfire smoke. With a little luck he could make it to the top before the stars began to fade. He didn't mind the extra burden of gold coins. At least the Indians wouldn't be getting any gold now if they succeeded in massacring the people in the Fancher Company.

Chapter 38

After all the discussing, praying, and crying, the main idea, the single thought that seemed to umbrella everything else, was Lee's conviction that the responsibility for what was about to happen was on the heads of those giving the orders, Lieutenant Colonel Isaac C. Haight and Colonel William Dame. The orders carried added weight because these two men were also the religious leaders in southern Utah. Haight was the stake president at Cedar City and Dame was the stake president at Parowan.

"We must obey our leaders," said Lee. "No matter how unpleasant the task, we must understand that this small battlefield is just a small piece of a much larger problem. The future of the State of Deseret is hanging in the balance, with hostile armies at the door. Our leaders must make hard decisions if our state is to be preserved. We must follow orders, knowing the responsibility for what we do rests on the shoulders of those giving the orders. None of you will be held accountable before God for what you do here today, if you carry out the orders as outlined."

With the chiefs and most of the white men gathered around, Lee laid out in detail the plans of the day. Lee, accompanied by William Bateman carrying a white flag, would approach the Fancher Company and present the plan. If it was accepted, Bateman would wave the flag back and forth, the signal for two empty wagons and the white militiamen to come to the circle of wagons.

The surrendered arms would be placed in the wagons, as well as the small children and the wounded who were unable to walk. The wagons would lead out, going north to join the road to Cedar City. They were to hurry, widening the distance between the wagons and the group of women and older children who would follow on foot. The men herding this group were to hurry them along, too, widening the gap between them and the last group, the men who would be marching single file. An armed Mormon would be on the right side of each of the men.

Most of the Indians were to hide in the brush where the trail passed between two hills at the bottom of the meadow. The rest of the red men were to surround the entire area, ready to intercept any person trying to escape.

Phillip Klingonsmith was to ride between the last two groups, and when the women and older children were in position between the two hills where the Indians were in hiding, he would turn toward the men and shout "halt," the signal for each Mormon man to turn and shoot the man at his side. Any militiaman who at the last second could not do this was to fire into the air and sit down, allowing the Indians to do the job for them.

Upon hearing the shooting, the Indians would come out of hiding and kill the women and children. The men up front driving the wagons would finish off the wounded. Lee was to ride in the first wagon and help with this task.

Those who had spoken out against the slaughter during the night were quiet now. Everyone seemed soberly resolved to do his duty.

When Lee asked if Ike and I were going to help, I politely declined, saying we were not part of the militia and as civilians would just watch from our camp on the hill. When we were satisfied that Boggs was dead, we would leave, taking Susannah and the girls with us. Lee would never hear from us again.

I had just said good-bye to Lee and was about to return to Ike and Susannah on the hill when a new group of Mormon reinforcements arrived. There were about ten men in the group, and they seemed relieved they hadn't missed any of the action. They hadn't spent the night searching their souls and consciences like the rest of us.

"When your courier shouted in passing," said the leader to Lee, "that he couldn't stop because he was taking an urgent message to Cedar City, I figured we had missed the fight."

"I didn't send a courier out this morning," said Lee.

"You sure did," responded the man. "We passed him just a few miles back, and he was riding like Satan himself was on his tail."

"What'd he look like?" asked Lee.

"Older man with a patch over one eye, and an excellent rider, even with a wooden leg."

"That's Boggs!" I shouted to Lee. "He's escaped from the wagon train. Ike and I'll get him."

I ran up the hill to where Ike was already beginning to saddle the horses. On the one hand, I was upset that the man most deserving to die had slipped away. On the other hand, I was glad for a reason to leave this godforsaken place before the business of the day began.

Chapter 39

I lied to Susannah. At least, I didn't tell her the whole truth when she asked what all the white men were doing at the meadows. I asked her how she knew white men were there. She said she could hear iron-shod hooves striking against rocks, and men's voices speaking English.

I told her some men had ridden out from Cedar City to try to convince the Indians to let the Fancher Company go. I told her the Indians were planning another attack and that I didn't think the chances were very good of talking them out of it. Ike and I had avoided talking to Susannah about the events of the previous night. She didn't know about Lee's orders or the plan.

I was torn between her right as an adult to know the fate of those she had traveled west with and my desire to protect her from the horrible truth of what was about to happen to these people. For her own good, I decided to shield her from the truth by lying, and I felt guilty for doing it.

I couldn't help but wonder how many other people would tell lies too as questions began popping up about the fate of the Fancher Company. How many good men would have to swallow their sense of honesty and integrity in their well-meaning attempts to cover up what happened at the meadows?

At least I was not going to see what happened there. I would always be able to say I was not at Mountain Meadows when the

Fancher Company was wiped out. It felt so good to be leaving.

Ike was riding on one side of the road, me on the other, with Susannah in between. Ike and I each had one of the little girls in the saddle with us.

Ike and I were watching the sides of the road for fresh horse tracks leaving the beaten path. We knew Boggs had been seen galloping toward Cedar City, and we figured he would not enter the city where he would surely be recognized as the man who had convinced a local merchant that a dead Indian was Parley P. Pratt. Boggs was not the kind of man who could go through a town unnoticed, not with a wooden leg and a patch over one eye.

"Stop," cried Susannah, after we had covered three or four miles. Ike and I whipped our rifles out of the scabbards as we reined in the horses, scanning the nearby trees and brush for any sign of an ambush from Boggs. Neither of us could see anything out of the ordinary.

"Hold your horses still," she said. "Be quiet."

I couldn't hear anything, and neither could Ike, but realizing Susannah had a more highly developed sense of hearing because of her blindness, we quickly obeyed, making the horses stand still.

She was standing in her stirrups, twisting sideways in the saddle, as if she were looking back the way we had come.

"There was a lot of shooting a moment ago," she whispered. "Now it's almost stopped, but I think I can hear screaming, not one person, but lots of people, maybe horses. I'm not sure." Ike and I couldn't hear anything, but we both knew what Susannah was hearing.

"Do you think the Indians will succeed this time?" she asked.

"All I know is there is nothing we can do to change what is happening back there, so let's keep moving," I said, irritated by her comments.

"Wait a minute," she said. "Maybe I should be back there with those people. I feel like a deserter, sneaking away with you while the rest have to stay and fight. Maybe I should go back."

I moved my horse close to Susannah and put my hand on hers.

"Susannah," I said. "I can understand how you feel, having

traveled that far with those folks. But remember, your husband is dead. You were forced to make a choice as to who you wanted to be with—Dick Boggs, Henry Dunlap, or these two little girls. Of your own free will and choice you selected the girls. That's all. Nothing more. This is where you belong right now."

We resumed our journey toward Cedar City, trying to concentrate on horse tracks and not what was happening back at the meadows. We kept a closer eye on the west side of the road, thinking Boggs would probably head in that direction, toward California.

Later in the day we found a set of tracks heading off to the north along a brushy ridge, but unable to reason why Boggs would go that way, we continued along the road until we reached Pinto, a small community with just a few homes.

Some women were in a front yard discussing all the Indians and Mormons they had seen riding toward the meadows the last few days. When they said they hadn't seen anyone fitting Boggs's description heading toward Cedar City, or anywhere, for that matter, we turned around and headed back the way we had come, figuring those tracks heading north must have belonged to Boggs.

We considered leaving Susannah and the girls at Pinto, allowing us to travel faster after Boggs. But on second thought, with all Susannah knew about the meadows, we figured the farther we could get her away from there the better, even if it slowed us down some.

I could only think of two reasons Boggs would head north. First, it was the last direction anyone would expect him to go, so there would be a smaller chance of being followed. Second, Johnston's Army was only a few hundred miles beyond Salt Lake. If Boggs succeeded in getting that far he would be safe from the Mormons, with an immediate contact to the eastern press, with a story to tell that would make him a national hero. Boggs would like that, all right, especially if he could benefit at the expense of the Mormons. But this was only speculation. All we could do was follow the trail and see where it led.

That night, after we had finished supper and the girls were sleeping, Susannah startled me for the second time that day.

"Why did you lie to me?" she asked in a calm voice.

"Why would I lie to you?" I responded, trying to sound calm, too.

"I don't know, but you did."

"What'd I lie about?"

"You said the Mormons had come to try and stop the Indians from attacking the wagons. That's not true. They came to help the Indians."

"Why do you think that?" I asked cautiously.

"Because that's what happened. Nobody tried to stop the attack."

"Some wanted to," I said meekly.

"But the order was to help the Indians. Something to do with us seeing the bearded Mormon killing our man trying to get away on Wednesday. Your leaders were afraid that if we got away we would tell the world how Mormons were attacking emigrant trains. Your leaders decided we had to be silenced."

I didn't respond. I was stunned with a horrible reality. It didn't bother me so much that Susannah had figured things out. What stunned me was how quickly a blind lady with just a few facts had so easily figured out what had happened. I realized, for the first time, that the massacre at Mountain Meadows would not remain a secret, regardless of the oaths of secrecy made by the white men involved. Some of the facts would be made known, and others would arrive at the same conclusions that had come so easily to Susannah. The only thing she didn't know now was how the massacre was carried out, and I didn't plan on giving her those horrible details.

"What about me?" she asked.

"What do you mean?"

"Why did Lee allow me to go free? I could tell everything."

"I told him you were blind and hadn't seen anything."

"But I know what happened. I heard the gunshots. I heard the screaming. People will believe me. I have no reason to lie."

"Are you going to tell the world what you know?" I asked.

"How can I remain silent?" she sobbed, tears beginning to stream down her cheeks. "There were over a hundred people in that circle of wagons. I knew almost all of them. I'll be the first to admit that some of them were wicked, mean people, especially the men, but they didn't deserve to die."

"When Lee agreed to let you go," I said, still calm, "I promised him you would not cause any trouble."

"You had no right to speak for me."

"But I did have a desire to save your life, and that's what I did."

"And now I should show my gratitude by remaining silent?" she snapped.

"That would be nice," I said sheepishly.

"There's only one thing that will keep me quiet," she said coldly. "And that's six feet of dirt, Mr. Storm. Are you going to kill me?"

"No," I said.

"Because if you are, you'd better get your gun and do it right now."

"Not in front of de girls," said Ike, surprising both Susannah and me in a way that we began to laugh, but stopped quickly.

"I won't kill you, Susannah," I said. "That's a promise. There's been enough killing today, except for what Boggs has got coming."

"Don't make any promises you can't keep."

"That's one I'll keep. I'm a man who keeps his promises."

"I know one you are going to break," she said.

"Tell me."

"You promised Lee I wouldn't make any trouble and you promised me you would see that I got wherever I wanted to go. You can't do both."

"Where do you want to go?"

"Directly to Johnston's Army. I'm sure they have a *New York Times* reporter along who will be more than happy to hear and publish my story."

"Seems you and Boggs have the same idea," I said, looking over at Ike, who just shrugged his shoulders.

Chapter 40

Susannah hardly spoke to me the next day. Whenever we stopped, she fussed over the little girls like a mother hen, but she avoided any interaction with me. She was more open with Ike, though. I suppose it had something to do with his being the father of the girls.

Ike was quiet too, and there was little conversation as we followed the northbound trail. The knowledge of what had happened at the meadows hung over us like a black cloud, depressing our spirits, making it impossible to feel cheerful about anything.

About midmorning we found a spot in some willows by a spring where the horse we had been following had been tied up while the rider rested. The ground was soft and we found the unmistakable marks of Boggs's wooden leg. Knowing we were on the right trail, we made our horses travel faster.

The trail was leading us straight north, about thirty miles west of the main wagon road and the Mormon settlements. Later in the day, however, the trail began to veer eastward toward the settlements. Perhaps Boggs needed food and supplies.

That night we camped in sight of the town of Beaver. After camp was set up, I rode into town to see what I could learn. Perhaps someone had seen or talked to Boggs. Plus I was curious if news of the massacre had begun to travel north.

Stopping at four or five places, I couldn't find anyone who had seen anything of Boggs, but there was a lot of talk about the Indians attacking the Fancher Company at Mountain Meadows. News of the massacre had not yet reached Beaver.

I was about to head back to camp when James Haslem galloped in from the north, calling for food and a fresh horse before he even came to a stop. He was still wearing the same clothes he had been wearing at the Sunday night meeting in Cedar City when he was sent to Salt Lake to ask President Young about the Fancher problem. Having had hardly any sleep the entire week, he was now returning with Brigham's message.

As he dismounted from his weary horse, I pushed in just close enough for him to hear me and said, "I have just come from the meadows and would like to speak to you in private."

I have never seen such weariness in a man's face as he looked over at me, nodding for me to join him at a distance away from the others.

"What's happening down there?" he asked when we were far enough away so as not to be overheard.

"There was a lot of shooting yesterday morning as I was leaving," I told him. "I think the Fancher Company was wiped out by Mormons and Indians."

"Why didn't they wait for word from President Young?"

I gave him a brief account of the attempted escape on Wednesday and how that had changed things, forcing the leaders to feel an urgency to handle the situation right away.

"Then my journey was wasted."

"What did President Young have to say?"

"To let those people go," he said in a weary voice.

"There's a chance I might be wrong," I said. "I heard a lot of shooting but didn't actually see anything. You'd better keep going in case I'm wrong."

I asked him if he had seen a man fitting Boggs's description, and when he said he hadn't, I returned to camp.

I didn't say anything around Susannah about my meeting with Haslem. I figured as long as she was intending to talk to the eastern press, the less she knew, the better.

Later on in the evening, after the girls were asleep, she broke the silence of the day by asking me what we were going to do with Boggs if we caught him.

"Just give him what he's got coming."

"And what's that?"

"Three weeks ago those little girls had a mother," I said. "Boggs murdered her. The boy saw it all, and Boggs even confessed it to Fancher earlier this week."

"Will you shoot him?"

"Probably have to. Doubt he'll give up without a fight."

"You haven't considered taking him to Salt Lake for a fair trial?"

"Little Plume was a squaw," I explained. "Those eastern judges appointed to the Utah courts don't figure killing Indians is murder, especially not a squaw. They'll just let Boggs go. I'll pass on that kind of justice."

"What'll you do to him if you catch him?" she asked, insisting on getting all the details. This woman should have been a reporter.

"I won't do anything," I said, catching her by surprise. "I'll just turn him over to Ike, who's learned a lot from the Indians on how to handle people like Boggs.

She turned to Ike. "What will you do to him?"

Ike scratched his chin and gave her a thoughtful look.

"Been thinkin' lots 'bout dat," he began. "Maybe I just tie his hands and feet tight and stretch hisself over an ant hill. Den cut open his belly real careful, so he don't bleed much. Doan want him t' go too fast. Den slip out his innards and let de ants do de rest. Man usually last two days dat way. Second day magpies come. Gets stinkin' awful bad."

Susannah didn't ask any more questions that night, and the next morning as we were breaking camp, she didn't seem to be in as big a hurry to get moving. Ike and I were optimistic that this was the day we would catch Dick Boggs.

Chapter 41

About midday we stopped at a favorite camping place for travelers, called Cove Fort. Susannah asked when I was going to take her to Johnston's Army.

"We're headed that way right now," I said. "As long as the trail stays fresh, we'll stay on it, regardless of the direction it takes us. When Boggs is taken care of, we've got to get the little girls home. Then it will be your turn, not before."

"What do you mean when you say take the girls home? Their mother is dead. Who'll take care of them?"

"Ike has three more wives. They'll find a place for the girls."

"You mean the Indians practice polygamy, too?" she asked.

"Good thing they do," I said. "Wouldn't want these little girls ending up with strangers."

"Seems disgusting somehow," was Susannah's only comment.

* * *

We followed the trail into Fillmore, where we talked to a lot of people who had seen Boggs just a few hours earlier. Some had even talked to him, but they said he hadn't introduced himself as Dick Boggs. Instead, he'd told them he was Rulon James on the way to see his only daughter sealed to Apostle George Albert Smith in the endowment house.

"Even ugly old buzzards like that can have pretty daughters, I suppose," said one of the men we talked to. He said Boggs had bought some supplies, including a pistol to protect himself from Indians and gentiles. And a fresh horse, so he wouldn't be late for the wedding. The man said Boggs had paid for everything in gold.

As we left Fillmore we began to worry. We had been steadily gaining on Boggs, but now that he had a fresh horse, maybe he would start widening the distance between us. To make matters worse, black clouds were rolling in from the west. A good storm could wipe out the trail.

And that's exactly what happened, but not before we determined that Boggs was not headed north and east toward the main string of Mormon settlements, but north and west into the desolate desert where wild horses and Ike's people roamed, a land of remote, rugged mountains where a fugitive could hide for years without being found.

That night we camped under a rocky ledge. Rain fell hard until well past midnight, and the next morning the trail we had been following was completely wiped out.

There was nothing to do but continue, spreading out, hoping to stumble onto fresh tracks. We traveled all day, checking carefully the mouths of canyons, scanning flat-bottomed washes as far as the eye could see. There were no fresh tracks anywhere. That night we camped on the banks of the Sevier River.

I remembered Porter Rockwell telling me about a new cabin he had built just north and a little west of this portion of the Sevier River at a place called Cherry Creek. I told Ike about it, thinking maybe an Indian friend of Port or a herdsman might be there. If we went there we could ask them to be on the lookout for Boggs. And there was an outside chance they had already seen him. The next morning we headed for Port's cabin on Cherry Creek.

As we rode along, now with no tracks to keep our minds occupied, I thought a lot about Susannah and the promise I had made to take her to Johnston's Army. And my promise to Lee that she wouldn't cause any trouble. Even though Susannah had been hard to get along with since leaving the meadows, I was convinced she was a good woman. I could believe nothing else every time I watched her pouring out love and affection on those little girls.

At the same time, I didn't want to help get a story out that—once grabbed on to by the eastern press—would stir up even more hate against my people, hate that could easily result in the death of countless Mormons. I think I was becoming more concerned with what to do with Susannah than whether or not we caught Boggs.

"You are going to miss the girls," I said as we were riding side by side at a wide place in the trail. She nodded.

"If we don't pick up Boggs's trail again," I said, "we'll probably be heading west to take the girls home. Maybe you'd like to stay with them a while. I'm sure the Gosiutes would give you a warm welcome and let you stay as long as you like."

"That might not be a bad idea," she said coldly. "I'd like to see how the girls will be living for the rest of their lives, but not until I've taken care of more urgent business."

"And what's that?" I asked, already knowing how she was going to answer.

"Warning the world about all you cold-blooded murderers. People need to know about Utah so they will stay away."

"You have a lot of nerve for a totally helpless blind lady," I said. "If I'm a murderer, why haven't I killed you?"

"You don't scare me, Mr. Storm," she said. She always addressed me formally when she was mad. I was getting used to it. And I was getting tired of her.

By afternoon we found a little creek flowing north and began following it, figuring it was Cherry Creek and would lead us to Port's cabin.

By early evening we spotted the cabin in the shade of some big trees. It was a new cabin, made from unpeeled cedar trees, very solid-looking with a big porch on both ends. It appeared Port liked to spend his mornings and evenings sitting on a porch. We were pleased to see smoke coming from the chimney.

We were about a quarter of a mile away when a big bay stallion in a circular corral made of vertical cedar posts spotted us and began neighing to our horses as only a stallion can. Pretty soon a gray wolf-like dog came out from under the porch and began barking at us. The horse looked familiar, and so did the dog.

I could hardly believe my eyes when Porter Rockwell stepped out onto the porch, slipping a knife into a belt sheath. With the fight against Johnston's Army going on in Wyoming, Port was the last man in the world I expected to find at his own cabin on Cherry Creek.

"Susannah Stevenson, I'd like you to meet Orrin Porter Rockwell," I said as we dismounted.

"The famous Mormon gunfighter," she responded. "We've already met."

"In Salt Lake, after your wives patched her up," said Port, sounding mean and indifferent. "She's the one you backhanded in the fight with that skinny maggothead from the Fancher Company."

Port had remembered her, the woman he had taken back to her wagon.

"I heard they were surrounded by Indians outside Cedar City, in real trouble," he said.

"That's right. We were there. Except for Susannah and Boggs, I think the whole company was wiped out."

"Thanks to the Mormons," she added. Port gave her a hard look.

As Susannah and the children entered the cabin, Port and I walked down by the stream. Ike was taking care of the horses.

I told Port the whole story, about Mountain Meadows and how Susannah was determined to take the story to the reporters accompanying Johnston's Army. I also told how we had been following Boggs.

"Too pretty to shoot," said Port matter-of-factly, "but you can't let her do that."

For the first time, I noticed that Port's hand was bandaged. He said he had injured it changing a wagon wheel. Since General Johnston had taken the fighting troops to Kansas, and only teamsters were with the main army, he had taken a few weeks off from war to finish the roof on his new cabin before winter set in. Lot Smith was handling things in his absence. He said in a few days he would be heading back to Wyoming.

"Look," he said. "Just shot an antelope up that draw, a mile or so back. Came back for my knife. Got to take care of the meat before it sours. Make yourselves comfortable. I'll be back in an hour or two, and we'll have antelope steaks for supper. You'll spend the night, won't you?"

I said we would, fighting to keep from grinning over a crazy idea that had just popped into my head.

While Port headed up the draw to get his antelope, I hurried over to Ike, who was just beginning to unsaddle the horses. I told him to leave the saddles on, and as we tightened the cinches I explained my plan, Ike grinning in total agreement.

We led the horses back to the cabin. I told Susannah we had spotted a bunch of Gosiutes out in the desert who appeared to be heading toward Ike's home camp, and that we intended to take the little girls out to them immediately, saving us a longer trip later on.

She barely had time to give the girls a good-bye hug. We tossed them onto the horses, swung up behind them, and turned the horses west.

"When will you be back?" cried Susannah.

"Maybe a week," laughed Ike.

"Maybe three," I said as we galloped into the desert.

"I hate you, Mr. Storm," she called after us, but I didn't care. We were taking Ike's little girls home before resuming our search for Boggs. Port could figure out what to do with Susannah.

Chapter 42

It was dark when Port returned with the antelope over his shoulders, the wolf dog trailing close behind.

"Why ain't somebody lit the lantern so a man can see where he puts his feet?" shouted Port as he stepped onto the porch.

"Because until you came along there was no one for whom the light would do any good," said Susannah quietly from a chair at the far end of the porch.

"What?" asked Port, not understanding the meaning of what she said.

"Until you came along there was only me," she said, "and lanterns certainly don't do me any good."

"Where's Dan and Ike?"

"Taking the girls home to Ike's camp."

"That's over a hundred miles. When will they be back?"

"Ike said a week . . ."

"You can't stay here that long."

"Mr. Storm said three weeks. Maybe never."

"I'm heading back to Wyoming in a few days. What'll I do with you?"

"I'm going to the same place, so you can take me with you."

"Hell will freeze over first," growled Port. "Dan told me about you, how you want to tell them reporters about Mountain Meadows. You won't get any help from me."

"You can't just leave me here."

"Don't bet on it."

"You wouldn't dare."

"Look, lady . . ."

"My name is Susannah."

"Lady, I'm not sure what I am going to do with you," he said, ignoring the reference to her name. "The only thing I know for sure right now is that next time I see Dan Storm I'm going to kill him."

"You Mormons find killing an easy solution to a lot of your problems, don't you?"

"It might be the best solution to the problem Dan Storm just dropped in my lap."

"Mr. Rockwell, you don't scare me."

"In that case, why don't you join me for a supper of fresh antelope steak? We can figure out tomorrow what to do about you."

"Sounds good. I'm very hungry."

Port stomped into the cabin and flopped the skinned antelope on the plank table. Taking two wooden matches from a drinking glass on the windowsill, he first lit the lantern hanging from a wire above the table. Then, striking the other match, he ignited the paper and kindling through the open door of the pot-bellied stove. Already on top of the stove was a black frying pan, its interior white with the bacon grease of several breakfasts.

After closing the stove door and adjusting the draft, Port moved to the table, removing the skinning knife from the sheath on his belt. By this time Susannah had entered the cabin and was seated on one of the wooden stools beside the table.

Carefully Port removed a long, narrow strip of red-blue meat from along the back, the tenderloin. He cut off both ends, which he tossed to the wolf dog waiting patiently in the doorway. The animal caught the first one in flight, gulping it down in one fast swallow. The second piece wasn't far behind.

When the entire loin was sliced into little steaks, Port sprinkled some flour from a red can onto a platter. After sprinkling a generous amount of salt and pepper over the flour, he began rolling the pieces of meat through the flour and dropping them into the now hot bacon grease.

When the interior of the pan was covered with sizzling steaks, he removed three clean potatoes from a bucket of water. and without peeling, sliced them over the meat, then covered the pan with a lid.

"Wait a minute," said Susannah when Port picked up the carcass, saying he was going to take it outside and hang it in a tree. "Cut off another piece for Abe. He's still hungry."

Port was surprised this blind woman even knew the dog was there. He hadn't said anything when he had tossed the meat to the animal earlier, and it had been perfectly quiet. Then he remembered how this woman had a sixth sense with animals. He remembered how she had calmed and petted this dog a month earlier, the only human being ever to get that friendly with this dog. He cut off a front leg and tossed it out the door. That would give Abe something to chew on all night.

"Thank you," said Susannah.

Port didn't like being thanked by a stranger for feeding his own dog. It was like she thought it was her dog, not his.

"Guess I don't need to set a fancy table with a cloth and all, with you blind," he said after he had finished hanging the carcass outside.

"As long as the dishes and silverware are clean, I don't much care about anything else."

"Seems funny, you caring about clean plates," he said.

"Why do you say that?"

"You're the dirtiest woman I ever seen."

Susannah felt herself beginning to blush. Then she became angry for feeling intimidated. She had every right to be dirty. No one thought much of washing and bathing during those four days the wagon train was surrounded by hostile Indians. And the last four days she had been on the trail with Dan and Ike, with no time for serious washing. Of course she was dirty, and if Rockwell didn't like it, that was his problem.

"At least I have good reason to be dirty," she said in partial defense of her appearance.

"There's some clean water in a bucket just to the right of the stove," said Port. While the supper finished cooking, she went over to the bucket and rinsed her face and hands.

Few words were spoken during supper. Susannah had forgotten how hungry she was. For over a week she had been surviving on jerky, dried fruit, and old bread. She couldn't ever remember anything tasting better than the juicy, tender antelope steaks and the salty brown potatoes, washed down with cold spring water. Port was hungry, too, and between them they didn't stop eating until everything was gone.

"Never seen a woman eat so much," he said when they were almost finished.

"Probably never seen a woman this hungry before," she responded, her mouth full of food as she reached for the last steak.

"Still some dirt around your eyes and on your left cheek," he said, watching her closely while she finished her meal. Even soiled, she was one of the most beautiful women he had ever seen. And there was no question but what a very beautiful womanly figure was hiding behind that filthy, ragged dress. Too bad she was blind. He would have to be careful not to get liking her too much or feeling very sorry for her. The news she was determined to take to the outside world represented a dangerous threat to his people. Somehow, she would have to be handled, and he wasn't sure how.

"Next time I wash I'll be more careful," she said pleasantly.

Sensing the food had made her more agreeable, Port mentioned the bathing tub he had out back, and offered to heat some bath water for her in the morning.

"I'd like that very much," she responded.

"As for tonight," said Port, "I'll be sleeping in the shed by the corral. You can sleep in the bed behind the door."

"I don't want to take your bed," said Susannah. "Let me sleep in the shed. Your dog can keep me company. I wouldn't mind that at all."

"I'll do just fine in the shed," said Port firmly. He wanted no more discussion on the subject.

"Of course, you probably don't sleep very well anyway," said

Susannah, bringing one hand to the side of her mouth, having just thought of something very unsettling.

"Don't you have a lot of nightmares?" she asked, "The faces of all the people you've killed, coming back to haunt you?"

"I'll be sleeping a lot sounder than you tonight," growled Port, getting to his feet and reaching for the lantern.

"I doubt that," said Susannah with a yawn.

"Haven't you heard about all the women murdered in their sleep by Porter Rockwell?"

Port blew out the lamp and stomped out the door.

Chapter 43

"Do you have anything I can wear while my clothes are drying?" asked Susannah while Port was pouring a steaming bucket of water into the wooden bathing tub.

He dropped to his knees and pulled a bundle out from under the bed and began unraveling it.

"No dresses or regular clothes," he said. "But I have some new buckskins a Ute squaw gave me. A little big, but they'll do. Here's some moccasins, too."

"They smell awful smoky," she said as he handed her the clothing.

"That's the way the Indians waterproof them. You get used to the smell. I like the soft feel of buckskins."

"Yes, they feel very soft. Thank you." Port went outside, closing the door behind him. A minute later as Susannah was beginning to unbutton her dress, she suddenly stopped and turned toward the cabin's only window.

"Mr. Rockwell," she said. "Being blind, I have a very keen sense of hearing. May I ask what you are doing outside that window?"

"Just picking up the ax to go chop some firewood," he said sheepishly as he turned to walk away.

"Listening to your continuous chopping will help me enjoy my bath a lot more," she called after him. He didn't answer, but the air was soon filled with the furious thunking of Port's ax.

A half hour later Susannah and Port were sitting on the porch, both in their buckskins. Susannah's freshly washed dress and underclothing were hanging on a rope stretched between two trees. Susannah's hand was resting on the wolf dog's head, her fingers scratching gently between his ears.

It was a clear fall day, the sun shining brightly beyond the edge of the porch. The leaves on the trees were rustling gently in a slight breeze.

"Port," she said, calling him by his first name for the first time, "I think I detect a distinct dirty sock odor coming from you. Maybe you should bathe too."

"The fact that you didn't notice that until now might be an indication of how you smelled before the scrub," he said. They both laughed.

"Maybe tomorrow I'll heat up some water and clean up—that is, if you are up to chopping the wood." Again they laughed.

"Can I ask a personal question?" asked Susannah.

"You can ask anything you want. Whether or not you'll get an answer, I can't tell you."

"Are you married?"

"Yes."

"And?"

"I have two wives and seven children. They're all at Lehi now, because of the war."

"Do you love them both? I mean, the wives."

"Sure."

"But how can you be in love with two women at the same time? That's not possible."

"You seemed pretty attached to those little girls when you arrived here yesterday. Do you love them both, or just one?"

"Both, of course."

"How, then, can you tell me I can't love more than one woman at the same time?"

"Romantic love is different than the kind of love a parent feels for a child."

"Maybe in some ways. But I love one of my wives all of the

time, and the other most of the time."

"Isn't it hard, living with more than one wife?"

"Sure, especially when both are under the same roof."

"You mean fighting with each other, trying to be boss, that kind of thing."

"No, my wives get along purty good," said Port, standing up to walk along the porch, looking thoughtfully across the desert. Susannah waited for him to continue.

"Women have tender feelings. Sometimes I don't remember very well, like who I kissed first the last time I came home, or which one I last took for a buggy ride, or who cooked the apple pie that I said was the best I ever tasted. A man's got to be on his toes and remember all those things. Otherwise he can't be fair. For a wanderer like me, it's hard to remember where I slept last. A man with two wives can't ever forget that.

"Sometimes I'll find one of them crying over somethin' I done, and I don't even know what I done. I hurt her and didn't even mean to. Sometimes I feel like just shooting myself in the head. I never mean to hurt them, but it happens, in little ways, because I forget, because I'm not on my toes. That's what's hard about having more than one wife."

Susannah could hardly believe what she was hearing. Words like that shouldn't come from the mouth of a hardened killer, the most notorious gunfighter in the American West. He seemed so sincere, so genuine. The seeming contradiction was too great.

"I have another question."

"As I said, you can ask anything you want."

"How does it feel to kill people?"

Port stopped and looked at Susannah, wondering how such boldness could come from someone so helpless.

He told her about the last person he had shot, the seventeen-year-old boy who had stolen two mules, how the boy had tried to run from him when he caught up with the lad near Salt Creek, not more than a day's ride from the cabin. The boy was still alive when he got to him, blood running from the boy's mouth. He didn't even have a gun. He said he was sorry about the mules. Then he died.

Port told her how he loaded the boy's limp body on one of the stolen mules and took him home, and how the boy's mother wailed like a squaw. "At first, I just felt sick to my stomach," he said, beginning to walk again, looking out across the desert. "Years ago I threw up a time or two, but not anymore.

"If I see 'em die up close, like with the boy," he said, his voice softer now, almost choking, "I feel pain, like rheumatism, all over my body, only worse. Almost like it's going to kill me sometimes. Maybe someday it will."

"Then why do you do it?"

"Can't stop."

"I don't understand."

"Started back in Missouri. Mobs burning homes, dozens every night. Raping women, beating and killing men. Tarring and feathering some, doing worse to others.

"Some of us decided to fight back. Called ourselves Danites. It helped. The mobs didn't quit, but they backed off some."

"That doesn't explain why you can't stop."

"I got good at it. Good with a gun, a knife. Learned to keep a calm head in a fight. I always won. Now I'm the best. When there's trouble, I'm the one they ask to fix it."

"Tell them to get someone else."

"Sometimes I wonder how many people in a day decide not to steal something, or hurt someone, because they are afraid that if they do Porter Rockwell will come after them. Deseret has less crime than anywhere west of the Mississippi. Fear of me is one of the reasons for that. I can't step down."

"That's a heavy burden. Does it have anything to do with your long hair?"

"I think you've asked enough questions for one day."

"Just one more, please."

"Go ahead."

"Have you decided to take me with you when you leave?"

"You'll be coming with me."

"Oh, thank you," cried Susannah, jumping to her feet and throwing her arms around Port.

"But I'm not taking you to Wyoming."

She dropped her arms to her sides and stepped back.

"I'm taking you to Storm's place, and when he gets home he can decide what to do with you."

A minute passed before Susannah spoke. When she did, her fists were clenched.

"I've been asking you questions. Why don't you ask me some?"

"Like what?" he asked cautiously.

"Like how well you get to know a group of people when you travel across a continent together in covered wagons."

"I've done that."

"Then ask me how it feels when you find out all those people were slaughtered like sheep in a pen, and you're the only survivor. How would you feel if you were me? Their blood crying from the dust for justice, you the only one left to tell what happened, and you can't get to anyone who needs to hear the story because you are blind?"

Susannah began to cry. Port grabbed her by the shoulders and shook her to silence.

"Your telling that story will bring more bloodshed," he said, "and not the blood of cold-blooded murderers, but lots of innocent people—men, women, and children. Those men who killed your people were afraid of the approaching army. Maybe the massacre is President Buchanan's fault because he sent out the army. The men you want to expose are hard-working farmers, tradesmen, men with wives and little children, men who go to church, who pray, who read scriptures. Men who help their neighbors and strangers too. Men who want to do what's right and generally succeed at it. I will not help you bring death and destruction to them and their families."

"Then take me to Storm's and I'll find my own way to Wyoming," she said, turning to walk back into the cabin.

"I've changed my mind," said Port firmly. "Too many people near Storm's who might help you. I'm leaving you here."

"You can't do that," she cried, turning back toward him.

"There's enough food in the cabin to get you through the winter," said Port, "if Storm doesn't come back. I'll leave old Abe with you for protection. Don't share too much food with him. He can catch rabbits. I'll probably come back before spring. Remember, it's almost a hundred miles to the nearest settlement. Lots of desert and rattlesnakes in between. If you try to leave, you'll die."

"Please take me with you," she cried.

Port grabbed his rifle and his heavy buffalo coat, then started toward the corral.

"Porter Rockwell," she called after him. "I hate you. You're nothing but a cold-hearted murderer!" He offered no defense as he bridled and saddled the big bay. After giving the wolf dog stern orders not to follow, he galloped away, following the trail heading east.

Chapter 44

"If Mr. Rockwell thinks he can leave me penned up in this cabin all winter like an animal in a cage, he's got another thing coming," said Susannah to the dog.

"The town of Nephi is somewhere west of here, and I have a hunch it's no hundred miles like Mr. Rockwell said. I'd guess you've been there a number of times and could find it in the dark. Abe, we're going to take a long walk."

After filling an old sack with sufficient supplies for several days, including plenty of antelope meat for Abe, Susannah felt around until she found a short piece of rope, which she tied to Abe's neck.

"Abe, you are going to help lead me to Nephi. I imagine you'll be pretty well trained by the time we get there. I guess you'll be an excellent bodyguard too."

Susannah thought about changing back into her clean dress but decided against it. The dress would be the desired attire once she reached the Mormon communities, but the buckskins would be more practical in crossing the wild country between the cabin and the first settlement. The buckskins would offer more protection from brush and rocks in the day and would keep her warmer at night. With the sack of supplies tied over her shoulders, the leash in one hand and a four-foot stick in the other, she was ready to begin the first journey of her life where she was not accompanied by another person.

Abe was not used to a leash and at first tried to pull away from her. But he quickly caught on to what she was trying to do and was soon pulling her as fast as she could walk along the same well-used trail taken an hour earlier by Port.

Susannah had never walked so fast in her life. The dog in front gave her a confidence she had never felt before. She wondered why it had taken her so long to make this fantastic discovery. They were going up a gradual incline through some kind of mountain pass.

It wasn't long before she tripped over a large rock, then a clump of sagebrush. When she fell down, the leash slipped from her hand, but Abe only turned and licked her face, urging her to get up. Gradually Abe seemed to get the idea that any obstacle in the trail gave Susannah problems. He began slowing down whenever something was in the path that might trip Susannah. She quickly learned to notice when the dog slackened his pace, and she felt more thoroughly with her stick for the cause of the slowdown. With time she stumbled less frequently. She could hardly believe what good time they were making.

In the afternoon the sky clouded over. Even though the sun was hidden, it was not cold, just right for hiking.

Several times they stopped for a snack and a drink of water from a jar in the sack. The walking became easier after they came down the other side of the pass. The ground became increasingly sandy, with less brush and rocks. She figured they would probably spend one night on the trail, maybe two, but no more than that.

Late in the day the sand began to give way to more brush and rocks, and Susannah was just thinking that she should start looking for a place to spend the night when the dog pulled her onto a well-used trail, which apparently led up into another pass. Feeling the ground, she could tell the trail had been used recently by horses, horses with iron shoes. Maybe she was getting close to a settlement.

She decided to put off looking for shelter, hoping she would perhaps find a town on the other side of the pass. Because she was blind, she had little concern about getting caught on the trail after dark. She was used to the blackness.

About an hour later, she noticed the sound of wind blowing through trees just ahead, and the unmistakable sound of running water, a small stream.

"Is anybody there?" she called out.

There was no answer. She continued on, letting Abe determine the direction. Finally he stopped. To her surprise, she reached out with her stick and tapped a wooden porch.

"Is anybody home?" she called out.

"Come in," said a strangely familiar voice.

"Your voice sounds familiar," she responded, stepping onto the porch.

"It ought to," said Port. "It's my cabin and my dog that led you around in the desert all day. Glad you had the sense to come back before the storm settled in."

"Come back?" she asked, beginning to feel sick. "Is this the same cabin I left this morning?"

"Sure is," he said. "I rode up on the ridge, thinking you might try something. When you got over by the dunes, I rode down close enough for the dog to see me, and he just followed me back to the cabin. Bet your feet are sore. You covered a lot of miles today."

Susannah didn't say anything, just walked over to the bed and collapsed, totally exhausted, totally discouraged. No further words were spoken between her and Port as he fired up the stove and cooked another meal of antelope steaks and potatoes. She sat up and ate the food he brought her, though she didn't feel like it. After Port blew out the lantern and retired to the shed, Susannah crawled under the blankets and cried herself to sleep.

Susannah didn't awaken until the sun was shining through the window. The storm had blown over. The stove was cold. Apparently Port didn't plan on cooking breakfast. She walked to the door and called to him. There was no answer. She walked down to the corral and shed. The horse was gone, and so was Port.

She called to Abe. She whistled. The dog was gone, too. Port had taken him.

Chapter 45

Susannah found the walking a lot tougher the second time. Without Abe to guide and pull her along, she traveled a lot slower and found it much harder to stay on the trail. Sometimes when she wandered away from the trail, the only way she could find it again was to crawl on her hands and knees, feeling for the softer dirt and horse tracks. She was carrying the same sack of supplies over her shoulder, and using a stick to tap in front of her. The only bearing she had to know if she was going the right way was the morning sun in her face and the evening sun at her back. Generally the winds blew from the west, but there were frequent changes, so she could not count on the wind to determine direction.

It was bad enough losing Abe as her guide. But what bothered her just as much was losing the dog's protection, which would have warned her of snakes, skunks, porcupines, and the like. He would also have protected her from bears, mountain lions, even Indians. Just the company of the dog was somehow reassuring—someone to talk to, to share companionship with.

Susannah's only protection now was her walking stick and a knife she had found in the cabin. Rather than carry the knife in the sack, she had slipped it down the front of her buckskin trousers, where it would be readily available in case she needed it to defend herself.

This time every obstacle seemed worse without Abe to share

it with. The rocks seemed harder, the bushes more scratchy, the badger holes deeper.

It took her most of the day to get over the pass, a distance she had covered in only a few hours the day before. Then she was in the sand, and somehow it seemed deeper. She must have wandered farther south or farther north during the middle of the day when she could not take bearings from the sun.

She remembered Port mentioning the dunes. She guessed she had been on the edge the day before. Now she was in the middle, amid seemingly endless sand hills growing increasingly steep—like giant waves in the sea, except the sand did not move.

Eventually the mounds of sand became so big that she frequently had to climb up the front side on her hands and knees, then slide down the back on her backside. No sooner would she get to the bottom of one mound than she would be confronted with another.

Though there were no rocks and limbs to trip over, she made slow progress through the sand. The footing was soft and required too much energy. Sometimes the hills were sufficiently steep to cause her to lose her forward progress and slide back the way she had come.

By evening she was beginning to think she had made a mistake leaving the cabin. At the cabin was food, shelter, and water. She could have waited for someone to come along. Dan and Ike had said they were going to return in a week, or maybe three. Perhaps she should have waited for them. That would have been the safe thing to do.

She knew it was too late to turn around. She could never find her way back to the cabin anyway. As the wind blew and the sand sifted, her tracks were quickly erased. There was no alternative now but to continue due east, hoping eventually to get out of the dunes and find help. She had enough food for several more days.

The sand warmed quickly whenever the sun came out from behind the clouds. When she was too tired to travel any farther, Susannah found a fairly warm little pocket facing the southwest where the evening sun had shone regularly. Using her sack for a pillow, she burrowed into the warm sand and rested. She was not hungry, just tired and worried. Sleep was a welcome relief.

She spent a restless night, burrowing deeper and deeper as the sand cooled. The only sign of life was the distant howling of prairie wolves. By morning she was totally covered with sand, except her face. She was grateful no rain had fallen.

Before resuming her journey, Susannah forced herself to swallow water from the jar and gulp down some antelope meat. She was not hungry, but knew her strength could not be maintained without nourishment.

She ached all over from the cold sand and felt as filthy as she had ever felt in her life. Sand was everywhere—in her ears, nose, mouth, eyes, down her trousers, and in her moccasins. The sand was damp with the morning dew and stuck to her like mud.

To make matters worse, it was a cloudy day. She could not feel the sun, though she could tell there was daylight. She knew which way was east from the position of the immediate hills in relation to the sun as it went down the previous evening. But she knew as soon as she began traveling, those bearings would be lost. All she could do was pray for more sun.

Instead, it rained. A drizzle at first gradually turned into a steady rain. The buckskin easily absorbed the raindrops, and soon she was soaked. The only way to stay warm was to keep moving.

The massacre at Mountain Meadows seemed a lifetime ago and a world away. Johnston's Army did too. Even the little town of Nephi seemed like a distant, unreachable dream. Her life was suddenly distilled to the simplest of terms as she put one foot in front of the other to stay warm. The heavy, wet sand was sticking to her moccasins, making travel more difficult than before. Still, there was no alternative but to keep moving.

Susannah had some matches in the sack, carefully wrapped in oilcloth to keep them dry, but the matches were no good to her in the dunes where there was nothing to burn. She also knew she could not stop at nightfall. The wet sand would not keep her warm. She must keep putting one foot in front of the other until the dunes ended, or until she could go no more. Then would come the time to court death—and maybe that wouldn't be so bad. Nothing could be worse than what she was going through.

Still, Susannah wanted to live, and whatever it took to stay alive, that she would do.

The rain continued for hours and felt so cold that she wondered if it might soon turn to snow. Because of the dry air, the rain was a lot colder here than where she had grown up in Arkansas. Oh how she wished she were back there now, sitting in the sun, chatting with friends, eating hot potato salad and barbecued chicken.

She was beginning to feel hungry and was thinking about stopping to eat when she was startled by a snort, possibly that of a horse or a cow, not more than twenty or thirty yards away.

"Is someone there?" she cried.

The only answer was another snort, no human voice. The thought occurred to her that she might be approaching a bear or a mountain lion, perhaps a wild boar.

"Shoo," she yelled, thumping her stick against the wet sand. She listened carefully. Nothing ran away.

Then she heard footsteps coming toward her. Not those of a person or a creature with paws. She was hearing hooves, probably those of a horse.

"Who is it?" she asked, beginning to feel frightened. "Port, is that you? Dan? Ike? Mr. Boggs?" The animal continued to come closer.

She felt like fleeing but knew that would serve no useful purpose. She couldn't imagine a wild horse, cow, or even buffalo coming up to her like that. It had to be an animal with a rider. But why didn't he speak to her?

"Please tell me who you are," she cried.

Still no answer. Finally the animal stopped right in front of her. Cautiously, after dropping the sack, she reached out with one hand while the other hand held tightly onto the stick, ready to strike.

She touched a soft, slightly hairy nose. It did not pull away. She decided it was a horse. Sliding her hand up its face, she could not feel the straps of a bridle. She was beginning to think she had come upon a tame stray horse. Then she decided to feel the lower jaw and found a wet leather cord. Now she knew she was petting an Indian pony carrying an Indian who apparently did not speak English.

She stepped back.

"Who are you?" she asked. She thought about the knife in the front of her pants. If the Indian was getting ready to scalp her, she might be able to defend herself with the knife. On the other hand, if the Indian were friendly, pulling out the knife might make him an enemy. She decided to leave the knife where it was.

"Me looking for Porter Rockwell," she said, slowly and deliberately. "He my friend." She figured all the Indians in the area knew Port and would be more likely to help if they thought she was his friend.

Still, the Indian did not say anything, but the horse began to move forward. Susannah didn't move. Suddenly the horse spun around and galloped away.

"Wait!" she cried. "Take me to Nephi."

There was no response, and soon the horse was so far away she could no longer hear the hoofbeats.

It wasn't until she reached down to pick up her sack that she realized why the Indian had left so quickly. Her sack was gone. The Indian had stolen it.

Susannah wanted to sit down and cry, but she was too cold. She had to keep walking. At least she didn't have to carry the heavy sack anymore. But she felt so hungry—more than ever, now that her food was gone.

Chapter 46

Susannah hadn't gone but a few steps when her stick detected an irregular indentation in the sand. Dropping to her knees and feeling with her hand, she realized it was a track from the departing horse. She found another. Galloping through the wet sand, the horse's hooves were leaving deep holes. The cold rain had almost stopped now, so the tracks were not washing in.

With the cloudy skies making it impossible to get bearings from the sun, Susannah decided to follow the Indian's tracks. She had to get out of the dunes, and she figured the tracks would lead her out. There would be no reason for the Indian to stay in the sand hills any longer than absolutely necessary. Hopefully he would continue widening the distance between him and her. She certainly didn't want to meet up with him again. But maybe, indirectly, he had done her a favor in leaving a trail that would lead her out of this awful place.

Once out of the dunes maybe she could find a warm bed of pine needles under a bushy piñon or cedar tree where she could rest until the sun once again allowed her to figure out which way was east—if only her strength would hold out.

★ ★ ★

Susannah was so occupied with trying to follow the horse tracks that she didn't hear the hoofbeats until the horses were almost upon her. When she finally realized she was hearing approaching horses, they were all around her and closing in. Taking a firm hold on her stick, she prepared to defend herself. There was no doubt in Susannah's mind but what she was being surrounded by the companions of the Indian who had stolen her bag. They had come to see the strange blind lady who lived in the dunes.

"Who are you?" she shouted, hoping one of them might understand English.

"Give me my supplies back," she said when there was no response to her first question.

She could hear some of them talking to each other now, in a strange tongue she could not understand.

"What are your names?" she asked, very slowly and deliberately. Certainly some of them understood a little English.

"Me Brigham," said a deep voice and they all laughed.

"Me Heber," said another, and they laughed even louder.

"Me John D. Lee," shouted a third as the laughter continued. In response to the third name, several said, "Yauguts."

Susannah had heard that name before. Storm had told her it meant "crying man," and it was the nickname the Indians had given John D. Lee at Mountain Meadows.

These Indians had come from Mountain Meadows, probably on their way home. They had helped slaughter the people of the Fancher Company.

Susannah felt a rage welling up inside her chest, partly a result of her total helplessness and the hardships of the last few days, and partly a result of the lingering torment she was carrying over what had happened at the meadows.

The decision to attack was not logical, just spontaneous, something she had to do.

Cocking back the stick, she lunged toward what her ears told her was the closest horse and swung the stick with all her might. It caught the horse on the side of the neck just as it was spinning away.

Without taking any time to think, she lunged for the next horse. This one she barely missed. Letting out an angry scream, she spun around and lunged at a horse she had heard approaching from behind. This one she caught on the side of a hind leg as it lunged away.

The Indians were all yelling now, totally delighted at the sport of avoiding the crazy blind lady. Hearing the laughter and shouting, Susannah realized they were playing with her. She dropped to her knees, totally exhausted, gasping for air. She felt the urge to cry, but refused to give in to it. Never would she give them that satisfaction, even if they scalped her.

"Give me stick," said a voice not very far in front of her. Still breathing hard, she got to her feet, cocking the stick again, ready to strike when the man was close enough.

"Give me stick." He was getting close. He had dismounted.

She was about ready to strike at the voice when two strong hands grabbed her arms from behind. Twisting her right arm forward, she automatically reached down with her mouth and sank her teeth into a dirty finger. The hand jerked way, almost pulling her teeth from her mouth. She spit a piece of skin onto the wet sand. Another hand wrenched away her stick, and others grabbed her arms. Someone grabbed her hair and jerked her head back.

The skin on the top of her head was pulled tight, ready to tear free at the touch of a sharp knife. She jerked, squirmed, and kicked with all her might, but there were too many hands holding her—strong, rough hands.

She kept waiting for the knife to touch her head, but it didn't. Instead, some of the hands let go of her arms and began pulling at her wet buckskins. Suddenly she realized they had something else besides scalping in mind. She wanted to throw up on them, but she couldn't. Her strength was gone.

★ ★ ★

Even with all the noise the Indians were making, the gunshot was loud, shaking the ground. The Indians were more startled than Susannah as they turned their heads to see who had fired the shot.

Even with the brim of his hat down over his eyes, the Indians didn't have any trouble recognizing the longhaired man wearing the heavy buffalo hide coat. He was mounted on a tall bay stallion accompanied by a big wolf dog.

"Porter Rockwell," said one of them, very respectfully.

Susannah felt the hands let go of her. She remained on her feet, not sure what would happen next, just knowing Port was in charge, at least for the moment.

"My woman," said Port, riding forward, the dog close beside the big horse. "Ran away."

"I'm not . . . ," Susannah started to say, but decided to be quiet. Port could say whatever he pleased.

The big bay stepped up beside her. She grabbed onto Port's strong arm and allowed him to pull her up behind him.

"Thanks for catching her for me," he said as he dug his heels into the horse's ribs. They galloped off into the dunes, leaving the Indians to wonder among themselves how badly the famous gunfighter must treat his blind squaw to make her want to run off by herself into the dunes.

Chapter 47

It felt so good to Susannah to be seated on the powerful horse, holding tightly onto Port, feeling his strong back against her chest. It felt so good to know they would soon be out of the dunes, on regular ground. It felt so good not to be alone, but with three friends: the man, the horse, and the dog. All three with good eyes to see where they were going. Susannah felt like closing her eyes and going to sleep, except she was too cold and was beginning to shiver.

"Will they follow us?" she asked, her teeth chattering.

"No," said Port, pulling the horse to a halt. "I wasn't sure old Ammon and his boys were going to give you up. Those bucks have been away from women a long time. But I'll bet they're in too big a hurry to get back to the Uintah Basin to bother you anymore."

Without dismounting, he slipped out of the big buffalo hide coat and helped Susannah put it on. She was amazed at how heavy it felt. But it also felt good. It would take away the shivering.

"Three hides thick," said Port, explaining why the coat was so heavy. "Wear it all winter. Even sleep in it when I'm on the trail. That coat's got a lot of sentimental value."

She wrapped the coat tightly around her and tied it in place with a thick rawhide belt. Once again she reached around Port's waist to hang on as the horse lunged forward. It wasn't long until she could hear the horse's hooves striking an occasional rock. They were out of the dunes.

"Where are we going?" she asked.

"Back to the cabin. Get you in some dry clothes and fill your belly with hot food."

"But that's a long way."

"The way you travel, maybe. But this horse'll have us there in less than an hour."

Susannah felt more than a little foolish. Almost two days on the trail and she had only managed to get an hour's horseback ride from the cabin.

They rode in silence for a while, the horse now traveling at a fast walk.

"Why did you come back?" she asked, wondering what possible turn of events would cause Port to come back and save her from the Indians.

"Didn't," was all he said.

"Didn't what?" she asked.

"Didn't come back."

"Sure you did, or you couldn't have rescued me from the Indians."

"Couldn't come back if I didn't leave in the first place," he responded.

Susannah could feel the blood rising to her face. She wasn't cold anymore. In fact, she was beginning to feel hot, hot with anger.

"Where have you been the last two days?" she demanded.

"Sitting on ridges and sand hills, watching a blind lady wander around the dunes."

Susannah let go of Port's waist and pounded him angrily on the back. As she did so, the startled horse leaped forward, causing Susannah to slide backward and onto the ground. A second later she was flat on her back with Abe trying to give her face a friendly lick. Port was laughing as he pulled the horse to a halt and turned around.

"You just watched me wander around lost in all that sand and did nothing?" she shouted.

"Just kept an eye on things to make sure you didn't hurt yourself."

"But I was lost. How could you just let me sleep on the damp sand without a blanket or fire?"

"Wasn't around then," said Port. "When it started to get dark, I rode back to the cabin and crawled into that warm bed."

"But I suppose you were back in time to see that Indian steal my supplies."

"Just barely. It was raining so hard I almost decided to spend the day in the cabin. Figured prettier women than you had been rained on before. You're lucky I found this hat, or I might not have come at all."

"Porter Rockwell, you're a cold-blooded murderer."

"Don't say that, Susannah. I just saved you from being raped by all those Indians."

"For the life of me, I can't figure out why you bothered to interfere, not after practically letting me die, right under your nose."

"Would you like to know why I waited so long?"

"Of course."

"Then get back on the horse. I'll tell you while we're riding." He reached down and helped her onto the horse a second time. This time she didn't wrap her arms so tightly around his waist.

"When I left you at the cabin alone, without even the dog for protection, I figured that was one of the meanest things I had ever done."

"I'll agree with that," she said.

"But knowing you had tried to leave with Abe the day before, I didn't dare leave, not without making sure you didn't try something stupid like that again. If you had ever seen the country you would have to pass through on the way to Nephi, you would not have tried. The way is full of dry washes with thirty-foot drop-offs and box canyons. All the places to get lost in and never get out of again. The dunes were just the first of a hundred deadly places.

"But you left the cabin anyway. Literally blind, you left the safety of the cabin and marched boldly into the land of a hundred deaths. I have been in situations where men have died, and I have seen what men call courage, but I swear I have never seen courage to match yours when you started marching up that trail all by yourself.

"I kept waiting for you to sit down and cry. But you didn't. Sometimes when you were crawling up those dunes and would slide back, I just had to look away. But when I would look back, instead of sitting hopelessly in the sand because you couldn't go any farther, you were heading back up the same hill until you finally made it over.

"Then I left you for the night, knowing you couldn't go far. When I came back the next morning, in all that rain, there you were marching along, cold and soaked to the bone, one foot in front of the other, never stopping. I was beginning to believe that God was giving me a glimpse of greatness, something I have seen only a few times in my entire life. It was like I was watching a miracle, and dared not interfere, even when the Indian took your supplies. I knew you would just keep going.

"Then when the Indians surrounded you, when you couldn't go any farther, when it was time for you to die or be raped and carried off to some distant camp as a slave; instead of sitting down and crying, or begging for mercy, you attacked them with that silly little stick."

"That was a dumb thing to do," said Susannah, "but when they called John D. Lee 'Yauguts' I knew they had come from the meadows and had participated in the slaughter of all those people, and I just couldn't hold back."

"And neither could I," said Port, "when they began to pull at your buckskins. Suddenly I was no longer an observer, but a participant, and would have given my life, if necessary, to prevent them from harming you."

Susannah wasn't sure how to respond. No man had ever spoken to her that way before. No one had ever expressed such respect or esteem for her before. People had always been nice to her, but no one had ever held her in such awe; no man, or woman for that matter, had ever expressed such high regard for her—never. Port had set her up on a pedestal much higher than she deserved. She savored every word and wished he would continue. But he didn't.

They rode in silence for a while, the late afternoon sun, warm and penetrating, eventually breaking through the thinning clouds. Susannah slipped out of the heavy buffalo coat, and Port laid it over the horse's neck.

After a lot of thought, Susannah decided to put Port's newfound reverence for her to the test.

"Will you take me to Johnston's Army now?" she asked.

"If that's what you have to do," he said without hesitation, "I'll see that you get there. But first, you're going to get some dry clothes, hot food, and a good night's sleep.

"I'll even take you to Lehi," he began a minute later, a note of hesitation in his voice, something Susannah had never noticed before in Port. "You'd be welcome to join my family."

"And become your third wife!" exclaimed Susannah.

"There's two in front of you. Can't change that."

"But I'm blind."

"You don't think I'm aware of that, especially after the last two days?"

"I'm not a Mormon."

"A little water can change that."

"Don't be so sure."

"When you understand the pure doctrine, you'll join."

"You seem awful sure."

"I am."

"Mormons believe a lot of strange stuff," she said. "I don't know how you can believe it yourself, let alone expect me to believe it, too."

"Didn't used to pay a lot of mind to the doctrines," he said thoughtfully. "Not until Joseph started teaching this celestial marriage business."

Port paused, gathering his thoughts. Susannah waited for him to continue. "You've got to understand what it's like coming home on a cold wintry night, your face frozen by a north wind and your bones hurtin' with the cold after you've been on the trail a week or so. So cold and tired, at times you wondered if you'd ever see your family again."

Susannah wasn't sure what coming home on a cold night had

to do with Joseph Smith's mysterious doctrines, but she waited for Port to continue.

"When you open the door the little ones attack you, climbing all over you like cubs on a mother bear. Maybe you lay yourself down on a rug in front of the fire, the little ones still all over you. One of the older kids puts your horse away.

"Pretty soon you get up and go to the table, where your woman has scooped you up a big bowl of stew or fried up a hunk of meat. She butters a piece of fresh bread, pours you a mug of cold milk. The children are gathered around, some wanting to sit on your lap, some wanting bites of the food even though they have already eaten, and all of them just wanting to talk, tell you what they been doin' and ask what you been doin'.

"The woman can't hardly get a word in, so she just sits there, not eating, but just looking at you, smiling, so glad to see you.

"Then when the kids are in bed, you and the woman go into a cold bedroom, blow out the lantern, and slip under a big down quilt, so cold that it makes your bodies feel hot when you put your arms around each other, holding tight like you are never going to let go. You lay there talking, enjoying each other in the dark like there's nothing else happening in the whole world."

Port stopped talking. Susannah sensed that his mind was in another world far away, that he could see the things he was talking about, forgetting he was riding double with a blind woman. After what seemed a long pause, he resumed his monologue.

"A few hours earlier you were so tired and cold you didn't know if you could make it home to your family. Now you feel so good, so happy, so content, you can't begin to sleep, just talking, holding each other, for hours.

"The best life has to offer," continued Port. "Nothing better."

"What does this have to do with Joseph Smith and celestial marriage?" asked Susannah, not wanting to spoil Port's dreamy mood, but curious why he was telling her these things.

"Until Joseph received his revelation on marriage," responded Port, "the only heaven I ever heard preached in churches was a place where everybody sings in choirs and you get hit by lightning for even looking at a woman. I'd rather be in hell with a good woman any day than be a eunuch in somebody's choir."

Susannah couldn't help but laugh.

"When Joseph said men and women and children should be together forever," continued Port, "I decided to get religion. Joseph said being in the highest heaven was like coming home to a family on a cold night and having the feeling last forever. That's worth dying for—living for, too."

To Susannah, Port's concept of heaven sounded very desirable but almost too earthy, too simple. Yet tears had come to her at his description of coming home. She couldn't imagine anything better, either. Still, she couldn't just abandon a lifetime of religious instruction presenting heaven as a place with white robes, golden streets, choirs singing glories to God, and lots of nice people being very kind and polite to each other. She would have to think about Port's heaven. In the meantime, she had to deal with Port's offer of marriage. She changed the subject.

"You are probably old enough to be my father," she said.

"Now, that hurts," said Port. "But it's true, and if you're more suited to want to warm my lap instead of my bed, I'll understand. I'm just tossing out an invitation. You're free to reject it, accept it, or just think about it for a while. I won't push you."

"I'll think about it," said the shaken Susannah. Too much had happened in one day.

A few minutes later the horse stopped beside the corral. Port slipped into the heavy coat to avoid dropping it in the mud, then quickly unsaddled the horse and turned it into the corral. Together he and Susannah walked to the cabin.

"You're still going to have to sleep in the shed tonight," she said, taking hold of his arm.

"I never presumed anything else," he said, his voice sounding nervous for the second time that day. The sun was just disappearing beyond the west desert.

"Hold it right there," ordered a gruff voice as they opened the cabin door. Port did not recognize the voice, but Susannah did. It belonged to Dick Boggs.

Chapter 48

With his pistol aimed at Port, Boggs handed Susannah the looped end of a rope, ordering her to twist it into a figure eight, making a double loop around each of Port's wrists, then pulling it tight. When that was done, Boggs ordered Port inside the cabin.

Using Susannah's walking stick, Boggs worked the free end of the rope over the center pole, then pulled it tight until Port's hands were stretched high above his head and only his toes were touching the floor.

After securing the free end of the rope to the corner of the windowsill, Boggs slammed the door and turned to Susannah.

"I was hoping Storm would come along," he growled, "but catchin' the great Mormon gunfighter ain't half bad. He's the one that shot my cousin, Lilburn Boggs, back in Missouri. But what I can't figure is why you're here."

"Storm dropped me off here," she said, not sure she wanted to tell Boggs anything. "Port was going to take me to Johnston's Army."

"So you could tell a reporter all about what happened at Mountain Meadows, I suppose," sneered Boggs. "Don't believe that."

"It's true," said Susannah. Boggs just laughed, then asked, "Where's Storm?"

"Looking for you," said Susannah. "Ike, too. And you'd better hope they don't find you. In fact, they're due this way any day."

"Guess I'll not hang around here long," said Boggs. "My horse pulled up lame a while back. Guess I'll be borrowin' yours, Mr. Rockwell."

"Horse thieves don't live long around here," snarled Port.

"Maybe I'll take the woman, too," said Boggs. Turning to Susannah, he said, "Come with me. Got a nice little hideout where we can stay until General Johnston gets here to shoot things up. Then us that ain't Mormons can do as we please."

"No thanks," said Susannah. "I prefer the company of Mr. Rockwell."

"How about the dead body of Mr. Rockwell?"

"You wouldn't," said Susannah.

"Always heard a man's got to be crazy to get in a gunfight with Rockwell," said Boggs, turning to Port. "You got too many tricks, they say. Only way to beat you is with your hands tied. Now that your hands is tied, maybe I'll see if I can beat you."

"Want me to turn around so you can shoot at my back?" scoffed Port. "That's the way most yellerbellies like to do it."

Susannah couldn't believe that Port was actually daring Boggs to pull the trigger. Maybe Port wasn't as smart as she had supposed. She wondered why men always seemed to be trying to prove something. Why didn't Port just shut his mouth and hope, with her, that Boggs would go away?

"Where do you want it, Rockwell?" asked Boggs. "Between the eyes or in the heart?"

"Them's awful little targets," said Port. "How about the butt? That's the only target big enough you probably wouldn't miss."

Boggs cocked back the hammer. Port spit across the room at him. Susannah stepped between them.

"Git out of the way," ordered Boggs.

"I've changed my mind," said Susannah.

" 'Bout what?"

"About going with you," she lied. "I think I agree with you that perhaps Mr. Rockwell wasn't serious about taking me to Johnston's Army. I might like spending the winter with you in your hideout."

"That's more like it," grinned Boggs.

"But I might change my mind," said Susannah, "if you were to kill Mr. Rockwell. Let him live and I'll go with you—right now—and make it very much worth your while."

She winked at Boggs. If only Port would keep his mouth shut, she would soon have Boggs out of here, and Port's life would be spared. But Port would have none of it.

"Boggs," he warned. "If you take that woman I'll personally see you are hunted to the ends of the earth if necessary. Course you'll never get that far, not with a wooden leg and a bad eye. You're only half a man, and when you're caught, I'll bring you back and turn you over to Ike's Indian friends. You know what they'll do. You have my word on it."

Without warning, Boggs shuffled sideways so Susannah was no longer between him and Port, then pulled the trigger. Inside the cabin, the report of the pistol was deafening. Boggs cocked back the hammer and fired again.

Port's head dropped forward, his eyes half open. There were two holes in the front of the big coat. A second later, blood began dripping from the corner of his mouth. Except for a twitch in his left leg, his body was still.

Susannah gasped in disbelief, her hand over her mouth. Quickly, she stepped toward Port, feeling his limp body, using her sleeve to wipe up the blood she felt running from his mouth. It had happened so quickly. A second ago Porter Rockwell was a living, breathing human being. Now he was no more.

"Shoot me, too!" she screamed, turning to Boggs.

"Had to do it," said Boggs, coolly. "Now let's git going before some of his friends drop in." With one hand he reached down and picked up a pair of saddlebags he had left by the door. With the other he grabbed Susannah by the arm.

"I'm not . . ." she began to say, then stopped. She didn't pull away, but let him lead her behind him as he opened the door and shuffled onto the porch.

It wasn't until both of them were on the porch that Susannah turned on Boggs with the fury of a wildcat, hitting and clawing, kicking at the wooden leg, finally succeeding in pushing him from the porch.

"Abe, Abe," she called. "Get 'im boy, get 'im."

The wolf dog was onto Boggs before Susannah finished calling for him, snarling, snapping, seeking the soft skin beneath the chin. Had Boggs not gotten his forearm to his chin first, he would have died in front of Port's cabin. As it was, the dog sank his teeth into the forearm, jerking and ripping as the blood began to flow.

★ ★ ★

As Susannah crawled about the porch in search of Port's gun, which he had dropped, she could hear Boggs backing to the corral, fending off Abe with the saddlebags and a club he had found along the way. By the time she found the gun, Boggs was too far away to be worried about getting shot by a blind woman. Almost before she knew it, Boggs had looped a rope around the horse's neck, opened the gate, and was galloping away to the north, the growling, barking dog close on his heels.

Susannah walked inside the cabin, quiet as death now. She walked up to Port's limp body, still hanging from the center pole. She put her arms around him and began to cry. For a moment she wished she had accepted his marriage proposal.

"Shake the coat," said a hoarse voice in her ear. It was Port! He was alive.

"Shake the coat," he said a second time. She pushed away, wondering what in the world he was talking about. At least he was alive. She must get him down.

"Don't you have ears, woman? Shake the coat."

This time she obeyed, and two hard objects clattered onto the slab floor.

"Remember when I said this coat had sentimental value?" said Port. "Today's the third time it's saved my life. Pistol balls simply won't go through three buffalo hides." Susannah realized that what had fallen to the floor were the balls from Boggs's gun. She threw her arms around Port.

"But there was blood running from your mouth," she told him.

"Bit my tongue," he said. They were both laughing as Susannah, with Port's direction, found where the rope was secured at the edge of the windowsill, and let him down.

A minute later Abe trotted onto the porch, panting from the chase but proud he had done his part in driving off Boggs. Susannah collapsed on the bed. She had never felt more weary in her entire life.

"At least Boggs doesn't have a gun now," said Port, looking across the desert. It was almost dark now. "Wish Dan and Ike were here with their horses. Could have that man in chains by tomorrow night."

He walked to the edge of the porch, then stepped down and started toward the shed, occasionally bending over to pick something up. A few minutes later he returned to the cabin.

"Gold," said Port as he walked inside. "Found a couple of hundred dollars in gold coin. Must have fallen from the saddlebag while Boggs was swinging it at Abe." Port dropped the handful of gold coins on the table. He turned toward the open door, thoughtfully scratching his chin. "He thinks I'm dead," he said. "I don't think a dog and a blind woman will keep him from coming back for his gold. Sure you want me to stay in the shed tonight?"

Susannah didn't respond. Sound asleep, she hadn't heard anything he had said. Port removed the heavy buffalo coat and gently laid it over the sleeping woman. He thought about changing her out of the damp buckskins but decided against it. The heavy coat would keep her warm enough.

He reached over and gently brushed several strands of stray hair from her closed eyes. His hand finally came to rest against her now pale cheek, soft as a child's. He wondered at the strength behind that angelic face. A few minutes earlier she was offering herself to Boggs to save a friend. Behind that beautiful face was a spirit with enough courage to attack an entire band of Indians, armed with nothing more than a stick.

He remembered his foolish marriage proposal, so clumsy, so unromantic, her sitting in the mud having just fallen off the horse. Bad timing. He wished he were as good with words and women as he was with guns and horses.

It was dark now, but Port didn't light the lantern. He deposited the gold coins in an empty can on a shelf by the stove.

Opening the door, he called Abe inside. He didn't want the dog running around outside where it might run Boggs off. Should Boggs return for his gold, he wouldn't get away a second time.

Port tied one end of a string to the door latch. He tied the other end to the bottom can in a neatly stacked column of empty cans. Anyone attempting to open the door would make plenty of noise.

Taking the dog with him, Port went to the back of the cabin and seated himself on the floor, partially hidden by the stove, his back against the log wall. The dog curled up beside him. With a loaded pistol in each hand, Port tried to get some sleep.

Chapter 49

"Probably afraid to tangle with Abe again," said Port while they were eating breakfast the next morning. "Thought for sure he would sneak back during the night to fetch his gold."

"Unless he had a lot more gold in the saddlebags and didn't lose enough to miss," added Susannah.

"Could be," said Port. "At any rate, he's gone. I've got to be getting back to Wyoming, and we don't have a horse."

"Ever thought of walking to Nephi?" asked Susannah.

"Not alone."

"Then let's go together, you, me, and Abe."

"Are you up to trying it a third time? That wandering around in the dunes had to have taken a lot out of you."

"More up to traveling than staying here alone."

"Would you like me to fix a harness for Abe?"

"Yes," she said, suddenly getting excited about the trip. "He was getting pretty good at it the other day. I have a way with animals, you know. I would like to train dogs for other blind people. I could make a living that way."

Port stopped what he was doing and looked at Susannah.

"Does that mean you've decided against joining my family?" he asked.

"Port, do you remember what I did the first time Boggs was going to shoot you? I offered to go with him in exchange for your life."

"Only those who know Boggs could fully realize how much that means to me," he said. "Why, then, this talk of supporting yourself?"

Susannah sat on the bed trying to gather her thoughts.

"Port," she began. "I want you to listen real careful. I don't think what I am about to say will be easy for you to understand since you have never been blind."

Port sat down beside her. "Shoot," he said.

"When Seth asked me to marry him three years ago, I had some serious doubts. I didn't want to become his wife, but I couldn't say no."

"Why not?" asked Port.

"Because I was blind."

"That doesn't make sense."

"I told you it would be hard to understand. All my life people have been giving me things—clothing, music lessons, food, money. Poor blind Susannah couldn't take care of herself, so all the people around her were obligated to do it for her. And it was good of them to want to do that. But it wasn't good for me."

"Would you please explain that a little better?" asked Port. His elbows were on his knees, and he was toying with one of the gold coins. The rest had been dumped on the table in front of him.

"All my life people have been giving me things because they knew I couldn't take care of myself. Because I was blind, I had to depend on others and needed their generosity to survive. My parents believed that and so did I.

"Before I married Seth I was abused by a neighbor, a good friend of our family, because I was never taught to say no, only to give people, especially friends, whatever they wanted in the hope some of their generosity might come my way."

"Do you mean," Port began, carefully picking his words, his back stiffening, "he used you the way men use women?"

"Yes, that's exactly what I mean."

"Did your parents know, I mean, what he did?"

"No. I never told them, knowing it would hurt them and they'd be angry. I had been taught never to do anything to make people angry at me."

"Then why did you allow him to do it? Did you want it?" he asked.

"Only a man could ask a stupid question like that. Of course I didn't want it. I hated it. I was ashamed."

"Then why did you allow it?"

Susannah got up and walked over to the open door, as if she were about to look for something out in the west desert.

"I couldn't say no. Even though I was practically an adult. I suppose, because of my blindness and the resulting dependence, I still perceived myself as a child, obligated to do whatever adults told me to do. To say no would be like asking lightning from heaven to strike me down.

"When Seth asked me to marry him, I simply could not say no. In my parent's eyes, and mine too, in asking me to marry him he had made the ultimate sacrifice. He was worthy of canonization. He had accepted the burden of this helpless blind girl for life. I could not say no to what people thought was such a wonderful sacrifice.

"Deep inside, I had a feeling that by bearing and rearing children, maybe I could somehow improve my position, justify my existence, free myself from that childhood prison. As time passed and no children came, this last hope began to fade. I had a growing feeling of being lost forever."

"That's how I felt in the St. Louis jail," said Port, not really serious but just letting her know he was still listening. "When did things start to change?" he asked.

"I suppose when I was allowed to care for Ike's little girls. I called them Ruth and Lucy, and loved them as my own. Still do. They needed me. For the first time in my life someone really needed me, instead of the other way around. I was coming alive again.

"Then Seth was killed. The first attack at Mountain Meadows. Things really started to change."

"How?" he asked.

"Mr. Fancher said I could not go on alone, not since I was blind. He said there were two men willing to marry me, Henry Dunlap and Dick Boggs. I had to choose between them. Both of them reminded me of the big sewer rats that live underneath the streets of St. Louis. I suppose if Mr. Fancher had told me to marry one or the other, without giving me a choice, I probably would have done it. That's the way I was trained.

"But when Dan Storm presented me with a third alternative, a chance to turn my back on both of the rats, to say no to both of them, I did it. And I got away with it. There was nothing they could do about it, and I was not struck by lightning."

"Susannah finally said no," said Port, "and it felt great."

"That's right," she said. "Maybe you do understand."

"I'm trying."

"Then when Storm," she continued, "wanted to put me away in American Fork where no one would ever hear what I knew about Mountain Meadows, I said no again. And you know, no matter how he tried, he couldn't make me change my mind."

"He might have killed you," suggested Port, "getting in the way of a secret military operation and all."

"I know that, but I did it anyway." She turned to face Port. He looked up at her.

"Through all this I learned something else. Do you want to know what it is?"

"Sure," he said.

"Some things are worse than death. I was perfectly willing to let Storm kill me rather than fall back into my old way of doing things—taking gratefully whatever people wanted to throw my way when they got to feeling charitable."

"So that's why you went after all those Indians with nothing but a stick?" asked Port.

"I probably overdid it there," she said. "Extremes in anything can be dangerous."

"Now I think I can understand why you were so determined to set out for Nephi, even by yourself."

"Can you understand now why I can't marry you?"

"Too much like charity; you being widowed, broke, and no family around."

"That's right, Port. Marrying you would be an easy solution to all my problems, like a handout. I'd be back in the childhood world where adults don't belong.

"Next time I marry," she continued, "if I ever do, it'll be because I am in love and that's what I really want to do, more than I want to do whatever else is available."

"What do you want to do?" he asked.

"As I said, I couldn't believe how easy it was teaching Abe to lead me along that trail." There was enthusiasm in her voice. "For the first time in my life I was moving along with speed and confidence without the help of other people. Every blind person should have that experience. I believe I can train dogs to do that for others, and that I can make a good living doing it."

"Do I fit in anywhere?" he asked.

"When I'm established, in my own home, you may come calling with the other men who wish my hand, if there are any. If I like you better than the others and want to spend the rest of my life with you, and your other wives, then that's what I'll do. Because I want to, not because it's the only alternative for a poor blind lady. If I marry you it'll be because I've fallen in love with a famous gunfighter and want to share my life with him."

Susannah leaned back on the bed. Without getting up, Port reached over to the table and scooped the rest of the coins into his palm.

"Here," he said, handing them to Susannah. "Boggs left you some seed money for starting your business."

She accepted the coins.

"What about talking to the reporters?" he asked. "Are you still determined to get to Johnston's Army?"

"I've thought a lot about that, too," she said. "I think I understand now why Lee cried so much, why the Indians named him Yauguts, or 'crying man.' "

"Why?"

"Because in his heart he knew that killing all those people was wrong. I think that's why he cried."

"Then why did he do it?" asked Port. "If he knew it was wrong?"

"Because he was trapped, just like I used to be."

"I don't understand."

"Johnston's Army marching across the plains to invade Utah, threats by the Fancher Company to send more troops against Utah from California, the new treaty to stand by the Indians, the threats of the Indians to turn on Mormon settlements if the Mormons didn't help them at the meadows, the Mormon killing the man trying to get away so the settlers thought the Mormons were behind the attack—all these things created a situation where the only logical, practical thing for the Mormons to do was to help wipe out an entire wagon train. It was logical and sensible. Circumstances demanded it.

"Lee was trapped, and so were Haight and Dame. Life played a cruel trick on them. Their oaths, loyalties, sense of responsibility and practicality, even their reasoning, told them to do it. Their sense of right and wrong, their consciences, told them not to do it. They turned away from their consciences and did what circumstances seemed to demand, not what they knew in their hearts to be right."

"Are you sure it's that simple?" asked Port.

"I felt the same way when my neighbor abused me. I knew it was wrong and hated it, but I had been taught, and I believed it was my duty, to accept without question whatever people wanted to give me or do to me because I was somehow dependent on them for the very air I breathed. I was so dependent on others for the very crumbs to survive, that there was no place for me to make my own decisions, to do what I knew to be right, if others wanted me to do differently.

"I was trapped as those men in southern Utah were trapped. I know why Lee cried, because I have cried like that, too, many times.

"Today I think Lee and Haight and Dame would agree with me that some things are worse than death. I can't speak for them, but from now on I am going to make my own decisions, follow my own conscience, or die in the attempt."

"Where do the reporters at Johnston's Army fit into this marvelous plan?" asked Port.

"I think the world deserves to know what happened at the meadows, but I don't think the news will be coming from me."

"Why not?"

"If those Indians know enough English to say, 'Me Brigham,' 'Me Heber,' or 'Me John D. Lee,' I think they know enough English to tell what happened at the meadows. Lee may be able to keep his men quiet for awhile with an oath, but there is no way he can keep three hundred Indians hushed up. I have a feeling the story is already out, that when we get to Nephi everyone will already be talking about it. First the Indians will start talking; then some of the white men will figure that since the bull is already out of the pen there's no sense in keeping secrets any longer. Do you agree?"

"We'll see when we get to Nephi," he said, standing up and stretching.

"Come here, Abe," he called. "Let's get you harnessed up."

Chapter 50

After dropping off the little girls, Ike and I headed back the way we had come, toward Port's cabin on Cherry Creek. We were still wondering whether or not to bypass the cabin where Susannah was when we came upon a fresh set of horse tracks headed north.

The hoof marks were larger and less round than the ones we had followed out of Fillmore, but there was always a chance Boggs could have changed horses. We decided to follow the trail, knowing that sooner or later the rider would have to dismount and when he did we could tell very easily whether or not the man had a wooden leg. If he didn't, we would return to our original course.

With cold weather setting in, Ike and I both felt an urgency to get back to our families to make preparations for winter. We had more or less decided that if we couldn't wrap this thing up with Boggs in three or four days, we'd just have to wait until spring. If Port put the word out that he was looking for Boggs, it would be pretty hard for us not to eventually find out where he was or where he was headed when he left the area.

The rider went a long way without dismounting, and it wasn't until we reached Simpson Springs on the California stagecoach road that we found the unmistakable mark of Boggs's wooden leg. We hurried our pace, following the trail north and east along the road leading back to Salt Lake City. We pushed our horses hard, knowing that when Boggs reached the more populated areas outside of

Salt Lake, the trail would be impossible to follow, since there were too many other tracks on the roads.

Boggs's trail wasn't very old, so when we didn't catch him, the only thing we could figure was that he had picked up an excellent horse.

Upon reaching Faust's Station, the attendant told us a man fitting Boggs's description had passed through three or four hours ahead of us. He said the rider had a wooden leg, a patch over one eye, and an arm that had been bleeding quite badly. He said Boggs had seemed to be in a terrible hurry to get to the city.

"Did you notice anything else?" I asked. "Did he have a gun?"

"No gun," said the man, "but I'd swear the big bay stallion he was riding was a full brother to the one Porter Rockwell rides."

We hurried our pace even more, wondering how Boggs had managed to get Port's horse. Since Boggs's trail had come from the Cherry Creek area, where we had left Port and Susannah, there was little doubt but what the big bay belonged to Port. We hoped Port and Susannah were still alive.

By the time we reached the Jordan River, Boggs's tracks were completely mixed up in hundreds of others, so we headed straight for the Salt Lake police station, figuring the police would cooperate with us in looking for the man. It was dark.

"What do you want him for?" asked the officer at the front desk when we described Boggs to him. He was a big, burly man with a thick mustache and mutton-chop sideburns.

"For stealing Porter Rockwell's horse," I said. We had already decided not to mention the killing of Little Plume, figuring the police wouldn't get too excited about a squaw getting shot.

"Amazing," said the officer. "You're the second person in fifteen minutes with a report on Rockwell's horse.

"A lady of the night from Molly Skinner's place," and he winked at me to be sure I understood his meaning, "just stopped by to report that a customer was riding Port's big bay stallion. I told her it couldn't be because Rockwell wasn't even in town, but down at his new place on Strawberry Creek, I believe.

"If you saw the same big bay, it's probably a full brother to Port's horse. Nobody steals Port's horse and gets away with it, especially not an old man with a wooden leg."

"Was it the lady from Molly's that told you he had a wooden leg?" I asked. He nodded.

Ike and I charged out the door, leaving the officer to wonder about all the crazy people who thought they had seen Porter Rockwell's horse.

I knew exactly where Molly's place was. Port and I had ridden by on our way to Wyoming.

As we approached Molly's house the air was filled with the rank odor of a wet pigpen. Right next to Molly's place was a huge corral filled with squealing, grunting pigs, up to their bellies in mud. The pigs were making so much noise because a man with a whip was wading through the mud, sorting and driving the pigs to the back of the corral, where they were being loaded into wagons, probably for shipment the next morning.

When we reached Molly's place, Port's big bay was tied to the front railing, still saddled. Ike drew his pistol and backed his horse into the shadows across the street, while I dismounted and went to the front door. Ike waited outside in case Boggs slipped past me. If he did, we were certain he would go to the horse.

"I'm a friend of Port's," I said when Molly opened the door.

"I remember," she said, smiling and inviting me in. "Dan Thunder, I believe."

"Dan Storm," I said, correcting her. She laughed at her mistake and invited me to be seated at a round table. There were two big books, law books, opened on the table.

"Going to sue that Jake Smith," she said, nodding toward the open law books. "I try so hard to maintain a clean respectable place, and he goes and puts a hundred pigs right next door. The smell is sickening, bad for business. I can prove damages."

"I believe that's Port's horse outside," I said, resisting the opportunity to be drawn into a conversation about pigs.

"I know," she said. "I sent a girl down to the police station. She hasn't come back yet."

She said the man with the wooden leg had some pretty nasty

cuts on his forearm, like a dog had been chewing on it.

"Where is he now?" I asked.

"Upstairs," she said. "Sleeping off a drunk."

I started to get up, reaching for my pistol.

"Easy," she cautioned. "Let's wait for the police. He's not going anywhere."

"How can you be so sure?" I asked. "Boggs is awful slippery."

She reached down beside her chair and began placing things on the table, among them a wooden stump with a leather harness for strapping it on, a pair of trousers, a single boot, saddlebags, and a gun I guessed he had purchased upon entering Salt Lake.

"There's several thousand dollars in gold in the saddlebags," she said. "I don't think he would leave without his gold, and I know he won't leave without his pants."

"I don't think the police are coming," I said. I told her about our visit to the police station immediately following the visit by her girl, and how the officer in charge hadn't been inclined to believe either report.

"Guess we'd better roust him out ourselves, then," she said. "But please, no shooting. Bad for business, you know."

She led me to the top of the stairs and down a narrow hallway brightly wallpapered but almost dark, with just enough candlelight to avoid tripping over things.

"Is anyone in there with him?" I whispered when she stopped in front of a door. She shook her head to indicate he was alone.

With my pistol ready, I slowly turned the brass knob. The door was locked.

I stepped back and raised my foot to kick the door in. Molly quickly stepped between me and the door, reaching into a side pocket in her dress for a key.

Very quietly she slipped the key into the lock. A moment later the door swung wide. The room was dark.

"Git up and come out of there, Boggs," I ordered. There was no response, not even the rustling of bedcovers. Molly handed me a candle. The room was empty, and the window was open.

I ran down the stairs and out the front door. The big bay was still there. Ike trotted up, leading my horse. Said he'd just heard a horse gallop away from behind the next building. I swung into the saddle and we raced after the fleeing rider.

We hadn't gone far when we caught a glimpse of the man as he passed under a street lamp. He was not naked. Apparently Boggs had found a coat to cover himself.

He was riding a good horse, and because ours was weary from the long ride into Salt Lake, we were simply unable to catch him. He was heading southeast, away from the more populated area of town.

Realizing he was going to get away if we didn't get some help, I called to a group of four young men, mounted on horseback, casually watching our midnight chase.

"Thief!" I yelled. "Help us catch him."

Eager to join in the excitement, they urged their horses into full gallops. Two of them had fast horses and were soon gaining on the fleeing Boggs, who, to my surprise, seemed to know the area unusually well, darting in and out of darkened lanes, seeming to know which gates were opened and which were closed.

It was a long chase, but eventually the two young men caught up with the fleeing man and pulled him from his horse.

★ ★ ★

When Ike and I arrived, he was sitting in a clump of grass, hands over his face. It was not Boggs. This man had two legs. It was discouraging to think we had spent nearly half the night chasing the wrong man. All of a sudden I felt very tired. Nevertheless, I got off my horse to see who it was we had been chasing, to find out why he had run from us, and why his hands were over his face.

"I didn't go in," cried the man and suddenly the puzzle pieces fell into place. He was a local citizen who didn't want anyone to know he had spent an evening at Molly's.

I got back on my horse without bothering to get a look at the man's face and thanked the boys for their help in catching the wrong man. Ike and I headed back to town to find a livery stable where we could rest and feed the horses while we caught a few hours of sleep for ourselves.

In the morning we rode back to Molly's and started asking around the neighborhood for any information on Boggs. It wasn't until we located Jake Smith, the man with the pigs, that we got some answers.

"Yes," he laughed, "I saw him. Naked as a jaybird, covered with mud, the old drunk crawled right into one of the wagons with the hogs. Didn't notice him. Looked right at home in there with the hogs.

"After we got moving, I guess one of the boars got him with a tusk. Instead of squealing like the hogs do, he yelled like a man. That's when I found him. Out by the hot springs.

"Strangest thing I ever saw. Made him get out. Only had one leg, a bad eye too, and his arm looked chewed on, maybe by one of the hogs. A real sorry sight. I felt bad for the old drunk.

"Next thing I knew, he had spit a ten-dollar gold piece out of his mouth and bought a change of clothes from one of my teamsters. Only took one of the boots. Last I saw of him, he had spit out two more of them gold pieces to buy a horse and saddle from a drifter and was headed north. Damnedest thing I ever saw."

Ike and I rode back to Molly's and picked up Port's horse. Molly gave us the gun and gold too, after taking out what was owed her. As we rode away, we kept wondering what had happened to Port and Susannah. We had a hard time deciding whether to go after Boggs or head back to Cherry Creek. Maybe Port and Susannah were dead or wounded and didn't have a horse to go for help, not that a horse would do Susannah any good.

We decided to go to Cherry Creek. Boggs would keep until spring. We would settle the score with him when we weren't so pressed to do other things.

I felt funny about riding past American Fork without stopping to see my family, but we couldn't justify any delays in the fear that Port or Susannah might be seriously wounded and unable to get help. We had left the extra horse and the gold at Port's stage station at the point of the mountain.

We weren't too far past Lehi when we spotted two riders coming our way, one wearing a heavy buffalo coat like Port's. A big dog followed behind. The other rider was wearing buckskins. As they got closer we could see that both had long hair. When we finally realized we were watching Port and Susannah, we galloped ahead to meet them.

Seeing them well and unharmed was good. What surprised me was how friendly they seemed toward each other. Port didn't even seem upset with me for leaving her with him at the cabin, so I didn't bring up the subject.

We turned around to ride back north, recounting what had happened since we had last been together. I was relieved when Susannah said she no longer wanted to go to Johnston's Army. Everyone already knew about Mountain Meadows, and she just wanted to forget the whole thing.

She asked if she could come home with me and spend some time with Caroline and Sarah while she made plans for the rest of her life. I couldn't get over how much she had changed. I said she could stay as long as she liked.

"You've got to take the dog, too," said Port.

"Why's that?" I asked.

"That's too long a story to tell here," said Port as he turned his horse toward Lehi. Waving good-bye he urged his horse into a gallop. Ike said his good-byes, too, galloping off to the west. Susannah and I rode on together toward American Fork, the wolf dog close at our heels.

Author's Note

Storm Testament IV is a historical novel set in turbulent 1857 Utah Territory when twenty-five hundred federal troops were marching west to Utah to unseat Brigham Young. The setting for this story is as accurate and authentic as I could make it after much research. Porter Rockwell, Lot Smith, and others really did go eastward to harass Johnston's Army. At the same time, the Fancher Company, led by Charles Fancher, was heading south through the Mormon settlements. The massacre of 120 California-bound emigrants at Mountain Meadows by Mormons and Indians actually took place under conditions and circumstances very similar to those presented in this story.

The main characters in this story, however—with the exception of Orrin Porter Rockwell—are fictional. Dan Storm, Ike, Dick Boggs, Susannah, and several others are fictional characters.

This story makes no attempt to cast blame or determine guilt for the massacre at Mountain Meadows, only to present what happened in an accurate and authentic historical setting so the reader, hopefully, can better understand how that unfortunate tragedy could have happened.

My two primary sources of information on the Mountain Meadows incident were *The Mountain Meadows Massacre* by Juanita Brooks, certainly the most authoritative and widely accepted book on the subject, and a typewritten copy of John D. Lee's confessions made available to me by a member of the Lee family. I am grateful to Provo historian Bruce Elm, who made many other volumes available for further checking of names, dates, and events.

My personal conclusions—after finishing the research and sorting out what happened in order to put this story together—are that when U.S. President James Buchanan ordered twenty-five hundred troops to march against Utah, he set into motion a chain of events that led to unavoidable tragedy. History played a dirty trick on William Dame, Isaac Haight, John D. Lee, and others who in their narrow interpretation of events and sincere religious zeal acted as they felt the situation demanded.

In producing this historical novel, I attempted to place my fictional characters in an authentic historical setting, hoping that as the story unfolded, readers would begin to feel and understand the circumstances and events that led otherwise good men to engage in a horrible blood bath.

This book is not an apology, nor is it an attack on the men who carried out the massacre or on their church, but merely an attempt to present a much publicized and controversial event in an authentic and realistic setting—brought to life by fictional characters engaged in their own problems and strivings.

My main objective in writing this book is not to teach history, but to tell a moving story, hoping that in the process an accurate and perhaps sympathetic understanding of an important historical event will settle in the reader's mind and heart. Whether or not I have accomplished that purpose only you, the reader, can judge.

About the Author

Until someone else steps forward, it appears *The Storm Testament* series author Lee Nelson is the only man in modern times to kill a bull buffalo from the back of a galloping horse with a bow and arrow. No, Lee is not a lunatic bent on suicide, but a best-selling author intent on gathering authentic research. Digging through dusty journals, starting fires without matches, and even chewing on raw buffalo is part of Nelson's research in writing historical/adventure/romance novels unparalleled in authenticity and originality.

Lee was born high in the Rocky Mountains in Logan, Utah, later graduating from high school in California. After studying at the University of California at Berkeley, he served a mission for the LDS Church in southern Germany. Lee has a bachelor's degree in English literature and an MBA, both from Brigham Young University.

Lee Nelson has more than thirty published books, including ten historical novels in *The Storm Testament* series.

0 26575 74132 2